THE PORT

OF MISSING MEN

Alain Prévost

THE PORT
OF MISSING MEN

A Novel

FIVE AND TEN PRESS INC.
Washington, D.C.
2001

In memory of Alan R. Stuyvestant

Originally published in France as *Le port des absents*
by Éditions du Seuil, Paris, in September 1967.

Privately published in the United States
in English translation on the occasion of
the Fiftieth Reunion of the Class of 1951,
Princeton University, Princeton, New Jersey
June 1, 2001

LIMITED EDITION

Number **590** of six hundred copies

International Standard Book Number: 1-892379-13-9
Library of Congress Control Number: 2001-131465

This is a Black Sheep Book
published by Five and Ten Press Inc.

Manufactured in the United States of America

I

My father was old. I realized this one rainy day at the end of the war. I was waiting in the shelter of a doorway for the worst of a downpour to end. An American shook me by the shoulder: "I got a son your age." He did not have gray hair like my father. The American had to be mistaken. In my high school English I asked him:

—What age has your son?

—Fifteen.

Without any doubt that meant *quinze*. Fifteen year-old boys had fathers who were soldiers? In the two months since we had been liberated I'd learned the American ranks. This man was a corporal. He was a fighting man, no armchair general. His son would be getting letters in which his father described his battles, his conquests, the countries he was passing through. My father deployed paper flags on a map of Europe and strung a thread of red yarn in zigzags, running over the steppes, the tundra, the deserts.

The flags had passed by Rouen without stopping at La Chêneraie, without even stopping in the valley seen from the terrace of our house. For a few days, though, through our binoculars, we had followed the Germans in full retreat. They crossed the river in small boats or on doors wrenched from barns; they paddled with planks. This exodus was of less interest to my father than the damage inflicted on the cathedral, the courthouse, at Saint-Ouen and Saint-Maclou. He took back the binoculars, focused them on the city, chest thrust forward, jacket stirred by the breeze. He studied each monument, each street, he briefly reported new ruins.

For a long time these bombardments had bathed the foot of our hill. Night after night, day after day, the planes attacked Rouen and, especially, Sotteville. The glow of the fires flowed down the current of the Seine. The old outline of the districts that had been annihilated was only a black spot in the morning mist.

Rouen, always before our eyes, had been put out of bounds by our parents for the last fifteen months. Rouen whose fireworks we watched. Rouen where the English burned Joan of Arc, where, if we disobeyed my father, bombs lay in wait for us. Rouen dangerous as an explosive, a city as small, seen from our terrace, as a scale model you could carry in your hands. Rouen life and death.

Perhaps death for Fabien whom my father sent to the high school to take the first part of the baccalaureate examination after a year of study at home. June 1944. My mother and I watched the sky and its bombers for two days in a row. Would Fabien die or would he pass his baccalaureate? What kind of life was this, at the foot of the hill, that was not worth living without a baccalaureate?

On our property, not a bomb gone astray, not an oak wounded; a few traces of an encampment of Senegalese troops barely remained at the foot of the park. Five years of war and all we had lost were our city ways.

When, for the first time in fifteen months, I went down the hill to Rouen, I was less surprised by the ruins than by the houses still standing: by the sidewalks and cafés, new objects in the window displays, objects more important than the shattered walls, the cellars open to daylight and the bricks piled up by survivors.

Ah, these strangers in the streets, these dozens of pocket-knives in the windows, these movies, these restaurants, these American soldiers, these jewelry shops!

—Look, Fabien, three hairdressers in the same street!

—Of course!

In six days we saw five films; all American war films. Cargo ships exploded in the open seas off Murmansk, planes crashed on the palm trees of Guadalcanal. Nurses, blondes and brunettes, cared for the ill-shaven wounded. And, always, at the beginning and at the end of each film, in the curiously flat streets of American cities, young men waited patiently for the right time to enlist, in the navy, the air force, or the infantry. My heart was broken, I had missed the chance to be a hero. I wouldn't be wounded or decorated. I wouldn't be worthy of the love of the nurses. I had missed the war, finished for me. I was sorry not to be American, not to be twenty, not to be a soldier, an aviator, an amputee, loved. I felt a hatred for the Germans I had never felt during the occupation; I even hated the Japanese. For the first time in my life, I was not happy, and for the first time too I saw a world divided between the good and the evil. My father had refused to send me to learn my catechism: five movies had taken its place. For the good I invented a paradise where Veronica Lake let herself be kissed in a convertible. The evil, bloated caricatures exploding in mid air, hurled their guttural curses from the midst of the flames.

In the days following the Liberation, I had my first glimpses of peacetime. The autumn was warm. We had our breakfast on the terrace. Pink hollyhocks held for a long time the morning dew. Our goings and comings from the house to the stone table furrowed paths in the overgrown grass; my mother was hesitant to have it mowed, just as she hesitated to send us to the barber, expecting that my father would complain. We were served eggs, porridge, apple sauce. Dread of the mid-day meal at school doubled my appetite.

My father's gray hairs: between spoonfuls I searched for the words to ask him his age. Yesterday that would still have been easy. Besides, he had surely told us and each year on his birthday told us again without my paying attention. Today, after this encounter with the American, my voice wouldn't be normal. My father would look up at me with surprise and anxiety in his eyes.

At the front of the house Fabien was getting irritated: "Hurry up, Grégoire, we're going to be late!" Since the beginning of the term he yelled every morning that we would be late. That was because he wanted to have time to play his game.

Fabien called this game "Shot down in flames." As soon as we left the rough road of La Chêneraie , when our bikes hit the smooth asphalt and gained speed on the great slope towards Rouen, Fabien turned to me:

—Are we going down in flames?

We became German and American fighter pilots. Our school bags served as machine guns and the ringings of our bicycle bells were bursts of gunfire. We died ten times, first one, then the other, in the quarter of an hour it took to ride to school. Fabien laid down the rules: shoot only when our bikes were in a precise line-up. The damaged plane "crashed" and, without touching the handlebars, we threw ourselves into a ditch or onto a bush. Sometimes we had time to "hit the silk" while the bike, abandoned at full speed, rolled in a somersault.

At the end of November, Fabien broke his ankle. I was left alone. Alone on the road and alone at school or in the park; from eight in the morning to six at night, ten hours a day of solitude. Until then Fabien had dreamed up all our games. Pirate, he commanded the oak tree that served as our ship. Explorer, he led me to the end of the park to civilize the Senegalese. With them we had shared chickens stolen from neighboring farms and roasted on a spit between two stones; but one night in the spring of '40, on the outskirts of Yvetot, the Germans killed our Negroes. Fabien became an animal trainer; I was his lion, his bear, his Indian elephant. Sioux chieftain, he initiated me into the mysteries of the tribe; I raced through the night across our park where branches and fear whipped my face. We searched for gold on the banks of the Seine. We swam among the crocodiles. Fabien rewrote history, we helped Vercingetorix conquer the Romans. Everywhere, from Africa to Asia, from the past to the present, from the Atlantic to the Indian Oceans, Fabien commanded, decreed, made the laws, wrote the reports or kept the log. Now, without him, I had to find my own game; I invented friendship.

—How is your son?

On a sidewalk of Rouen I recognized the American I had run into in the rain. "What news of his son?" He brought out some photos. In the beginning it astonished me that he understood my English.

The next day, I hailed a dock worker in front of a shopwindow full of fishing rods.

—It's a beauty, that big one!

—It sure is! But we won't go fishing this year!

—As for me, I've never been fishing.

This time he winked at me.

—That's right! You kids, with the war, you don't know anything about all that!

In the evening , after school, I would hang out in the streets of Rouen, my bicycle at my side. When I spotted a passer-by pausing , I would re-tie my shoelaces.

—Ah, what fine weather!

Men or women, expressions numbed by the wait for a bus, roused themselves and studied the sky. The best days were those when it was full of fat white clouds.

—Do you think it's going to rain?

At this question, faces became animated. Head raised, forehead wrinkled, my pedestrian would look for an answer. A dialog was begun. Was France less distant than the Amazon? Its inhabitants less savage than the Zulus? First I noticed clothes: tattered jackets, fabrics worn at the elbows and the cuffs, scarves wrapped twice around the neck with their ends tucked under the straps of overalls, leather belts that were much too long (remembrances and hopes of better times), berets stiffened by bad weather, short dresses, galoshes clop-clopping along on the sidewalk. Then I discovered hands, worn out like old tools, broken fingernails blunted by labor, hands with black motor oil greased into every fold. The well-groomed hands of shopkeepers, warmed in the pockets of their aprons, appeared only with a handkerchief and quickly plunged again to shelter from the cold.

The days grew shorter. I now left school as night fell but tricks I had learned took the place of the darkened sky; no need to look up at the clouds, I already had so many friends! Every evening I ran across half a dozen. I greeted them, I stopped . A crowd of unknown faces that I could surprise at will with a smile. My thinness aroused their pity. One woman offered me her ration ticket for a hundred grams of bread. Wonderful people: they had gone without milk and meat all through the war while on my hill I had eaten my fill, supplied by my father's farmers . . . and yet they were offering me their bread!

My American friend introduced his comrades to me. Their uniforms marked them as a breed apart; like spaniels, dock workers, Negroes, percherons, soldiers, peasants. I learned that the different species display an infinite variety of faces as well as an array of uniforms showing their origin or occupation. Their mouths, thin, broad, supple, thick, smiling, pouting or sad, and their looks, light from the green and khaki-colored fabrics under the khaki helmet; two spots of light of an intensity and color that conjured up a name: Sam, Bill, the lieutenant, Dick, Tex, George, Harry. Sam, his beard a haze of undergrowth, father of a son my age; Bill, with yellow eyes like the headlights of a car; the lieutenant, a glint of reflected light behind his spectacles; Dick, afternoon gray; Tex, summer-sky blue; George, eyes like candles; Harry, also the color of the summer sky, but a summer less violent than Tex's, a northern summer. All these lights from the uniforms, flaring up, dying down in a brown and green barracks, among the gray-green bunks with their earth-colored blankets. Jeeps, motorcycles, even flashlights had this color of the fields and a factory smell.

I spent my Thursday school holiday in America; three hours in the lieutenant's office as an interpreter. Sentences in English broken up into words, into expressions that could be reshaped to suit new sentences. They lent me detective stories: *Black Jack, Killing Time, A Hole in One.* With this brand new language, I welcomed each noun like a gift. At first I understood nothing of the rapid-fire dialog, shorn of the official formulas of grammar. Then scraps of conversation, whole sentences became familiar. At first a stranger in the life of the barracks, I learned its routines at the same time as its vocabulary. When they laughed at a joke launched from the other end of the room, I was able to laugh also. I came to understand better both the language and those who spoke it, to the point where I became upset with them because I discovered a contempt for French customs. Ways I'd never noticed: we were dirty, our streets narrow, piles of manure gave off a stench at the gates of the farms, men urinated on the walls. One day I told them about my American uncle. Immediately they surrounded me. They called to each other, opened the doors, spread the news: "The kid has an American uncle!"

—Where does he live?

—Is he married? Got kids?

—Is he in the war?

—What's his name?

None of them, of course, knew my uncle. However, my prestige skyrocketed. Thanks to him, I became their cousin, almost one of them.

Thursday afternoons we took to the motorcycles. Harley-Davidsons, lumbering and nimble as Percherons, rolled across the hills, between the hedges of sunken country roads. Rouen, Yvetôt, Le Havre: seated on the luggage rack, both hands clutched on Tex's belt, legs thrust into leather saddlebags, I refereed the races. The Norman countryside no longer existed. With exasperating sluggishness, Dick's motorcycle caught up with George's, ours, lost twenty meters again in a bend from which we emerged triumphant; my eyes returned then to the countryside which was rocking from side to side. Fear made me cry out, my voice lost in the howl of the sirens.

Military Police: my friends enforced the law. They overtook convoys, checked the documents of the tanks, stopped the trucks. Often we emptied the bordellos: obstinate soldiers let themselves be subdued. Through me as the intermediary, the lieutenant lectured the whores for obstructing the war effort. My father didn't worry: I would get a better mark in English on my baccalaureate. He understood too that my innocence was without limits, with reason, because I was amazed that in these strange bistros the women were still in bathrobes so late in the afternoon.

Besides, Marie Godefroy was more on my mind than these girls.

"Three minutes!" I had called to her, "Three minutes!"

Front tires could be patched quicker than rear tires. I upended the bike, took off the wheel, the tire, all the while counting in a loud voice: "Twenty-six, twenty-seven, twenty-eight." At "one hundred and fifty" I was obliged to count more slowly; already, the coupling of my air-pump was giving me trouble. But at "one hundred and seventy-three," I handed her back her bike: "Seven seconds to spare." She was still weeping.

—Look, it's fixed!

Who was she? Thirteen? A school bag on her carrier.

—Do you go to high school?

She didn't answer. Obviously she went to school.

—Where do you live?

—At my grandfather's.

No handkerchief. I tore a page from my notebook:

—Here! You can't go into school looking like that. We're going to be late.

Finally, she got back on her bike. I followed her.

—Who's your grandfather?

—Mr. Godefroy.

Her grandfather? The friend of my father? How old my father was!

—I know your grandfather well. Last year, since the bombings kept us from going to school, he taught us math and physics, Fabien and me.

She said nothing.

—Fabien, that's my brother. He's a senior, but he broke his ankle. I'm a junior. And you? You live near us. Our parents know each other. That is, our parents and your grandparents. We'll be seeing each other. What's your name?

—Marie Godefroy.

Twice I had her repeat her name, she spoke so softly. At each curve she put on her brakes. Surely we would be late.

At home, when I told them about my meeting with Mr. Godefroy's granddaughter, my mother asked:

—What is she like?

—She has pigtails.

I didn't see her again for several days.

That same week I had a real reason to worry: Fabien and I. We weren't getting on together. Every time I crossed the living room he said to me, "I don't like you anymore." Or, on his chaise longue, he turned away so as not to see me.

I had planned a great adventure: together we would leave for America, together we would make a fortune. Usually this plotting was at night before I went to sleep. One night we would cultivate millions of acres of wheat; another, we would strike gold and oil. In the cities we would make a name for ourselves using our wits. Crowds hailed us along those curiously flat streets. War broke out: Fabien in one airplane, me in another, always a team, decorated the same day in the same ceremony. Sam, Bill, Tex, Dick, George, Harry, they were all there. The lieutenant, now a general, pinned on the *Croix*. In a convertible, Veronica Lake smiled. In this America there was never any rain. We passed without a transition from horses to cars, from towns to endless forests. Snow was acceptable, we hunted wolves. We traveled by plane or canoe. Skyscrapers and log cabins, friendships swiftly made and never to be forgotten.

At the first words Fabien interrupted me:

—And what language would they speak?

—English, of course!

He responded with a burst of exasperating laughter, his new invention; a theatrical cry, a cry of rage that made me grow nasty.

—You would like me to stay with you on Thursday's holiday to bring you books, change your records for you, listen to your poems . . .

Fabien was going to be a poet. That was his daydream. He the poet and me the journalist . . . in Paris. Which might as well be a suburb of Rouen, less than a couple of hours away by train. There we would write all day long. What was the point of going away? Why not a whole life in school . . .

"Not in America yet?" Fabien would taunt me every time he saw me.

He thrust one of his crutches in my face.

17

—Come now, boys, said my mother.

She took me by the arm and drew us together to embrace.

"Since your brother can't get around," said my mother once again, " you should play with him more." What an exasperating word! Were we at an age to "play"?

—Grégoire would rather beg chocolates from the Americans!

—You filthy redhead!

—Grégoire!

My mother was furious. My father laughed: before his hair turned gray, he had been a redhead like Fabien.

—I think redheads do have the worst temperaments. Grégoire must have the soul of a redhead in spite of his black hair.

The situation improved when Fabien was able to return to his piano. With one leg on a footstool, he played for hours. During Christmas vacation his music pursued me all over the house. My father, and especially my mother, were too pleased with his progress to be annoyed.

Fabien also took correspondence courses. In spite of everything, he would pass his second baccalaureate in June. My father helped him with philosophy, history, geography; Mr. Godefroy with math and science.

Mr. Godefroy came in all kinds of weather without a coat, without even a muffler, while my father would wrap himself all winter in a cape. My father wore corduroy vests that puffed out his suits, their pockets already out of shape due to his packets of tobacco and his pipes. Mr. Godefroy's jackets hung straight over trousers that were always newly pressed. As soon as Fabien's studies were over, they both installed themselves next to the fireplace for their game of chess. My father lit the fire. When Mr. Godefroy came to the house, I would bring in an extra load of wood. The next day I told Marie:

—Your grandfather paid us a visit yesterday afternoon.

I could scarcely hear her response. I would like to have known her words in order to remember them, she spoke so rarely! A girl almost without words and almost without expression. I followed her every morning; for her sake I had changed my habits when I saw that she left earlier than I did. On the road, I saw her coming, I waited for her, I rode next to her, I asked her precise questions in order to obtain an answer.

—Have you had a letter from your mother? Are there gardens in Paris?

Each day, at the end of January, the sun was a little higher in the sky. Its rays struck the slope of the hill at a horizontal angle as we descended towards the town still in shadow. Marie sat straight up on her old-fashioned girl's bicycle with upturned handlebars and wooden grips, her two blonde braids flowing down either side of her neck and in front of her shoulders. I, slightly behind, sat thin and dark on my forest-green bike. If it hadn't been for the war I would have had long trousers; the shortage of cloth condemned me to short pants, shorter still because of my sudden burst of growth. I bent over my racing handlebars, hunched down and aerodynamic, capable of getting down the hill much more quickly than she and conscious of never daring to overtake her.

With Marie on the slope down to Rouen, the sun sparkled on the damp trunks of the oak trees, then a few fields of very pale green where three cows grazed on the right, a horse on the left; finally, the first café, *le Bout du Monde*; again into the shadows, and the first of the wooden barracks built in haste to replace the houses that had been destroyed. I left Marie on the quay, slipping left towards the boy's school, pedaling then with all my strength.

In the evening I rarely returned home with her. I did not forget my friends of the streets, old women with pointed elbows who offered me their little dogs to pat, shopgirls whose voices called out to me from the back of their stores, silent factory workers who smiled at me just to say hello, old men in woolen gloves. Without knowing their names, I learned their quirks. They all had an animal, a child, a cousin in an important job, an armoire, an illness, a memory, a hope, a fear, a complaint or a hatred that, remembered, animated them. Their life was spread out around this unique event which they described with passion and in minute detail. I sympathized, I admired, I encouraged. From six to seven, every evening, I sighed or laughed with them, always filled with wonder at their monotonous tales. Finally they had a patient listener! A blind man knew me by the sound of my bicycle bell. A young woman offered me her father's rosary. He had been killed in the bombing. A hardware dealer wanted me to become his employee; I would marry his daughter and inherit his shop.

Often, I went up to the barracks of the Americans. I returned their books. They lent me others that I read at night. *Gone with the Wind, The Grapes of Wrath, For Whom the Bell Tolls.* Sometimes flat on my stomach, sometimes on my back, feet tangled in disheveled sheets, I told myself: "Just ten more pages, just one more hour, just one more paragraph."

At school my comrades were astonished. From being mediocre I became a good student, not only because of the year of special study with my father and Mr. Godefroy—I was afraid a bad mark would threaten my freedom. To gain more free time I absorbed everything even without understanding it. I was amazed to find that sooner or later I ended up understanding everything I had learned.

Standing still made me uneasy. I needed movement. I might have broken my leg too and then remained like Fabien on a sofa, never meeting the Americans, Marie, the passers-by in Rouen. The fear of missing such moments haunted me. Where would the adventure be this evening? At the school gate? In the street? On the quay? With the soldiers? Sundays and Thursday mornings at home seemed interminable. How was Fabien able to stay there with only his books and his piano? I crossed the living room. He pretended not to hear me and I could watch him closely: he hid his mouth with his hand, a new gesture that concealed what kind of a smile, what bitterness?

One day, when he had left the door of his bedroom ajar, I went in. It was a prettier room than mine since he, of course, was the older. It had two windows, a fireplace, a real bookcase with doors of lattice work , things I didn't have. But I recognized the mess, our mess: pajama bottoms on the parquet, dirty socks on the hearth, bed unmade, papers and books strewn on the desk with a shirt and a notebook, DIARY drawn by hand in capital letters. In the salon he was playing the piano. I opened the notebook:

November 10. Last week the trees were still yellow and red. Now, after three days of wind, the leaves have fallen and I have all this color at the end of my foot, I stir it about.

December 23. Musset pisses me off. "The handsome knight who hastens off to war . . . " He recited this in the salons with a lock of hair over his eye. He must have looked a fool, this young man . . .

21

January 5. What a change in my life because of one bad spill. But what does one single change matter among all the changes that are going on? A life altered. It's hardly worth turning around to look back. If I were in Greg's place I would probably do as much. Especially since he is only a kid . . .

"Kid," yourself! What does he know about what I think and what I feel?

Below, the piano became silent and I closed the diary. I met Fabien on the stairs. He was climbing, backwards, sitting down on each step, dragging his crutches behind him.

—Want me to help you?

—Don't bother!

If only he had wanted to listen to me! I would have gone to Paris a hundred times, even been a journalist, just to please him . . . if he had been willing to go along with me from time to time in America, to discover oil, to share in my adventure.

This America pursued me even at home. One Thursday morning, a letter came from Aunt Laura. My mother called the family together and opened it solemnly. Uncle Henri was fighting in the Pacific. Maman wept: her little brother. For her, the war began all over again. We consoled her.

—You remember her, Fabien, your Aunt Laura?

—Of course!

Fabien believed that he remembered everything. Mother read the letter in English and he was the only one who didn't listen. He was not very good in foreign languages. Aunt Laura asked if we were all alive. She promised a package of sugar and coffee. She asked for two photos of the family, one for Uncle Henri and one for herself. We could answer her in French; she understood French very well even though she didn't write it.

—Why doesn't she send her photo? asked Fabien.

We passed the envelope around. We examined this first letter from a country that had not suffered in the war. A second liberation. The ink, the stamp, the paper came from America. A blue envelope, transparent and strong; decidedly, the Americans knew how to make everything— airplanes, wars, and transparent paper.

They sent me off to Rouen. An hour later I returned with a roll of film. Papa dusted off his camera. Everything was ready.

Fabien asked:"Who's going to take the photo?"

I went to find Mr. Godefroy.

In another forest of oak their house also had its lawn but no hollyhocks; a lawn that was mowed regularly. Windows, doors painted dark green; my mother believed in gray paint. I noticed the differences between the two houses: four steps to their front entrance, three to ours. How small my universe was! The difference in age between two wisterias bewildered me. In a photograph I would hardly know how to tell the difference between our house and the Godefroys': slate roofs, walls of rose-colored brick, stone lintels and jambs, old houses held together by climbing plants, by roots buried under the turf. The almost identical houses were transformed by the habits of the two families. Not one dead leaf was lying on the Godefroys' lawn. In their house the insides of the fireplaces were glazed; in our house cinders and charred logs awaited the next fire. In our house, no rugs on the parquet floors and the tiles. In their house I couldn't hear my own footsteps. Did Marie hear me?

Seated near a window, partly hidden by the high back of

her armchair, she was reading a novel. I recognized the pattern of the pages. White space surrounded gray text and, at the very heart of the lines, the name of the heroine: Martha. So, Marie was reading a book I had mentioned a few mornings before, proof that she had been listening to me. Pride followed by fear—it would bore her—then embarassment; the main character of *Devil in the Flesh* seemed to me dirty, vicious. Marie would believe I thought about her as he thought about this woman. A week before, I had cried reading Radiguet. Now he disgusted me. I was soiled. I would pay for this mistake. I would change my life, run in the woods every morning, take two cold showers a day, learn pure sayings by heart. To chase away the bad thoughts I would say to myself: "The torrent washes the stones," "The flax flowers turn to the sun," "The winter breeze . . . "

—Grégoire! What are you doing here?

She had clapped the book shut between her hands. Marie stood in front of me. I didn't dare to look at her. I saw only her legs, gray socks in blue slippers.

—It's beautiful, said Marie.

—What?

—Your novel.

She pointed to it, thrown on the table, cover exposed, pardoned by this verdict. I, too, was pardoned, mute, happy to hear the voice of Mr. Godefroy.

—You are even thinner, Grégoire! Or else you are growing . . .

—We need you to take a photograph.

He freed me from my paralysis. My voice returned to normal. My legs carried me towards him. I explained about the letter, told him about my uncle in the Pacific, my American aunt, every word meant for Marie, so she would know we were not just farmers, that, in a way, we crossed frontiers. I turned back to her long enough for one au revoir, accompanying her grandfather, two men on the lawn. I was the tallest in spite of my short pants. Was she watching us from the window? Had she already taken up her book?

"Hurry up! Hurry up! The sun's out!" cried my mother when we arrived.

I tried to pay no attention to them in order to hold onto the memory of Marie.

—Where do you want to take the photos?

—On the front steps, answered my father.

For once he did not wear his cape and kept saying:

— Hurry it up. I'm going to catch cold.

"*Ton* novel." Did she tutoyer me for the first time? If I had only raised my eyes I would at least have seen her face in full daylight, the color of her eyes.

Mother didn't want to use the front steps, the wisteria had lost its leaves.

—You think they don't know in America that wisterias lose their leaves? Come on! I'm surely going to catch a cold.

Fabien proposed the laundry room.

"Idiot!" Mama suggested the living room, everyone seated around the fireplace.

—Not enough light . . .

—But we can light the fire!

Marie vanished. I could not even hear her voice. I could scarcely recall the gray socks. We walked through the wet grass towards the little steps of the studio. A photograph at the foot of the ivy. Papa posed the family: Fabien on the left, then Mama, himself, and me.

—A redhead, a brunette, a redhead gone gray, a black . . .

—However, this photo is not in color! said my mother.

—No, but I separate the Engivaines from the Cahans!

Fabien snickered:

—It's true Grégoire looks like the women in the family.

—Is Fabien going to be photographed with his crutches?
I asked.

—Ah! No! said Mama.

—Then how am I supposed to stand?

—Fabien, put a hand on your mother's shoulder and
throw away those ridiculous crutches.

Fabien protested. Papa raised his voice:

—You want me to get bronchitis?

—I'll pay you back for that, Fabien said to me, throwing
his crutches aside.

We waited for the sun.

The photograph taken, the family returned to the living
room and I noticed that Mama was wearing a hat, Fabien a
tie, Papa his green tweed English suit. While I was looking for Mr. Godefroy they were dressing up and were now
uncomfortable with their elegance while waiting for lunch
to be served. Seated on the edge of the sofa, her hands on
her knees, Mama told the story of Uncle Henri's departure
for America.

— . . . because he always hated war. Oh, he knew very
well that Germany would take over Europe. He wanted
us to leave with him. In the United States, he said, Italians,
Germans, British, had found their melting pot. There's the
future! And now poor Henri is in the war! Grégoire looks
like him, you know. He will be as tall and thin as his uncle.

My father opened an old bottle of port and Mr. Godefroy,

glass in hand, listened to my mother.

—It will be all right. It will be all right. The war is almost over.

On the sideboard the little blue envelope from America stood up among the family photos. It hardly affected our routine: Papa smoked his pipe; seated at the piano, Fabien read a musical score. However, everything seemed changed, their clothes, their meditations. Papa and Mr. Godefroy didn't play chess, they hadn't lit the fire, the piano remained silent. I thought that this kind of letter should be opened only on Sundays.

At lunch there was a scene. Mother had not had time to think about hors d'oeuvres, usually offered before lunch, so soup, which by custom always opened the evening meal, was served. Fabien refused to touch it.

—At noon! You want me to eat leek soup at noon?

—You should be ashamed! Don't you know that millions of Chinese are dying of hunger?

—Then send them my soup! he shouted.

The soup bowl slid across the table, dropped to the floor in front of my father, and cracked. Fabien left the dining room, crutches, legs, arms every which way—a spider.

—Come back this minute!

My father rose in his chair, sank back, rose again.

—Perhaps Fabien is not all wrong," he said, finally. "Except for throwing his plate."

—So it's the Chinese who are to blame?

My turn to get up. But I didn't know how to get myself angry. By chance I hit on the right words. I sat down again, slamming my chair to the floor. "People are dying and we make fun of them!" Not enough conviction. I felt foolish in the silence that followed. The silence went on. With the

cheese Mama declared:
—The Pacific isn't far from China!
My father went to look for a map.
—If you like, I'll pay more attention to the news. We will put some flags on the islands as they are retaken.

At the end of the afternoon I carried the film to Rouen, then I went up to see the Americans. The lieutenant called me into his office to translate a letter. A wretched letter, disfigured by misspellings, from a poor woman complaining about a brawl. Some soldiers had broken a dozen glasses, some chairs and windows in her café. She asked for payment for the damages, begged for protection. The lieutenant took notes. I thought to myself: "Is this what war is about?" I imagined my uncle conveying the official apologies of the American government to a Polynesian bistro.

—How dumb they are, said the lieutentant when I told him about my uncle. The army has someone who knows France and they send him to the Pacific. That Pacific is a son of a bitch!

He repeated, "a son of a bitch, a son of a bitch." Behind his glasses, he closed his eyes against the light.

—Does he have children, your uncle?
—A daughter.
—After the war you must go there, Grégoire.

The lieutenant was the only one who called me Grégoire. The other Americans called me "Greg". He took off his glasses and his eyes became minuscule. I would rather he called me "Greg" like the others.

—This is your house?

I recognized the post card. My father had hundreds of them that he sent instead of letters.

—Your father is thanking me for some cigars . . .

—Yes. That's our house.

—In America almost all the houses are brand new . . . not old and pretty like yours.

Seated behind his desk, the lieutenant played with his glasses. When he had something to say to me, my father sat behind his desk and played with a ruler.

—In America, Grégoire, in New York, Boston, Philadelphia, many children have never seen the country, never seen a cow. Do you know that, Gregoire? You are a lucky fellow. Ask Sam. He has a son your age who plays in the streets and doesn't know what a field of wheat looks like, or a field of snow.

Since the lieutenant had taken off his glasses, I could not read his expression, I saw only his eyes. I tried not to hear but I didn't know how not to hear. Thousands of children, in my mind's eye, played in the flat, white streets of America. A few emaciated cats, like the cats of Rouen, were their only animals since they had never seen a cow.

—You like America, Grégoire?

If my father had asked me: "Do you like Marie Godefroy?" I could not have blushed more.

—You ought to go to America, Grégoire. I will help you go there, to the university where I teach. It's so you won't be disappointed that I'm talking to you about your house, your good luck. America is not like it is in the movies."

My father also said: "Novels are to be read, not to be lived."

—If you go to America you will help Americans to understand the French . . . and when you return to France . . .

I wasn't listening anymore. I didn't want to be French in America. I wanted to be American like George, Harry, and the others. And I didn't want to come back to France. If I was going to return, why leave? I wished the lieutenant would keep quiet. His words offended me. If he wanted me to go to America, why discourage me with stories of ugliness and poverty? What was he thinking?

Until that morning I had never thought of leaving for America; I had dreamed of it, that's something else. In making my dream a possibility the lieutenant destroyed it. Out of a hope that was faint, malleable, he constructed a reality.

"I will go somewhere else," I thought. "To Chile or to China . . . "

Would I be condemned to leaving for America, but without glory, merely to study?

—I will give you my address at the university," said the lieutenant. "If you have good marks in France, I will get you a scholarship. Your uncle will help. The war will soon be over."

Discouraged, I went through Rouen. I didn't hear the voices of the passers-by. I wanted to see Fabien. Perhaps he would persuade me to go to Paris with him. America.

A quiet afternoon. I listened to the tires of my bicycle on the road, on the driveway, and soon the house was in view. I heard Fabien at the piano. It was music without rhythm, a passage of clear notes weighed down by deep dissonant chords. He was improvising? I paced in front of the house, no longer daring, no longer wanting to go in. There was no room for me in this music. A few weeks had been enough to split us apart? "There we were," as they say in books, "at a crossroad." Fabien headed for Paris and me, in spite of everything, bound for the United States.

With night coming on, the scenes I had imagined for

weeks regained their potency. They marched at the foot of the terrace, along the Seine again covered in winter carpet. They appeared, without labels, without order, without measure. Only colors remained: hopes as gray as American steel, Flying Fortresses, Liberty ships, gray as the rain of Normandy, the road to Rouen, gray as the Atlantic swell, the waiting rocks, the hour of counter-attacks, the tears of widows, gray like those white streets of America dulled by the lieutenant's veiled stare, gray like my mother's winter dresses; green hopes of spring at La Chêneraie, of runs through its woods, of the forests of London and Curwood, green against fresh snow, green of the Amazon, on the islands of the Pacific and in the jungles of Burma; red dreams of airplanes in flames, of the sun setting or rising, of a glorious day, of fires spreading along the Seine, red flags on the Russian front, hollyhocks on our terrace, the curtains in the living room, red yarn separating the steppes, wounds, sacrifices and revolts.

The parade ended in the night. The clouds were put out and the city lit up, first along the quais, then a few boulevards in dotted lines. Down below, the school, my street friends, my Americans. What a distance! Would it be possible to cross it? Yes, if I carried it in me . . . and lived by this gentleness: the kindness of my mother, the beauty of the trees of La Chêneraie, the peacefulness of our hillside. Seen from the terrace, the war and its miseries were only faint colors shaded by the changing light of the sky. "You're lucky, Grégoire," said the lieutenant.

And yet, how to depart? I had to leave myself behind. But already the lieutenant's plans, the blessings of my father, and an infinity of memories would go with me to America, where my Uncle Henri was waiting for me. What was the use? I would never leave since I no longer had anything unexpected to hope for.

This passing depression lasted only a few days. The ice storm rescued me.

A coating of sheer ice under the reflection of the sun. Each blade of grass, each tree held its color encased in the ice, under a sky of pale blue that the cold veiled with a luminous film. No more wind, no more insects, no more birds. An end to the sighs and murmurings. The countryside crackled in the silence and I could easily hear everything that Marie said.

I followed right behind her, holding out my hands. Without touching her, I carried Marie to Rouen, ready to break her fall. Could I still love her if she fell? And when she fell, relief that nothing was injured: neither her ankles nor her dignity since darkness had come.

An hour to get down to Rouen, an hour to return. Six days of ice and five times I accompanied Marie. It was official. Madame Godefroy had made this request of my mother because she was afraid "for the girl, alone and on foot." I carried our two notebooks in a backpack. Daybreak. I saw myself clearly as bigger than she; she was so thin, even in her cloak. Soon I could make out colors: a red bandanna on her head, a green scarf, a green cloak with a black velvet collar setting off her yellow braids, motionless in spite of the movement of her shoulders. When she spoke to me she hardly turned her head.

—That morning, she said, I wasn't crying because of a flat tire. I was crying because I miss my Papa and Mama and because I was afraid of my grandfather and grandmother. I hadn't seen them since the war began . . . I didn't know they would be so old! I couldn't cry in front of them so I waited to be alone.

—How old is your father?

—He'll be thirty-eight on the seventeenth of February.

We walked along on the shoulder, not as icy as the road. Below, Rouen was smoking; smoke that did not change form but only grew thicker, trapped by the freezing cold.

In the evening, climbing the hill, I walked at a distance from Marie, afraid of bumping into her by mistake in the half light. Each evening as the moon waned, it became darker.

—Grandpa is certain that, with the new moon, the wind will change.

—What wind?

—The wind that brings this ice storm.

—The Americans are on the offensive again.

—Then the war will be over and I 'll go back to Paris!

—And we won't see each other anymore?

—You'll write to me, Grégoire.

Marie stopped. Perhaps she turned towards me. I thought I saw her face.

—Actually, you can write to me now.

We arrived at her house and she explained.

—Not in the mail. You can give me letters from hand to hand.

Singing, I went back to La Chêneraie. I sang badly? So what. "You're a lucky fellow, Grégoire." Tomorrow I would write to Marie. To say what? Anything I liked; it would be so much easier than talking to her! I would explain that I would love to follow her as I had followed her this week, to follow her to Paris or wherever she wished. And America? Would she understand? Why not? Some day . . .

Through the trees I saw the lighted windows of our house. Usually we closed the shutters at nightfall. What a shame! The lights shone on a few branches glazed with ice. Behind this screen lay the warmth of our living room. I heard a few notes on the piano in a high register. A melody was cut off and then gradually recovered its flow as I approached.

Fabien was playing Bach. Easy to recognize, Bach, always the same. Poor Fabien. The same piano, the same music, the same Bach. If only he knew that Marie . . .

—Grégoire?

He went on playing, looking at me over his shoulder:

—Maman has gotten some news.

—Well?

—Uncle Henri has been killed.

—Ah?

What else was there to say? Fabien examined me. What was he hoping for?

—Well, of course, you don't remember him at all, do you?

—Where is Mama?

—With Papa in their bedroom.

He turned back to the piano, continuing his music. How was he able to play while thinking of something else? From the top of the stairway I watched for a moment, then I hesitated. Should I go to my mother? Fabien's door was open, his diary on the bed.

January 17: In five days the doctor will take off my cast. In a month I return to school, after the Mardi Gras vacation. I was so happy by myself. Finally, only a few more months . . . (later) Mother has just learned of the death of her brother, her "little brother." A great sadness for her in which I can't take part. I don't remember him. Will

Grégoire pretend to? Basically, I would rather have had a sister.

For several days I composed letters to Marie. I didn't write any of them. I wrote to Aunt Laura. The words of the lieutenant came back to me as I faced that blank page: "That Pacific is a son-of-a-bitch!" That would not console my aunt who must be as grief-stricken as our mother. Maman asked Fabien to play for her on the piano and she wept when he stopped. "Love each other now!" she told us. She turned to me as her confidant: "You're the one who looks most like Henri, even your eyes."

Papa had me read his letter to Aunt Laura, "because you know American customs better than I do." In seven pages he told how he had known, loved, understood Uncle Henri. "... twenty-eight years younger than me, Henri could have been my son, and I often treated him as a son ... He loved our Normandy so much, the dogs, the horses, the farming. His intelligence didn't allow him to remain like me, humbly hidden away. I wanted him to avoid my mistakes and I encouraged him to pursue his studies. He was brilliant and yet he knew how to remain simple ... this overgrown boy whose ideal was peace but who did not draw back from war ... " Poor Aunt Laura, after a letter like this she would never be able to recover from her grief!

Even the American soldiers talked to me only of my Uncle Henri. They asked me about the spelling of his name, his date of birth, the date and place of his death. Then they appeared one Sunday at three o'clock, the lieutenant at their head, all in white helmets and white gloves, surprised that we were still at table. "In America we have lunch much earlier!" Dick explained. "Translate, Greg," said Sam. "Tell your folks that we have lunch at 12:30 in America."

The lieutenant gave a short speech. This ceremony was his men's idea, approved by the commandant and the colonel; my mother was to consider their visit as a tribute paid by the American army to her brother. I translated. George gave my mother two little flags, the American and the French, tied together with black ribbon. She placed them on the mantelpiece. She did not cry. She was wearing one of her winter dresses of gray wool. At the time one didn't buy mourning clothes; for some years we hadn't bought clothes of any kind. However, mother wore her mourning on this everyday dress and I searched for a sign of it: a black ribbon? Only her black hair against a pale brow. How young my mother seemed! Yet her expression made a mourning veil of her hair. Her voice was different, too. She asked the soldiers to sit down and they sat around the living room on sofas, armchairs, straight chairs, their white helmets on their knees, like empty bowls.

—We don't have any more coffee, said my mother. Would you care for some tea?

Tex slipped me a package.

—Tell your mother, Greg, that the sister of an American hero mustn't be short of coffee.

Behind the piano, Fabien tapped out rhythms on his cast. We listened.

We listened also to the rain. With the new moon the wind had changed. I imagined Fabien's thoughts. For the first time he was meeting my Americans. Oh, how he must be delighted to see them so ill at ease in our living room! He wouldn't understand; he wouldn't want to understand. He played Bach on his cast, but his half smile didn't go with the music.

Next day I read in his Journal:

(later) A visit from poor Grégoire's famous Americans. Handsome élite troops in Sunday best. One could believe oneself to be at the movies (Hollywood-special-hero's-death). A nice series of clichés. Being ridiculous doesn't kill you. The proof!

What a bastard! I would have sworn it . . . These guys thought only of pleasing us. If he had put himself in their place, Monsieur the poet? And if I were to throw his Diary in his face? A good opportunity to punch him in the nose.

Below he was playing an innocent air. Mozart, no doubt. Carefully, I put the diary back on the shelf where I had found it. One day I would pay him back for that . . . One day he would need me . . . One day . . .

I went downstairs. Fabien at his piano, shirt unbuttoned; hair in his eyes, down his neck, behind his ears, a red mop of two months' growth; dirty hands, dirty nails, even his cast was a dirty gray.

—Grégoire. Would you do me a favor?

As usual, he did not stop playing.

—Your Americans. They have wonderful high-button boots. Just what I need to support my ankle. Would you ask them for a pair? They look so fine . . .

—Listen, you could use a bath!

—Don't worry . . . as soon as this damned cast is off . . . OK, then, for the boots?

—Sure, sure. I'll try.

It was almost too easy. With the lieutenant, I went to a military hospital, an old chateau in the midst of fields of sprouting wheat and ash trees. Here, the soldiers wore the uniform of blood, red bathrobes, faces as white as the bandages, red packets in the little carts pushed around by the nurses.

—I meant to ask you, Grégoire. What's the matter with your brother? On Sunday I noticed his leg . . .

—It's his ankle.

—If he needs treatment here . . .

I told him about the boots.

—Certainly, this very evening.

Fabien would find this the natural course of things. I imagined myself coming home: "Here are your boots . . . " "Right!"

—Grégoire, since we're talking about this visit last Sunday . . . I know that your family . . . well, they're sophisticated but kind. Your father and mother will have understood that my men are like kids. Even you, Grégoire, are more mature than they are. Oh, yes. I want to mention this childish scene ("childish," he put it well, "childish") with the flags. Obviously it was their idea. A sweet, touching and childish idea . . . They're not used to foreigners, nor death, nor the ways of the world.

We got back in the jeep. Premature warmth with a sky half-rain and half-sun. The jeep followed a narrow road between plowed fields and stands of wheat. Everywhere, larks caught the light in the beat of their rushing wings. I seemed to hear their song.

—We don't have larks in America, said the lieutenant.

. . . No larks, no cows, no houses like ours . . .

—You know Shelley? When you come to Princeton I'll teach you to love Chaucer, Shakespeare, Keats, Shelley: *Hail to thee, blithe spirit! Bird thou never wert* . . .

He quoted several poems, a professor in uniform, almost an impostor. I scarcely listened to him. I thought of George with his little flags, Tex with his coffee, Dick, Bill, Harry, Sam, father of a son my age and yet as "childish" as the

others . . . Anyway, I liked them. Too bad about the lieutenant, about Fabien, about all the complicated ones. I preferred the kids, their motorcycles, their laughter, their joy
as simple as their sadness. I loved their sweet, touching,
and childish idea. It was not in me to be ashamed of them,
even if I was to learn poems at Princeton about the birds.
That was to be my adventure . . . to learn about Shakespeare
. . . But one day, during vacation, one day I would take a
motorcycle and go across their country from one ocean to
the other, across the plains, the forests and the deserts, over
the Rockies. Since they were kids, I would play with them.
In towns and cities I would stop the passers-by. "Isn't it a
nice day?" Farmers, workers and shopkeepers, Negroes
and Indians, sailors and cowboys. From one coast to the
other they would learn to recognize my red motorbike. A
country tailor-made for speed, a young country for the
young.

Here, an old country for the old. Who understood me?
Not even my brother. Only Marie understood me and yet
. . . she knew only a Grégoire made to order, a Grégoire
invented for her, a copy of Grégoire.

I said to myself, "Grégoire, perhaps you shouldn't have."
But time was pressing. Soon Fabien would be back on his
bike; an end to the daily walks with Marie. I must write to
her before that, at once.

Dear Marie,
  It surprises you that I want to leave for America. I so
love our Normandy, the horses, the farms, the hedges. It's
Europe and its wars that I want to leave behind. In the
United States, French, Germans, and Italians have found
their melting pot . . .

Why not? Mother herself said that I looked like Uncle Henri. His ideas suited me too. After this first letter, Marie said to me:

—You're very nice, Grégoire .

. . . and on the eve of the Mardi Gras holidays, after my third letter:

—You will come back to France all the same? Some day?

I think those were her last words, the last that I remember. Perhaps one morning she called out to me. "Grégoire!" A flash of surprise, my name written in full detail in that voice. Just time to turn around in my saddle to see her silhouette on her outdated bike; scarcely time for a wave before Fabien disappeared; I also disappeared, hidden, like Fabien, by the falling away of the road, by its steep slope. What an effort to catch up with him! What pain there was in this race with inner regret: "Farewell, Marie!" With shame: "You understand that I must go with him?" With fear: "You understand that if he knew, if he guessed, he would make fun of us?"

A few days later, after a game of chess, Mr. Godefroy said to Mama as she offered him his port:

—The house seems empty without my granddaughter.

—She'll be back in the summer . . .

—Oh, not so soon. My son has been sent to Rabat.

Then it was the Americans' turn. An abrupt departure without saying goodbye. The day before Easter, I went up to pay them a visit but found unfamiliar soldiers unloading a truck in front of the barracks.

I went towards them, searching for a friendly face. One of them, with the jaw of a prize-fighter and a Southern accent, called to the others:

—Hey, guys, here's a froggie looking for a man for his little sister!

They laughed.

—If she's as pretty as he is I wouldn't pay two packs of cigarettes.

Answer in English? Show that I knew their slang? Ask, at least, for my friends' address?

I went away, half angry, half sad. So, they had gone off without warning me. What was a friendship like that worth? As for their replacements, this aggressive vulgarity? Childish . . . the lieutenant would have said "a childish attitude."

A few days later I received a package from the lieutenant. The postmark read "Colmar." I pictured him standing in line at the post office among the housewives. The package contained a pair of long trousers in khaki and, in one pocket, a card with his address at Princeton University.

A return of good weather. Again we had our breakfast on the terrace, tracing a new path in the untrodden grass. As always, Fabien became irritable.

—We'll be late. Hurry up!

He had not reinvented our game but we still biked too fast down towards Rouen. Was it only a race? Never a challenge at the start. At the finish the victor was silent. My bicycle hung up in the schoolyard, I got the shivers and again saw Fabien on the road, ankle broken: my ankle one of these days. But I didn't want to be the one to say: "OK, you've got more guts than I have."

He wanted that too much. I wouldn't admit it for anything in the world. Since he had thrown away his crutches, put on his boots, and resumed his usual place among us, one detail confirmed our falling out: a few centimeters was my revenge, for when I spoke to him my chin was level with his eyes. In the end I would have forgiven him his contempt for the Americans, the loss of Marie. I would have granted him everything , except my fear, but that was the only thing he wanted of me.

—Have you thought of your exams, Grégoire? Still two months to go!

How slowly time passed!

—Grégoire, only one more month!

At the beginning of May, the armistice was signed and that evening , from the terrace, we watched the fireworks over Rouen. Blue, white, and red rockets, a joyful remembrance of the bombings, they made a bonfire of cartridges and bombs that from now on were useless.

One morning , Fabien handed me a post card from Marie, palm trees and minarets. "Hold on, this is for you!" No hint of mockery in his voice. Had he read the text? 'To each, his own America."

—It's in three weeks, boys.

Twenty days like twenty Mondays. Fabien didn't play the piano any more. Dates, formulas, theorems, definitions, Q. E. D. In our books, pages of text looked like lines of insects that flew away as the eyes grew tired.

After great forebodings, the small joy of being successful candidates. Then the distress of idleness. What to do?

To leave the grayness of books, to be dazzled by the June sun. From the terrace you could barely glimpse the Seine through the foliage. I listened to nightingales for an hour; I went down to Rouen: the passers-by no longer diverted me. I knew them all and they were no longer passers-by. Ride my bicycle? After races on motorcycles? And the countryside, much too green, made me sick. Fields of wheat, of barley and oats, peasants who spoke only the language of horses: "Whoa! Gee! Giddup!" I waited for a thunderstorm that would restore fragrance to the grass.

Dream, of course, but of what? Of the past? I could hardly remember Marie's face: an adventure seen dimly in retrospect. As to the future, a year of patience before America, and what America? The land of a professor and a dead uncle.

A curious summer: I no longer knew how to play, I didn't yet know how to interest myself in things. This boredom came to me not so much from the world around me as from within myself. I carried it under my skin, it weighed me down, slowing my movements and slowing down time. My thoughts didn't matter because they didn't surprise me anymore, I saw them coming. "It's my fault," I said to myself. " I've learned to know myself because I haven't been able to change quickly enough."

Finally, the last luncheon for Fabien. His two bags waited upstairs in his bedroom, put in order. On the white tablecloth lay the menu for grand occasions. A luncheon of sun and rain; I saw, through the windows, the passing clouds , some white, some gray, and a few drops of light on the wet panes. Wood fire and roast chicken.

—You, too, Grégoire, more quickly than one would believe, said my father.

The wind stirred the leaves of the oaks and I judged its strength by the number of window panes it caused the branches to sway across.

—Today, Fabien. In a year, Grégoire! my father repeated.

—Yes, but America is so far away, said Mama.

—Oh, not that much farther, my dear.

A drop of white wine on the lip of the glass. Would it

fall? Wine from before the war, carried up from the wine cellar in its dusty bottle. Strawberry tarts. My father and Fabien covered their slices with crème fraîche, a cloud of powdered sugar.

—When is the train?

No need to respond. Papa knew the answer, as we had all known it for a week. The gold of his watch, placed on the tablecloth. A bottle of champagne.

—And then, there will be hunting this autumn . . .

A new shower rattled against the windowpanes. Bubbles rose in the clear crystal flutes of champagne.

—My children . . .

We waited. Papa said "my children" several times, rose and sat down again, his hands spread flat at each side of his glass. Freckles, veins, nails. His little finger touched his watch.

—Let's hope . . . in the end you will hope one day . . . you'll see when you are sixty-four . . . that this life we have lived may not be a special page of history and that you lived years like mine, like ours. To be sure, you will work, though I have had the good luck and the bad luck of not working. But not in an office! Just a few journeys and much happiness . . .

He held the flute of champagne between his fingers and went on talking without drinking from it. He described a mysterious life, a permanent examination to succeed in each day. He sat upright in his chair; between his back and the cushion were a few centimeters of space, or rather of habit, his discipline.

II

Chapter 1

A bird floated on the breaking wave: a sea gull, a herring gull? Why did it stay on the water? "Take to your wings! Find a bird of your own kind!" The September sea, sunlight on the spray in the wind from the west, three rays of light under the clouds. The moon between the clouds. The ship's bow plows from one wave to the next, one harbor to the next, one day to the next. I was waiting for a storm. What 's the good of crossing the ocean without experiencing one? What is the average life of a bubble of foam? Will this one get all the way to the horizon? Bubbles in the wake, light on the dark waves. Among the bubbles, a rain that had not come by way of the rivers. A drop of water in the sea. Fresh water squandered on the froth.

On the deck of the *Columbia* I thought about my family at our parting, planted in a row of three on the dock at Le Havre. That afternoon I had summoned up enough pride to hide my panic, sure, however, that the parting was not worth the pain: my illusions had drawn me away from them and now I had abandoned my parents to try to make a few games of childhood come true. At a hundred meters, already their absence left me with a tearful emptiness. It was the liner that disappointed me. On a sailing ship I would have left joyfully, giving up this beautiful memento of pain.

"He'll see New York before Paris."

"Who?"

"Engivane!"

"Engivane's never seen Paris? At seventeen?"

"He went directly from Rouen to Le Havre."

They looked at me with kindness.

"That's the modern world for you," said the general.

"That's only the beginning, " said the engineer.

"He'll be American in a month," said the women.

Certain traces of democracy left behind by the war lived on with the *Columbia*, a steamer of the Transatlantic Line transformed into a hospital ship and not yet restored to its class system. The men slept in a dormitory and took their showers in a common bathroom. I borrowed the general's bar of soap; tufts of black hair were scattered on the diplomat's back, the engineer was knock-kneed; the nuclear physicist, a mountain climber in his spare time, won the prize for the "least revolting."

"The other, the prize for the 'most revolting,' I award to myself," explained the organizer of the contest. Fingers posed in the shape of a tulip, he raised his hand, and his eyes, his upper lip promised such a retort that no one contradicted him. A minute of silence celebrated his victory. Then, cheeks puffed up, Perrault performed an imitation of a hunting horn. Taking up his brush again, he scrubbed every fold of his skin. "Do you think, General, that this obesity will make me exempt from military service?" Imitation of a trumpet. "I would be devastated!"

Finally, bad weather was reported, what the officers called "backwash from the tail of a hurricane." In the dining room the waiters fastened down the tables and chairs, more and more passengers skipped meals. Intimacy grew. "Always a good appetite?" We talked of Conrad. "Although I was in the infantry . . . " said the general.

The same room was used for all the games: bridge for the general and the diplomat, the engineer's chess tourney in which I participated every evening. At the end of the room , the bar and the orchestra. The ladies fought over Perrault. Small feet, black pumps, his agility in the waltz, in spite of the rolling of the ship, bore witness to his weight. I forgot my chess game to watch him enviously, surrounded by ladies with their perfume and their silks in fragile hands. A redhead with gray eyes asked him about the sea. He called out to two hazel-eyed sisters: "My name is Charles Perrault de Peygues, as in peg-leg, you know?"

In the afternoon, the women arrived by twos, sat down by fours. Their petticoats, their knees. Madame "You-don't-dance?" sat down in the interval between two walzes. The wife of the engineer " . . . never, never been to Paris?"

They all knew me: "Good evening, Grégoire." At the doors, on the stairs, along the corridors, they answered my greetings. But I knew only one of them, the only familiar person on this ship, her face devoid of make-up, her woolen dress, a woman of my mother's generation. At ten after five she greeted me in the salon, "I was waiting for you, Grégoire," and ordered tea for two. Peking, Shanghai, the Han dynasty, Confucius, she taught Chinese philosophy at Yale. An oriental profile though born in Châteauroux. To myself, I named her "Madame de Chine."

—I've written to my son, Grégoire, and he will phone Fabien. Since they like music, it's easy.

She talked to me about my family, about my house, forgetting nothing I had told her in the past few days.

—Since your father is sensitive to the cold, Grégoire, send him some wool shirts. They make very thick ones in America.

At a neighboring table, a young girl knitted some gloves. She had slipped off her left shoe and caressed the carpet with her foot.

—At the University they will ask you what career you have chosen. The military? The sciences? Politics?

I looked around me: the diplomat scolded the general who had not played clubs, the engineer sneezed.

—I don't know, Ma'am.

—Never mind. Tell the truth. It's worse to make up a vocation.

A pianist played *le Petit Vin Blanc*. The passengers assembled at the bar while the waiters replaced the empty teapots on the tables with platters of green olives . . . The lights were lowered and a reader closed his book. My eyes met those of Madame "You-don't-dance?" who took a cigarette from her lips and smiled. Madame de Chine gathered her bag and her needlework. The engineer called to me:

—If you have white, what attack this evening?

—Queen's pawn.

A discussion of chess. Other groups were being formed around us discussing politics, literature, music. I envied their assurance, their nonchalance when they interrupted themselves to sip a drink of gin or whisky. The hem of a dress brushed my leg and I lost track of the fine points of a gambit of the queen's pawn, distracted each time the roll of the ship brought the skirt back against my knee. In three days the *Columbia* would arrive in New York and I had not yet danced . . .

Outside, the night masked the wind. I walked on the deck of the *Columbia* counting the lines of waves, white rows more or less parallel, which advanced according to the familiar rhythm of this dress that I had just fled. The bell for dinner rang, distant behind closed doors. Back at La Chêneraie, what time would it be? Ten? Eleven? Goodbye, family, good night, family. What a shame they had no other child to keep them company. Mother talked about a daughter they had wanted in the past, a sister who would have taught me to dance like Perrault, to banter with girls as he did. After "good morning," what was there to say? I, who knew so well how to talk with the unknown passers-by of Rouen!

The waves sometimes slapped the prow, sometimes caressed it. Had the sea birds all gone before the storm? Gone where? The wind whistled in my partly opened mouth, producing different notes when I rounded my lips in a pout.

From its time as a hospital ship all the bulkheads were still white and the furnishings, a few posters, some curtains weren't enough to hide this whiteness.

Had the red bathrobes of the wounded Americans, seen at the Agricultural School, travelled here?

At a neighboring table the general bid six spades. The nuclear physicist, all the while chatting with Madame de Chine, tapped me on the head:

—With his talent for chess, this boy ought to make a scientist. What will you study at Princeton, Grégoire?

—Oh, surely math and English literature. I know an American lieutenant who gives a course on Chaucer at Princeton.

—Well, I'm not worried about you. Bravo, General! You bid the grand slam?

The pianist played *Tea For Two*. Sometimes Madame de Chine looked at me over her glasses, sometimes her eyes returned to her needlework. With a silk thread she picked blue stitches into her embroidery. We knew each other well enough now to appreciate this silence. The day after tomorrow the voyage would come to an end and this woman was my sole conquest, a dear old lady as tranquil as my countryside . . . Gray suit, a small cigar, Perrault approached, bowed over her, speaking with his accent from La Drôme:

—My father will be glad to learn that we have made this voyage together. Did you know that he has retired? An end to the university, he's returned to Peygues to eat rabbits and chestnuts. He wants to finish his famous book on Malherbe.

—You will come to visit me at Yale, Perrault. With Grégoire?

—*Oui, Oui.* (A tenor voice dragging out the "i.") Dear Grégoire, I've neglected him because I know we will have time at Princeton. Isn't that so, Grégoire? Every morning we take our showers together. We are very clean chaps! You will excuse me . . . I see a young lady who claims (the left hand raised in the shape of a tulip) that Kierkegaard is a pessimist. She must have read that in *le Petit Larousse*.

Perrault's buttocks steered around the tables as he crossed the room.

Madame de Chine had just stood up; she brushed a few colored threads, fallen on her dress, with the back of her hand, while speaking to me so softly that I had difficulty singling out her voice in the hum of the room.

—I know the Peygues well. They are Protestants from La Drôme, wealthy before the war from an American dowry which they've spent. When you are at the university, Grégoire, you'll take care of Perrault, won't you? He'll need your help.

What? Me, the poor Grégoire who had not danced, help Perrault? By what masquerade had I managed to make her think I would be able to?

—You don't like him, perhaps?

—But yes . . .

—He is all talk, like certain shy people.

She had taken off her glasses and tucked them in their case. When the lieutenant took off his glasses, he, too, spoke to a different Grégoire. The grey wool dress moved away, passing between the dresses of silk and rayon; I could make out, for a moment yet, her white hair among all the colors of hair. Would my mother have white hair when I returned?

A walk on the deck was already a habit. A warm breeze of summer's end hardly rippled the sea, calm as a field at nightfall. A tranquil hour during which the passengers remained hidden below decks, gathered in the salon, a town hidden from sight where they crowded themselves together, leaving to me this plain of green water. If only I had met a girl here I would have known how to speak to her in this almost silent place and I would have lent her my jacket since townfolk always feel cold in the country.

—So, Grégoire!

—Good evening, General!

—A breath of fresh air for the appetite?

—Yes, sir, every evening . . .

—Tell me, Grégoire, what are you going to study in America . . . and aren't you afraid of being alone there?

—I have an aunt in New York, General.

—Ah, these new generations! Let's go to dinner!

The return of the convalescents filled up the dining room. They talked again of Conrad. The sisters with the hazel eyes, returning to my table, picked at their food. A waiter brought them herb tea. To which one of them would I have lent my jacket up there on the deck? The elder smiled more often than the younger sister, fuller breasts, more cheerful, less mysterious. The older one for Fabien, the younger for me.

—You are from Rouen, isn't that right?

The older sister was speaking to me.

—Before the war we spent our summers at Étretat. That's not far from you.

Cliffs, tides, pebble beaches, the rain and sunny spells of Normandy, we traded memories. The younger sister preferred the pastures and the fields of flax of the Pays de Caux, while the older knew all the rocks on the coast. At the end of the meal, when we left the table, I took each by the arm, thinking "how easy this is."

—Are you coming to the salon?

—Please excuse us, Grégoire. If we hadn't been so seasick . . .

—Good night, Grégoire. See you tomorrow.

I remained alone, standing and smiling while an inner voice shouted "shit!" at these two saintly untouchables. Just one dance . . . If one of them had granted me one dance I would have been saved, vindicated. I would have been able to withdraw to the other side of the room where the engineer and the professor were setting up the chess boards.

The orchestra had hardly begun to play and three couples were dancing already. I watched the door, but the women were arriving two by two, followed by a husband or some man, a lucky lover, perhaps. With sweating hands, I strolled in rhythm among these couples, walking sometimes to a waltz, sometimes a fox-trot. Perrault had the redhead with down on her cheeks. Would he lend her to me just for one dance, a half of a tango, slow and easy?

—You don't dance, Grégoire?

—But yes . . .

Madame "You-don't-dance?" came into my arms. I moved at random. "The music," she said. I recognized the tune of *Sentimental Journey*, often heard in the American barracks in Rouen, and a few words of the song came back to me: *Seven, that's the time we leave, at seven* . . . Madame "You-don't-dance?" pushed me, pulled me, murmured "Pa-Pim-Pa-Pan Pa-Pim-Pa-Pan," She held me close and I breathed in her hair, dyed blonde with black roots. Almost all the other couples danced with their eyes closed. I tried to make my mind a blank but each time I lost the rhythm Madame "You-don't-dance?" called me to order "Pa-Pim-Pa-Pan Pa-Pim-Pa-Pan."

She didn't let me go. Waltzes: "Pa-Pa-Pim Pa-Pa-Pim Pa-Pa-Pim, Pa-Pa." Tangos: "Pa-Pim-Pa-Poum, Pa-Pim-Pa-Poum, Pa-Pim-Pa-Pèrrre." Paso dobles: "Ta-ta-Ti, Ta-Ta-Ter, Ta-Ti-Ta-Ti-Ta-Ter." In two hours I learned to dance, but when I regained my cabin I was shaking with fatigue and I had to take a shower. All through the night her voice pursued me: "Pa-Pim-Pa-Pan." The professor snored, the general coughed, Perrault was the last to bed and undressed in the dark singing .

After breakfast, as I left the dining room, a steward called to me:

—Mr. Engivane, you're wanted in Number One Thirty.

One Forty-eight, One Thirty-six, One Thirty-two, One Thirty. "Come in!" There, under the porthole, stretched out on her bunk, Madame "You-don't-dance?"

—Push the bolt, Grégoire, the door doesn't close very well.

Little Red Riding Hood. "The better to eat you, my child."

—How nice of you to come, she said. Sit here!

With her hand she patted the bunk. I tried not to hesitate.

—So nice this visit. So beastly to be in bed in such good weather!

Under her transparent nightgown, I saw everything.

—He blushes!

She spoke in a low voice now.

—You've never seen a woman's breasts?

She laughed.

In the cabin they were all there watching me: my mother, my father, Fabien, the lieutenant, and Marie Godefroy.

Chapter 2

"Are there men inside there?"

Stalks of concrete gilded by the sunlight. What a harvest! The inhabitants will look like the Statue of Liberty, giants in bronze robes. Seated at the foot of the island they play on these organs to welcome us: OOO . . . UUU . . . AAA . . . sirens.

The *Columbia* sailed through oil slicks, liquid flags on the flat water. Already America surrounded us. I held the sisters with the hazel eyes by the elbows, regretting, in the same moment, that the voyage wouldn't last another ten days and that the ship was so slow to dock. Madame "You-don't-dance?" was hastily giving out her address. The general said again and again: "What a country! When I think that I am seeing this for the first time . . . what a country!" Thus the general and I at this instant were the same age, two New World newborns on this beautiful afternoon in September.

The gangplank lowered, confusion began. From Customs to Passport Control, time grew ever more sluggish as the distance diminished. I spent two hours covering the last few meters, happy to have only one suitcase since a porters' strike condemned the passengers to carrying their own baggage.

I was in America. I crossed an avenue paved in gray where a policeman in marine blue, mounted on a chestnut horse, surveyed the green and yellow taxis. My bag on my shoulder, I went down a street, one of those curiously flat

57

streets seen in films. Where were the skyscrapers? Was this the same city as the one we saw from the ship? Dirty walls of pink brick, yellow paint scaled from a building where a washing of pink panties and blue undershorts hung from one window to another. Against a fence, debris, boards and a crate full of rusty scrap iron and broken bottles. Suitcase on the other shoulder now, I pushed forward from detail to detail, object to object, step by step, and everything was new to me, boxes for garbage and boxes for mail, intersections with their streets at right angles marked off by green and red lights.

Finally, I came across inhabitants, three men who were loading a truck, two women seated on some stone steps who were peeling carrots. I heard shouts whose sadness I recognized: the first autumn recesses, cries floating about by chance like dead leaves, school that begins again after summer. In a vacant lot, half-dirt half-asphalt, some boys were passing around an oval ball, red hair, black hair, blue denim pants, white tee-shirts illustrated in multi-colored designs.

The lieutenant wiped his glasses. "You're lucky, Grégoire! Ask Sam. He has a son your age. His son plays in the streets."

And these boys? Had they ever seen a cow?

The ball bounced onto the sidewalk. I threw it back.

—Have you ever seen a cow?

—A what?

—A cow.

He must have been ten. He turned to the others.

—Hey, guys! You know what he asked me? If I've ever seen a cow.

—A what?

—A cow!

The ball, forgotten, rolled up to the sidewalk. The boys came over , ten, thirteen, seventeen years old. A dog barked at the end of the street. A dozen boys, some fat, some thin, all with the same white teeth.

—... elephants, tigers, lions at the zoo, monkeys.

—... cows in the movies. In the Westerns, they're full of cows.

—... on TV.

Me too, me too, me too, me too.

—... who is this character?

—... the suitcase!

—... hey, kids! Seen his cap?

—... this guy's no American!

They followed me along the sidewalk: "His hat! His hat!" They pulled up at the edge of Tenth Avenue; when I crossed, their cries disappeared behind the trucks and buses.

How long did it take me to realize that I was wandering? First I noticed that it was hot, wiping the sweat from my forehead with my beret, opening the bag to put in my coat, opening it again to look in a pocket for my aunt's address: 97 East 38th Street . . . Then I saw that it was evening: vanished, the flaking walls. The dull gray of the sidewalks was replaced by an electric cleanliness in the blue and yellow glare of neon lights.

Whom to ask for my way? I looked for someone strolling by but all the pedestrians were in a rush and I had to go into a shop to get directions. In one thrust, I reached Broadway where the crowd and the light brought me to a halt.

The bottom of a goldfish bowl! The air was as heavy as water, saturated with shades of red, with mixtures of purple and orange. Times Square to the right. The square of our time. No facades, just words: WILD BETTER BEST SWEET TERRIBLE FAST FABULOUS AMAZING GOOD. On, off, on, each word cast a different color on the faces of the crowd, on the throng of girls, arm in arm, on families idling along, young men elbow to elbow. Necks drenched with sweat, wiped away with the swab of a handkerchief. Chewing on cigars. I walked along invisible because those who jostled me, those I jostled, didn't look at me and only the posters watched me, their smiles following each and every one of us. Eat us! Drink! Smoke us! Whiffs from the subway, from exhaust fumes, from meat grilled by Negroes in white shirts.

But as soon as I crossed 42nd Street no more people, the neon lights and the crowds disappeared. Soon I would come to my aunt's house. I put my coat back on. A man in livery walked a poodle. His patient pace kept up with the frantic scampering of the dog. Address in hand, I read the numerals on the door: 97. I had already rung the bell.

Imbecile! Too late now to think things over, to step back and measure the distance covered since that first letter from Aunt Laura, opened solemnly one Thursday morning at La Chêneraie . "But leave the past alone! Someone's coming to the door, take off your beret . . . How dirty I am! Should I say something right away about Uncle Henri? Not speak of him at all? Bravo, Grégoire, this is the first time you've rung a doorbell and already you're in a panic."

—Good evening, Sir!

—Good evening!

A servant, bald-headed, dressed in black, held out his hand: I offered him mine, but he took my suitcase. A door opened into the entrance:

—It's you at last, Grégoire! Where have you been?

Four meters of beige carpet to step across to the gray rug of the living room. They were three: a little girl, a man, and my aunt. Should I kiss them on the cheek or on the hand? Mother forgot to tell me. My aunt's hand, my cousin's cheeks: "You must be Jeanie?"

And Aunt Laura's father: "How are you?"

—Jeanie ought to be in bed. She wanted to wait up for you.

—She looks like my mother.

—Yes, and like her father.

That was the moment to say something about him. I ought to have prepared the words. But what was there to say? Above all, nothing about death. Evoke some memory? Which one? I have so few.

—But where were you, Grégoire? We looked all over for you at the boat.

—I came straight away. I haven't taken more than an hour . . . an hour and a half.

—An hour? Your taxi must have taken you to Brooklyn!

—What taxi?

—Surely you came in a taxi!

—No, on foot.

—Why? Didn't you have any money?

—I could have. Didn't think of it . . . I've never taken a taxi . . .

I was in the wrong. I had botched my arrival, my entrance. But I feel a warmth in the hollow of my hand and a child's fingers in my fingers. Jeanie is beside me. I ask myself what color are her eyes? This question becomes all-important, as if my fate depended on it, and I lean down to her.

—How old are you?

61

—Six and a half.

To answer me she looked up at me and I saw her gray-blue eyes, my mother's eyes, and mine. Her name was Jeanie Cahan, this cousin of mine. That helped, to be a member of the family. Meetings are so stupid when they are premeditated: an examination instead of an adventure. In a few weeks, a few months, the moves of this first meeting will seem ridiculous like the fumblings of a child in a blindfold who looks for obstacles, holds out his arms, raises his legs, deafened by the laughter of spectators who have pulled away chairs and sofas. But our spectator is silent in his photograph in uniform. Soon it will be two years since Uncle Henri died. Is Aunt Laura going to remarry? That is the most important question in this room, an invisible piece of furniture not to be blundered into, there, between the sofas and the tables. Unless this question is hung on the wall next to the Géricault in which two horses drink the white shadow from a trough. What color does this mourning have? Does it wear out with time? Black cats, when they grow old, become rusty and gray, gray like the rug where Jeanie has seated herself, an orphan in a yellow dress. For the widow, a green dress. The color of hope? She leans over Jeanie: both at the center of the mirror. *Widow*, the English word that I confused with *window*. I had written "the window puts on mourning," and the professor amused my classmates with this mistranslation. I had imagined black curtains. Here the two windows are draped in gray silk.

—Are you hungry, Grégoire?

—Yes. I haven't eaten since noon.

—Your English is good, said Aunt Laura's father. A little military, but the university will straighten out your accent.

We moved to the table and, seating himself, he said:

—Usually we dine at eight o'clock.

So! From one routine to another, a few thousand miles to dine a half hour later. A long narrow head, green tie and yellow mustache, my aunt's father looked like a mallard posed on the blue tablecloth. In a bowl, some red peonies. Silver forks with three tines, plates for salad, for butter, for soup, crystal glasses. I watched their hands and took my lead from their slow movements, sure that the butler was observing me to see if I was used to being rich. Ah well, yes! Poverty in Rouen? I'd never noticed it. It took this greater wealth to teach me. The lieutenant said: "You're lucky, Grégoire!"

This luck continued the next morning when the butler carried one of Uncle Henri's suits into the bedroom for me to try on. He must have been almost as thin as me, this unknown uncle, for I scarcely felt his presence in his coat on my back. My hands fell easily into the pockets where I found a train ticket. What was he going to do in Boston, my Uncle Henri?

They gave me everything: shirts, undershorts, socks, suits for summer, for winter and for between seasons, everything but his ties. Perhaps Aunt Laura wanted to preserve them in a mahogany chest, or did they frame the photo of the deceased in her room?

I walked on the streets of New York and the suit changed my step. The city no longer seemed strange to me now that I was dressed like its inhabitants. Besides I hardly saw the city because the suit completely absorbed me, wrapped me in a remembrance of mothballs and of sorrow for the deceased that I was replacing. Would he be pleased with me if he could see me? If he could see us? His gestures brought to life by movement: "Arise, and walk!"

—Usually we have lunch at one, Aunt Laura's father had said.

At noon I returned to the house. In the hall, I met the butler, his arms full of my dirty laundry. "It will be done tomorrow, Sir!" Something in his voice made me ashamed. A return to humility, to myself. I felt ill at ease with this suit. I hesitated in front of my bedroom closet. Put on my old clothes? Now they seemed to me to be childish and shabby but I didn't dare to go downstairs for fear of meeting my aunt, disguised this way in her husband's clothes.

In my hesitation, time passed. "So what! I'll see." I tried to reassure myself, to recover my usual manner as I entered the living room. A burst of laughter greeted me:

—Grégoire, you look like a Methodist minister!

Aunt Laura near the window. I thought, the Merry Widow . . . What sort of a widow? She didn't even have black hair like the little orphan, but light hair, the color of American tobacco: Chesterfields, Lucky Strikes, Old Golds.

—*I am sorry!* Do you know about Methodist ministers?

Her face held traces of laughter. I avoided the windows, looking for shade. At each step the trousers tickled my calves.

—Thank you for the suits.

---Oh no! It was my father who saw at once that you were just Henri's size.

Then in French:

—*Henri, ca lui ferait plaisir, n'est-ce pas?*

["That would make Henri happy, wouldn't it?"]

She spoke French in a graver voice than in English; the voice, the language, of her mourning.

—You sure do look like Mr. Henry, Master Gregory.

The Negro placed this observation in the bedroom with my suitcase.

—Thank you, Slow!

—But you're thinner and you speak better American. He spoke English, Mister Henry. The English of England.

An elm branch outside the window projected a green shadow on the white walls of my room, another souvenir of La Chêneraie to go with the smell of the musty stone and wood of old houses. The Negro had driven us there. Under his octagonal cap, gray hair. Had his ancestors come from Niger or from Lake Tanganyika? On the concrete highways crossing the marshes and the factory smoke of New York's surroundings, the Cadillac lulled us among the trucks. Then the roads became narrower and narrower until we reached a dirt and gravel road at the end of which stood a house of gray stone on a green lawn, as simple as a child's drawing.

—At the Port of Missing Men, we dine at a quarter to eight.

With his index finger, Aunt Laura's father wiped away an imaginary spot on his left hand. I had just rejoined him in the living room, where he stood in front of a great fireplace, his brow, almost bald, haloed by a bouquet of yellow chrysanthemums behind him.

—Call me Uncle George. We'll see each other often during the next few years. I'll be your *"loco parentis."* You've studied Latin?

On a table, in a leather frame, our family smiled in the photo sent to Aunt Laura almost two years ago. Fabien, Mama, Papa, and me: "Throw away those ridiculous crutches," my father shouted at Fabien. My father played with a ruler, the lieutenant wiped his glasses, Uncle George brushed at an imaginary spot on his hand.

—You know, Grégoire, when I say *"loco parentis"* that doesn't mean that I'm the one who pays. Your aunt is paying for your studies. It's her idea, a good idea to be sure. She has the money that her mother left her when she died and the Port is hers. The house in New York is mine. Not that it makes a great difference, but she is so young, she wouldn't have explained it. It's better when all this is explained.

He grew quiet when Jeanie came in.

---Greg! Tomorrow, will you take me with you in the boat?

Leaning forward, Uncle George filled his pipe. Since he was not paying for me his mannerisms seemed less menacing. They became vulnerable and benevolent. Perfect teeth on the black stem of his pipe. With his scarf of green silk and his gray hair parted to the left, he was a young man in retirement rather than an old man.

—Your cousin will take you in the boat, Jeanie, if you put on your life jacket.

Jeanie was my guide to the Port of Missing Men. Not worrying about the big picture, she showed me a thousand details: the burrow of a woodchuck, an overhanging rock where one could take shelter in case of rain, the oak knocked down by last summer's storm. Seated at the stern of the rowboat, she told me to go right, left, and again left. The creek passed through the fifteen hundred acres of the estate, flowed down towards the sea between two banks changing with the rhythm of the tides, sometimes the browns of the mud and the reeds, sometimes the greens and gray of trees and of rocks. In this landscape rock had as much importance as wood.

Great stones were strewn about or had been laid parallel to the slope by pioneers of another era; tumble-down walls marked out pastures, gardens, fields long since abandoned for the fertile plains of the Middle West.

—Faster, Greg! cried Jeanie. After ten strokes of the oars the rhythm slackened. I wanted this voyage of discovery to last as long as possible since only for this morning was the Port of Missing Men new to me. I was new to myself since I had come there.

—Look, Greg. Médor is waiting for us. Faster!

To have a Médor in her life. . . When does a name pass from the public domain to a dog, to his running, his swimming, his way of sitting on one haunch, to his black coat hanging loosely on his shoulders? Already Médor leaped against my chest at this first meeting and I almost fell over backwards.

—Sure enough, he's found you, said Slow.

The Negro had exchanged his chauffeur's hat for a butler's white coat. Shoes shined, face shining in a crown of pearls (his gray hair in the sunlight), he met me, his hands extended:

—Master Greg, I knew it! I knew it! You smell like Mr. Henry. The keeper, he had just unleashed Médor this morning when Médor went looking for you. I know his game. The same blood, the same scent. You see, this was your uncle's puppy. In the car, in their bedroom, hunting, in the city. It's one thing to look like a man, another to have his scent and Mister Henry, he was a good man. Right, Médor? Doesn't he smell like him? So, we'll have to show him our places, the places for pike, for ducks, for rabbits. He's one of the family, the young Frenchman. You'll find some blue teal for him, lay them out on the snow in front of him. Then, like Mr. Henry, he'll scratch your ears.

We went up toward the house, Jeanie and the dog ahead of us, Slow next to me, seemed to offer his remarks with the light-colored palms of his hands. I thought to myself: "Médor smelled the clothes, that's all," and this cold logic disgusted me; a vicious thought unworthy of the others' joy, especially unworthy of the sentimental image: beautiful child, fine Negro, good dog. I didn't want to belittle them, a pretty lesson in morality.

And what a lesson! A child of the rich, a dog of the rich, a Negro of the rich: happy, generous, warm towards one another, we often ate together in the kitchen, each time that Aunt Laura and Uncle George "went out." Then Slow took off his white coat. In his shirtsleeves, he fried chicken for us, made us raspberry shortcake.

—Your Uncle Henry. Jeanie's father here, he loved raspberries.

On all fours, behind a thicket, we looked for rabbits. A pistol stuck out of Slow's back pocket. Not a sound except for the quivering of Médor's tail in the dry grass.

—Fetch, Médor!

In a few bounds he caught the wounded animal, laid it in my hands.

—For sure, he's recognized his master, said Slow.

I was sorry when Uncle George and Aunt Laura dined at home. They often had guests, lawyers, Wall Street brokers, businessmen who also lived in New York and in the New Jersey countryside. Aunt Laura introduced me:

—This is Henri's nephew. Grégoire Engivane.

They poured me one, two cocktails.

—He needs to get used to them, said Uncle George. He 's entering Princeton in a few days.

I was fitting in badly. Where were "my" Americans: Sam, Bill, Dick, Tex, George, Harry? They spoke of rain or good weather in a world that I understood. Uncle George's guests talked about their business, their friends, politics. I knew only the names of Roosevelt, Stalin, de Gaulle, and I learned quickly that they didn't like these men who I thought were the heroes of the war. Churchill alone impressed them and they pitied the poor British who had deprived themselves of such a chief through their ingratitude.

I listened to them with a smile to thank them for the politeness they showed in speaking to me. And Paris? Paris hasn't suffered too much, has it? "What! You've never been there? A Frenchman who doesn't know Paris?" Aunt Laura came to my rescue:

—His parents live in a delightful Louis Treize house, in Normandy.

Standing at a window, I watched the birds on the lawn: orange and black orioles, red cardinals, blue jays came to eat the seeds that Slow scattered every evening at the foot of the elm. I finished my first cocktail. Aunt Laura had placed her hand on the wrist of a man, blond and well tanned, one of those Aryans whose photos were published in Pétainist magazines during the war. Would he take Uncle Henri's place? Just then Aunt Laura shook her head; she was much too pale beside the athlete. I read her lips: "No, Roger!" Silver shaker in hand, Uncle George went from armchair to armchair to offer a last cocktail before dinner, to say a few words to each guest: to the pale blue dress, to the mustard-colored suit, to the champagne dress, to the gray suit and to the emerald dress. None of these women aroused me like the nurses of the films. The available smile was missing. "America is not like it is in the movies, " said the lieutenant.

—And our student?

Uncle George filled my glass.

—Come on, one last effort!

Above the fireplace, a stuffed teal was in flight. Aunt Laura came toward me. I recognized the voice of her mourning:

—You're bored too, poor Grégoire! But you, you're a child. Time doesn't count yet.

Chapter 3

Get lost? Why not?

Not much risk of losing one's way on this "campus," this field of the University where the giant elms, the ivy, camouflaged a confusion of styles, Gothic, Colonial American, Victorian, Modern.

But to lose oneself in the confusion of ideas that the uniform of white shirts and gray flannels poorly disguised: atheists, Christians, bourgeois, anarchists, Marxists, scholarship students, millionaires, rebels, snobs, athletes, drunkards: all Puritans. Poets of eighteen, scholars of twenty, young libertines, young saints, the students scattered themselves on these sun-drenched lawns of autumn transformed into a market of ideas. The classic words came back to me, *Agora, Forum,* where everyone took himself for Socrates and Diogenes. To speak, to read, to write: words, each word disemboweled at its first encounter. What do they mean: freedom, faith, love, the future? Screw your dictionary! What are you trying to say?

—I mean the freedom to sit in the grass, the simple faith of the coal miner, love-hate, the future soon to come . . .

My thrusts didn't amuse and I realized I shouldn't laugh. These Puritans of language wanted a confession, wanted me to confide about myself just as they did at every opportunity. Man-to-man sincerity, a game for children who have already claimed the right to speak as men and aren't yet afraid to do so.

—Why did you come to America?

—To learn English.

—You speak it already.

—You never know a language completely!

—Then why not learn French in France?

I beat a retreat, the chess player, ashamed to admit I came out of love for Veronica Lake, by the accident of a living lieutenant and a dead uncle. A witticism, the truth raised too late: "I've come for a change of scenery . . . " That's the right answer!

Along a street lined with sycamores, I came on a wooden house painted yellow with pale blue shutters. A tiny woman opened the door and laughed when I asked for Lieutenant Harris.

—You mean Professor Harris, Grégoire.

She knew all about me. They had been waiting for me between these walls loaded with books and these children's toys scattered on the rug. They wanted to know everything: my family, the trip, Aunt Laura. I told them about my dirty underpants in the butler's arms.

—You've lost weight, Grégoire.

—These are my Uncle Henri's clothes. They're a little too big for me.

—Do you like your room, your roommates?

—I've hardly seen them. The very tall one said "Bonne jouar " and then laughed for five minutes. The shorter one invited me to lunch at his home on Sunday. But it's so different from France. Boys you've never seen before immediately ask questions that are so personal. They scare me a little.

The lieutenant handed me a plate, a gleam of light behind his glasses.

—You've nothing to fear, Grégoire. You're a solid boy.

In the center of the table, the spoon stuck in the vanilla ice cream gradually fell over. Why did the lieutenant think I was solid? Madame de Chine had put Perrault in my care. People didn't sense my cowardice? I would become an actor. I already wore the costumes of a dead man.

The Harris children went up to bed: one by one they kissed me good night, blue pajamas, pink pajamas. After this ceremony, silence.

—It's been a long time since Rouen, Grégoire. Not much more than a year, but the distance ... In fact, I didn't think you would come. These projects are so uncertain! Why did you come, Grégoire? What are you looking for in America? You must have thought about it.

—A change of scene.

We went into the living room. With his foot the lieutenant pushed the toys into a corner.

—Why not?

He uncorked a bottle of Calvados, "this also comes from Rouen, " and balanced two glasses on the arm of the sofa.

—And what do you want to study? Have you chosen your career?

—No!

Did he find me solid now? He looked into the bottom of his glass. To read my future?

— A good thing that there are boys like you, Grégoire ... But why, why?

— ... boys who are honest, ingenuous, or naïve. If you don't know what to do, you can always think it over. It could be literature, philosophy, mathematics, history. With your two diplomas, you'll enter here as a junior. You have two years to read, to talk. The change of scene will come of itself. Don't rush. See a little of America. The other one. Not the world of the butler and your dirty underwear . . .

After this lesson, I went back into an evening drenched with fog, with the sharp perfume of boxwood at the edge of the lawn. The smell of the country contrasted with the rhythm of the town each time that my heels struck the cement of the sidewalks. There was a line of street lights on the right where a dog trotted off and, beyond a house, the university library all lit up. " To lose oneself there, to lose oneself also in the landscape. I am free, free at every step and I don't even know what freedom means . . . except that in order to be free, one must lose oneself."

Several voices raised in song approached. A little group of Puritans of booze, somewhat the worse for wear:

> It was sad, Lord, sad
> It was sad, Lord, sad
> It was sad when that great ship went down
> To the bottom of the . . .

One of the singers fell on the grass. In attempting to lift him up the others also tumbled down, mouths open wide in a gay melody, half waltz, half polka:

> Husbands and wives
> Little children lost their lives
> It was sad when that great ship went down.

To lose oneself among the men. To play their game. To learn to be Christian and atheist, snob and rebel. To wear white bucks like the shadows that I met on the lawns. A voyage right here: "My new movie, my new adventure. I will know very well what freedom is on my return, if I return. "

Three of us shared an apartment in Foulke Hall, a Gothic tower with bathrooms and arched windows of leaded panes. From The Port of Missing Men, Slow had brought a rug, a lamp, a sofa which, with my two roommates' furniture, made for an apartment of many styles in beige, chestnut and gray. Three desks in the living room and three cots in the bedroom. . . I slept badly the first nights because I had always been alone in a bedroom and these new presences fascinated me. Can you tell the difference between two men by their breathing? For hours I listened to Peter Allan Stone and Peter Bull Graham sleep: Peter A and Peter B. The first was six feet tall and weighed two hundred pounds, the second had a white forehead between black hair and black eyebrows. My bed creaked. I didn't dare to budge for fear of waking my comrades. In the night, a churchbell rang again. A few voices passed beneath our window with a song:

> We are poor little sheep
> Who have lost our way
> Baaah, baaah, baaah
> We are little black sheep
> Who have gone astray . . .

In this university without women, night belonged to the Puritans of booze. Interrupted in his dreams, Peter B turned over: " I'm coming right away. " A voice hoarse with sleep.

Who was he talking to? To the drunks, to a woman, to God perhaps?

Before losing myself, it would be better to get organized and I registered for a course in contemporary history, a course in philosophy (aesthetics), a course on Shakespeare, a course in mathematics. I bought notebooks, ink, workbooks, a dictionary, and I felt new myself like all of this equipment. I went to the library to borrow some books and on this first visit I let myself wander: eleven floors of books, floors underground, buried books, interred standing up like dead noblemen, packed one against the other on their metal shelves and forming corridors without day or night, without seasons, corridors that I followed slowly, eyes half-closed to make it a matter of chance which book I picked. The one I pulled out opened and my finger pointed to a sentence: *that we should use our children, as we do our puppies . . .* Another book: *. . . may Congress make it a criminal offense against the United States—as by the 10th section of the act of 1898, it does . . . .* Still another: *Murmuraban los rocines a la puerta de Palacio . . .* From Russian, from German, from history, from Japanese, from music, from French. All these voices in the silence! Catalogued, filed in this silence! Seated on the tiled floor, I leafed through Rimbaud, Rivarol, Rivière, Rochefort.

When I left the library it was getting dark and I'd spent five hours choosing two books.

Peter A and Peter B had roomed together for two years so I was new to them. The first days, time passed too quickly for a confrontation. They, too, were getting themselves organized, having their meals in their club, paying visits to their friends. It was on the first Saturday that we found ourselves face-to-face, or, rather, conscious of one another, all three sitting in our room. I could feel that Peter B was not reading his newspaper, that Peter A was searching for an opener. I, too, searched, but what to say? To be intelligent without seeming pedantic, to be familiar without becoming too personal, to avoid prolonging this first silence, to avoid, especially, the truth game.

—Show us how your record player works, said Peter B.

He was right, action first, and we would get to know each other through these objects, these push buttons (" press that one and the record stops automatically.") Better to invent a routine than empty phrases . . .

—Greg, want to get out three glasses and the bottle of whiskey? I'll go get some water.

Peter A chose a Jelly Roll Morton record and picked up his clarinet: Ti-Taliata-Tip-Ta. He accompanied the pianist, a few notes at first, then more and more as he became sure of himself. A neighbor came in, then other students, one of whom was carrying a trombone.

—Call Bob! Call Banjo Bob! Call Bob!

From mouth to mouth the message was passed down the staircase and soon our janitor, our Negro, installed himself in the Gothic window seat with his banjo.

—Have a drink!

—Here's the trumpet!

—Shall we try *Chicago Mess Around*?

—Go on, Banjo Bob. Give us the note!

And jazz filled the room. Trombone-bear, banjo-monkey, clarinet- weasel running from one chair to the other, scrambling over the furniture, disappearing, reappearing: trumpet air and brass, riffs balanced on the rhythm of the banjo. The walls came apart with each blast: Jericho!

"Blow, man! Blow!" Faces open or closed to the music.

Indifference trampled underfoot. Alternating melancholy and fury. "Go! Go! Go!" Only the weight of the trombone prevented the trumpet from taking off. Biting words. Craziness, a prisoner of the clarinet, where fingers rushed up and down. The trombone is angry. The banjo laughs. "Sing, man! Sing!" Negro troubadour in his Gothic window, Banjo Bob:

> When the blues jump the rabbit
> They run it for a solid mile.
> Well, the rabbit he turn over
> An' cry like a motherless chile.

Clarinet rabbit, trumpet rabbit, banjo rabbit, whose paws took off, burned, but were recaptured by the trombone. Strings, silver keys, wood and brass, the music and the vibrations took their revenge on the man's voice. This time each word is ripped open by the music, buried in the rhythm, released again, and thrown against the walls. Tears of wood, tears of brass, the tears of the strings, the tears of the rabbit. "Go! Go! Go! We're all brothers and Old Banjo Bob is our dad!" *New Orleans Stomp, Saint Louis Blues, Frisco Ramble*, whatta trip! *Snake Rag, Balling the Jack*. Faster! "Blow, man! Blow!" *High Society*: the clarinet bragged so much you felt sorry for it. Each song a story, a mood. Each instrument an actor: trombone—comedian, trumpet—hero, clarinet—coquette, banjo—the setting. A new tune and new roles: trombone—simple-minded, trumpet—worried, clarinet—sweet, banjo—off to war . . . all interlaced. Music for each and for all, a laugh for Bob, a smile for Tom, a grumble for Harry, a drink for Peter A, to think or to dance, to move Peter B. Notes scattered, blown, pinched, taken up again, forgotten, rephrased, organized, and destroyed in the smoke of the room, humid with sweat, warm with noise which broke away, followed by the clarinet . . .

Pursued by the clarinet when the music stopped.

There was a silent retreat, hands in pockets the students went out. They abandoned the debris of the jam session on our rugs, empty beer bottles, empty glasses, overturned ashtrays.

—Let's go eat, said Peter A.

—Let's clean up first, said Peter B.

With a dustpan in one hand and a brush in the other, I was going over the rugs when Perrault arrived. He had a rolled-up newspaper which he held in his hand like a marshal's baton, puffing but with a smile on his lips. With agility he avoided a bottle, two ashtrays, crushed an armchair under his weight.

—I prefer . . . the waltz . . . to the stairs.

In the draft from the open windows the smoke blew in circles, thick as incense around this face delicately inscribed in the middle of pale cheeks. Still on all fours, I paid him homage, amazed that he had taken the trouble to pay me a visit, fulfilling a Chinese prophecy: "He will need your help at the University, Grégoire. "

—You're not going to introduce me, Engivane?

—Excuse me! Peter Allen Stone, Peter Bull Graham, meet my friend Charles Perrault de Peygues.

—As in peg-leg, you know?

A phrase, cast in his Oxford accent, that he let fall like a pearl before spreading out the *New York Times* in front of him. Still turned toward me, the dumbfounded looks of the two Peters hung in the air, looks which convinced me at once that Perrault already needed me. We resumed our clean-up in silence, interrupted now and then by an "oh!" an "ah!" or brief bursts of laughter from Perrrault inspired by the reading of his newspaper, so engrossed that he did not even move (perhaps not realizing their presence) when three young men in vest and tie came to invite me to join Slate Club.

Ceremonious visitors in their gray flannels, they stayed ten minutes and gave me two days to think about their offer, so sure of themselves that I was dying to laugh. Only the seriousness of the two Peters held me back.

—Congratulations, said Peter B as soon as they had left.

—Why so?

—That's the most prestigious club at Princeton.

—The hell with their club. I'd rather be with you. What's yours called?

—The Briar Club, said Peter A. I think it would be easy to arrange . . .

—What! You can't say such a thing to him, said Peter B. It's too good an opportunity. He needs to think it over. And he would make friends at Slate Club too.

—What's that? What are you saying? The Slate Club? Perrault folded his newspaper as he spoke.

—The Slate Club has bid Engivane, Peter A explained.

Perrault's face lit up and when he raised his hand his fingers formed a tulip.

—But that's the club of *my* grandfather.

— . . . and Engivane refuses!

—I prefer the club of the two Peters. And I say fuck these snobs, if you had seen their faces . . .

—It's not a question of snobbery, said Perrault. The important thing is not to be snubbed, that's the whole point.

—Students have hanged themselves because they weren't

invited to join Slate Club, added Peter B.

—Natural selection . . .

As soon as I said it, I regretted these words which could hurt Perrault. He seemed to take this business seriously and we all grew quiet. Perrault fished part of a sandwich out of his pocket, chewed ten times, twenty times, slipped the crumbs fallen on the newspaper into the palm of his hand. Perrault wore a vest and tie. He licked the crumbs from his hand. The silence was so awkward that Peter A began to play a tune very softly on his clarinet. Perrault rolled up his newspaper and kept time. I thought to myself: "What's he waiting for? Why doesn't he go back to his room? Perhaps those three young man are also going to his place? Have they slipped a card in his mailbox: 'The Slate Club requests the pleasure of Mr. Charles Perrault de Peygues *as in peg-leg . . .* "

Perrault plunged two fingers into his vest pocket and withdrew his American grandfather's watch . . . President of Slate Club 1898:

—Already ten o'clock! Are you coming to see my room, Grégoire?

I went down the stairs two at a time and waited for him at the bottom. He followed me slowly; in the confined space on the ship I had not noticed this dignity.

—Gray flannel pants and tweed jacket . . . You're superb, Engivane!

Paused on the next-to-last step, he lit a small cigar and looked at me through the smoke.

—These are my uncle's clothes, the one who died.

Perrault put his hand on my shoulder.

—You're such a peasant!

He set off, imposing his pace on me, going slowly in spite

of a light rain, stopping under a streetlight to pull up a fistful of turf which he sniffed, tasted, spat out:

—Sweeter than in Paris, he said. The bunnies here are
lucky.

 . . . And then . . .

—Naturally, I live on the ground floor.

Why "naturally"? Didn't he also rate a Gothic tower, a
chateau with stairways so wide that horses climbed three
abreast up to the salon? We arrived at his room; a bed, a
desk, a chair, were all the furniture in a room that was too
large for them. Unaffected by my presence, Perrault opened
his mail box: it was empty, no invitation from Slate Club.
He shrugged his shoulders.

—We'll take turns drinking, he said. Sit on the bed.

On the mantelpiece, a bottle of Bordeaux and a glass,
which he filled. Then he put the chair in the middle of the
room and sat. The only light was a desk lamp reflecting on
a few papers, some blank, some scribbled on. This light
didn't reach either the walls or the ceiling of the room and
faded away in the shadows. Perrault on his chair was a
castaway on an island in the center of this vagueness.

—If you would like some furniture, Perrault. At the Port
of Missing Men, Aunt Laura . . .

—Oh, no! You're not to beg for anything on my account!

The chair tipped: a sloop in danger. When it had regained
its even keel, Perrault added in a softer tone:

—Lucky you're a peasant.

He brought me a glass of wine ("Here, peasant") and
returned to his seat, bottle in one hand, pipe in the other,
drinking and smoking.

—The meek shall inherit the earth . . . And you refuse to
join Slate Club. I should say the hell with it, too. Except,

because of my grandfather . . .

Silent on my bed, a witness in the shadows, a chest of drawers. I am like that chest of drawers and Perrault lays away in me his disappointment, his disillusionment. From his mother's fortune only three thousand dollars remain and a memory: "They brought me up to be wealthy." The dollars were to pay for his upkeep for two years. "Shit! Why am I fucking around here? In Europe it's OK to be poor, or in Slate Club if need be . . . It just goes to show you, my dear Grégoire, a living aunt is better than a dead grandfather. " He told me about the tumble-down village around the chateau of Peygues: " Some stones on sixteen acres and, at the foot of the hills, some chestnut trees, a vineyard, some olive trees." Rebuild the village as his father had rebuilt the chateau? Or free himself from the past? "But to be free these days takes money. " He didn't mention his obesity, he kneaded it, his hands on his belly, on his thighs, under his jowls. He paced up and down in a cage with three dimensions: money, the past, freedom. I yawned, too near a bed. No need to hide it, he didn't see me; he looked around, his head pivoting on his necktie, his eyes on the shadows. I didn't dare fall asleep or leave. My luck obliged me to respect his misfortune and Perrault took advantage of this superiority. All of that went on for some hours. Three empty bottles, two standing, one lying down, formed the beginning of a game of skittles on the parquet floor. "The role of the confidant, so useful in tragedy . . . " Memories of my courses in literature: I played *Pylade, Phénice, Arcas*:

> Frail daylight shines upon you as it guides me,
> Your eyes alone and mine, are open in *Aulide*.

At dawn I went home to bed. The farther I went from Perrault's room the greater his unhappiness appeared to me. What imbeciles, these guys from Slate Club! How could they not recognize one of their own? This boy alone in America, alone in that vast room. If ever . . .

Perrault didn't hang himself. He bought a dressing gown. He wore it as the symbol of his retirement; Perrault, naked under his blue robe with white polka dots. Early in the morning, late into the night, he wrote longhand, fly specks on yellow, pink and green pages stacked by color on his desk. On the mantle, bottles of beer replaced the too expensive Bordeaux and a few forgotten sandwiches dried up next to a new toaster. "My kitchen," he said, for he had refused to join any other club than the Slate Club and ate in his room. He took off his dressing gown only to go to his classes and to come, every afternoon at six, in suit, vest, and tie, to read the *New York Times* in our Gothic tower.

—May I? he said, picking up the newspaper.

He sat in his chair (we spoke among ourselves of this leather chair as "Perrault's armchair") interrupting his reading only to correct, with a short laugh, some comment from our conversation. At nine o'clock, when we returned from the club, he laid down the newspaper, to debate Peter B.

—If God exists, he must have a white beard.

. . . and left about ten. Sometimes I went with him. As soon as we got to his room he carefully hung his clothes in the closet and put on his dressing gown. "A silkworm," I thought. "At least in his cocoon he doesn't get lost. "

I didn't lose myself either, those first weeks. On the contrary, I found a place for Grégoire in this new geography. My feet knew the measurements of the landings of at least ten buildings and found their first step without hesitation.

At the club, I automatically lowered my head when hanging up my coat to avoid a pipe that was in the way. The silhouettes of five "proctors, " part policeman, part watchmen, in raincoats and felt hats, inspired in me from afar the same defiance they did in the three thousand other students that they monitored. I fed a few squirrels, two pigeons, a cat: the fauna of this park of a university. If I wanted to know the time wherever I was on the campus, I raised my head and immediately my eyes met Nassau Hall's clock.

Grégoire the student organized himself like his course notebooks. Paragraphs in a regularly slanted hand leaning towards titles underlined twice and subtitles underlined once. Three hours of math, one hour for a meal. Two hours of history, an hour of philosophy, three hours of reading, an hour for friends, an hour for a meal, two hours of reading, nine hours of sleep. The weeks followed each other like chapters in a book and every Sunday was a conclusion. Rain, sun, a fall of yellow leaves on the morning frost.

I also thought I knew the characters in this new setting. Peter B recited his morning prayers under the shower. He served a God with a white forehead like his own. Peter A didn't like to get up: "Since the army, I hate to get up. " That's all he said to me about his two years of war. Seeing him, almost as young as myself, a beardless face, no hope of a wrinkle, I imagined two years as a Boy Scout. Probably he was a hard drinker to give himself a certain style, to replace the razor? Was he studying Japanese out of dilettantism? Aunt Laura found them " very nice, both of them."

Passing through Princeton, she paid a visit to our rooms, congratulating us on our arrangements, promising to come back to see us on the "Harvard weekend," that Saturday in the fall, which everyone awaited, when Princeton and Harvard played their annual football game. Seated with her back to the Gothic window, gloves, shoes and purse of the same matching leather, scarf the color of Virginia tobacco, comfortable but in a hurry, Aunt Laura was amused by this silence of the two Peters. "Cute little chick," Banjo Bob observed to me when she left. " Hey, look, she's my aunt! " Banjo Bob's laugh came up the stairwell, a jazzy laugh, bass theme, soprano variations.

Roast beef, vanilla or chocolate ice cream . . . always the same menu on Sunday whether I went to dinner at the lieutenant's (this life without adventure) or at Father Graham's. He said grace with his eyes closed, a finger hooked in his starched clerical collar, standing between his son, Peter B, and his daughter, Jane.

Monday, the gray mustache of Professor Braintree: "Engivane, do you prefer Racine or Shakespeare? " Tuesday, the black wig of German Meyer: "Aesthetics? It doesn't exist. I've been talking about it so long I finally realized it doesn't exist." Wednesday, the causes of the First World War. Thursday, the prime numbers. Friday, an essay on *Othello*. Saturday, " I prefer Corneille, why not?"

And every day I was on guard against the seekers of truth. I'd learned to know them the way game knows the hunters and the range of their guns: a nervous scent, clawlike hands, sentences in crescendo. In the club, in our rooms, walking along the avenues bordered with sycamores, I listened to them as the hare listens to the steps of the beater. Frozen, I let their words pass near me, trembling when they approached, reassured when they finally went away. I preferred tangible objects: books as objects, ideas as objects, professors as objects, launched at a set hour in dusty lecture halls. I put their lectures in notes to preserve them, in an even hand, to wait for the coming days of exams. Perrault, an object in his dressing gown, Peter A clarinet, Peter B white forehead, Banjo Bob banjo. A universe . . . within sound of a single bell.

Chapter 4

The world that surrounded me changed first. Just a little.
Nothing to worry about: the lieutenant changed his spectacles for dark glasses, I couldn't see his eyes against the
light any more; my old fountain pen broke, the new one
had a stiff nib and forcing it spoiled my handwriting; one
evening, in the course of a conversation, Peter B said to
me:

—You're lucky to be a Catholic . . .

—But I'm not!

—Oh? I thought almost all the French were Catholics.

The mailman brought the first important news. Good
news. Fabien announced a success. A song had made him
"a little rich." A short note: "Tell me, old man, how's it
going? As for me, a song made me a little rich. Your turn
to play now. When you come to Paris we'll show you."

My turn to play? To play what? Fabien played the piano. Listening to Banjo Bob and Peter A, I kicked myself
for never having studied music . . .

Two days later, I received a letter from my mother: "I'm
proud as a peacock!" In the envelope were the music and
the lyrics of Fabien's song.

My brother (just a boy),
Is in the U. S. A.

He paints the Iroquois
With red atomic clay . . .

Peter A played the tune for me on his clarinet. "Your brother? Your brother wrote this?" A tune for a polka. That evening, Banjo Bob whistled it in our rooms. "For sure, Greg, we'll drink to your brother tonight."

A great guy, Banjo Bob, barely black, with long arms, long fingers, long legs, all wrapped around the banjo.

Even Perrault was listening, his newspaper on his knees.

—So, your brother writes ditties?

After a couple of drinks, we went down the stairs to go to the club. Peter A stopped us:

—Tonight, I'm paying for dinner. Bob, have you got your car?

I raised my eyes towards our room. Perrault up there . . .

—Let's go! Your Frenchman can be a pain in the neck. Let him read his newspaper, said Peter B.

"Your two Peters are nice, but a little dumb," Perrault had said to me the day before. In the car I felt like a sheep-dog whose sheep had run away. A few philosophic clichés about human misunderstanding overwhelmed me.

—Let's go to Trenton, said Peter A.

On the road, the cars moved along quietly, anonymous machines of the night hidden behind their white headlights or their red tail lights. Suburbs, the industrial districts and the city gleamed under the clouded cover of neon. Trenton or somewhere else: it didn't matter which American city at nightfall. Bob was singing:

Sometimes I live in the country
Sometimes I live in town

Sometimes I take a great notion
To jump into the river and drown.

—Where shall we eat? asked Peter B.

—At Goldstein's, Peter A answered.

—We'll have a ball, said Banjo Bob.

The friendliness I sensed in these voices made me smile.

—Good! said Peter B. I thought you were mad at us on account of Perrault.

—Who, me? Not at all.

At Goldstein's, only the owner's gold teeth glittered; it was a wood-paneled restaurant, without copper pots or mirrors, the decor of pre-war America. High-backed banquettes formed booths that separated the tables where a few hidden customers heard the clatter of dishes coming from the kitchen along with the smell of onions. New Jersey law prohibited the sale of alcohol to those under twenty-one so only Banjo Bob ordered wine, putting his glass in the center of the table so that we could all take turns drinking.

One, two, three bottles of wine that the owner always put down in front of Bob with a knowing smile.

—Tell us about Fabien, said Peter A.

I told them about the piano, his broken ankle, his diary.

—You shouldn't have read his diary, said Peter B.

—I never said I should . . .

—The kid's OK, said Banjo Bob.

He cut his meat with precision, pushing the fat to the right, the lean to the left. Next to him, Peter A ate nothing, raised his fork and put it back, played with the fried onion rings. Peter B had already emptied his plate.

—We'll send Fabien a post card, said Peter A.

—When did he write his first song? asked Bob.

Every time I fell silent, a question or their silence forced me to continue hunting for memories which I unfolded before their eyes: the bulging eyes of Peter B, the beady eyes of Peter A, and Banjo Bob's eyes, black against his beige skin. I welcomed their smiles but thought it was Fabien's story alone that allowed me to carry off this friendly cross-examination. I would have liked to talk about Grégoire but I didn't dare. I described our house, our parents, Rouen during the war.

—You suffered a lot from the war? asked Peter A.

—Not at all. As you can see, it passed us by.

We got up to leave and, following my three friends, I was sorry never to have suffered. I could have been noble, courageous. I could have had something to tell them about.

Peter A had put his hand on Bob's shoulder and they were approaching the exit when a man pushed open the door. Bob and Peter A stepped aside to let him enter but he stood there, a small man in the doorway.

—Your draft card! He said to Peter A.

—What for?

—Police. They served you drinks?

A man without expression, with a face as immobile as the badge he uncovered stuck to his vest. All our faces seemed in balance against this shining insignia. In front of me, Peter A's back was also in balance but in a single move he turned, revealed a star-shaped scar, obscure in the dim light, stuck to white skin like the badge stuck to the vest. The move was made so promptly that I wondered later if Peter A had a habit of showing the wound in this way.

—This is my draft card, he said.

The man was silent.

—I got that in the Pacific, added Peter A. And if you'd like to see my papers (he let his shirt fall back in place) I'll be twenty-one next week.

—O.K.! O. K.! said the man.

He stepped back. Bob, the two Peters, and I followed him out onto the sidewalk.

—You understand, I have my duty . . . said the man.

Peter A's beardless face turned towards him, turned away. The policeman made a last effort.

—Those "Japs," all bastards!

We were almost at the car. Peter A left us, walked back towards the policeman.

—You were in the Pacific too, perhaps . . .

—No!

—Poor guy! said Peter A. Poor asshole!

He returned, climbed into the car as it started up. He said again:

—That poor asshole!

Anger accentuated his childlike appearance. How was it that the war had been able to brand his body and his spirit without aging his features?

—Sure, Peter, you sure told him, the cop . . . said Banjo Bob.

Between Trenton and Princeton these were the only words spoken. Bob stopped on Nassau Street. A last wave of the hand and we walked on, the two Peters and I, towards our rooms, watching Bob's old jalopy pull away.

—Who do you hate in France? Peter A asked me.

—What do you mean?

—You know, do you hate the Jews, the Germans, the Negroes, the Japanese?

—I'm not sure. I think people who liked the Germans

denounced the Jews and people who feel sorry for the Jews
hate the Germans.

—And you?

—Me? I never thought about it very much.

—You're lucky.

Lucky? I wondered. All of a sudden truth wasn't a game
any more and I felt myself compromised by the evening's
events. Too late for further thought. Then, what hatred
would I choose?

—You, Peter A, you hate cops.

He answered at once. Evidently he'd already thought
about it.

—Not to the point of denouncing a cop.

—How were you wounded?

We arrived at our entry. Peter A climbed the stairs first
and without looking back, scarcely slowing down, he explained:

—I saw too many war movies when I was seventeen. I
enlisted. One day, when a hero was needed, I didn't hesitate. The others had seen fewer movies than I had, they
hesitated and I found myself all alone, on the ground. It
was a Japanese who found me. In the movies he would
have cut my throat. There, he made me a bandage. I had
three months in the hospital to think about it.

—And the Japanese?

—Oh! He must have croaked like all the rest of them.

We went into our room and I saw that Perrault had waited
up for us. I felt ill at ease. I pictured his irony in the face of
Peter A's fervor. "I hope they don't get into an argument."
I couldn't see myself taking sides. "Couldn't he have gone
to bed, after all?"

Peter B sat down next to Perrault:

—Do you have a date for the dance tomorrow night?

—Why do you ask . . .

—Anyway, come to dinner at the club. You'll be our guest. The night of the Harvard game, you have to see Prospect Street. There's going to be dancing and drinking from one end to the other. Especially if we win.

—I'll bet Princeton takes these Harvard mugs by two touchdowns, said Peter A.

—If it's not too muddy, answered Perrault.

—Rain would bother them almost as much as us . . .

All three threw themselves into a long discussion of the teams: Princeton's offense, Harvard's defense.

What astonished me most? Perrault's grasp of American football strategy, or the frivolous conversation? I had thought us to be set out upon a mission, I had abandoned my ambitions (financial, amorous, familial, artistic). I was taking up the cause, I was dedicating myself, I was ready to follow Peter A wherever he wished to lead because he had suffered.

. . . and my new master was discussing the merits of the T formation.

Chapter 5

What a game! Princeton orange and black against Harvard crimson on a field of green. American colors so violent that they cancelled out the violence of the game, giving it a symbolic value. A vague symbol, however, that everyone defined for himself. Was this a contest? But the uniforms blended as in a ballet, each player forming a couple with his opposing partner. The helmets came together, scattered, regrouped. As at a celebration of Mass, the thirty thousand spectators rose or sat down in unison. I was always out of step. Peter A and Peter B took me by the arms, made me rise with them: parents ashamed of their child's ignorance. And when a player left the field on a stretcher, the other gladiators formed an alley while the public stood howling its admiration for the wounded hero.

—You don't understand any of it, Grégoire, said Perrault at halftime.

We had found Aunt Laura and formed a group in the middle of the throng. Next to her, Roger, more "Aryan" than ever in a long leather coat, had produced a silver pocket flask which he offered around. Peter B accepted out of politeness. In my turn, I took a swallow. Peter A threw back his head; he drank in long gulps, punctuated by a catch of his Adam's apple. Aunt Laura laughed. In her beaver hat and coat, she took the flask and drank to victory. Only Perrault predicted Princeton's defeat. "No score at halftime," he explained, "is always a bad sign for the team with a strong offense." We went back to our seats. Around us, people stamped their feet and rubbed their ears, complained of the cold. But the University band launched a Princeton marching song:

"Wow, Wow, wow-wow-wow, hear that Tiger roar!"

and the muffled crowd took up the chorus:

"Wow, Wow, wow-wow-wow, rolling up the score!"

Princeton won, three to nothing, thanks to a field goal. I could not have imagined this victory would be so important, even for me. On the way back to our rooms we congratulated each other, we congratulated the strangers who crossed the campus lawns with us. Slaps on the back, hoorahs. Perrault rubbed his hands together: "I was afraid, really afraid." Peter B hoisted his sister in triumph and poor Jane pulled his hair. "Put me down, Peter! You'd better put me down this instant!" It was pointless to be self-conscious; in the general rejoicing no one noticed us. The band marched by. For the first time in my life, I took part in the optimism of a crowd. Altruism, human warmth, a paradise of immortal angels, briefly.

Night fell quickly. The mood changed. Lights revealed the interiors of rooms where students received their friends. We hurried to Foulke Hall to welcome our guests, abandoning Perrault to his huffing and puffing on the stairs.

—Hey, no, Bob!

Peter B's protest rang out at the threshold of our room. He had just seen, behind two desks covered with a tablecloth and an array of bottles, Banjo Bob dressed in a white jacket. Peter B marched toward him with the zeal of a priest coming on an act of sacrilege. With both hands, he attacked the coat's buttons:

—You're not a flunky, for God's sake!

Bob submitted like a child caught in the act. Slow, astonished, paused in the middle of the room, a bucket of ice in his hands: Peter B had forgotten the other Negro and awkwardly bunched up the guilty jacket. Silence. Perrault came in: having heard nothing, understood everything:

—I'll serve, he said, with *Monsieur*, if that's all right with him.

He turned to Slow, took the bucket of ice from him, carried it behind the bar, took off his coat, hung a white towel on his wrist.

—Let's go, Bob, banjo! Peter A, clarinet!

Relief confirmed by the arrival of the first guests.

—He's a genius, this asshole of a Perrault, said Peter A, adjusting the reed of his clarinet.

—Not very well tuned, their democracy, said Perrault in French.

He served me a Scotch and soda with the majestic grace of a professional. He approached the guests with deference, using his Oxford English which he sometimes laced with a French accent. The room filled with students and their dates, a few professors, some bourgeois from Princeton, friends of Aunt Laura. Aunt Laura herself, I introduced to the lieutenant, behind his new dark glasses, withdrawing as soon as I could, for I supposed they would talk about me in the terms that adults reserve for children.

Our guests spilled out into the corridor, the bedroom, the study, sitting on the frames of open windows, sitting on the floor, stepped over by new arrivals. The students all knew me, as they knew Perrault, or Chan the Chinese, or

José the Chilean. Modest celebrity: they called me by name and I didn't know their names. "Watch it, Kate, or Emily, or Sandra," they told their dates, by way of introduction, "this is a Frenchman." And there I was, a bashful Charles Boyer. What to do with this national reputation of Don Juan? Put on a blasé manner and escape, until another Kate, or Emily, or Sandra . . .

Sitting on his leather coat, Roger pulled me towards him by the cuff of my trousers. "Come here, Greg. I want to talk to you!" He talked to me about Aunt Laura, posing questions I was unable to answer: "Behind this facade, she's a serious person, isn't she? Has she gotten over your uncle's death? Did they meet in France or in America? They say you look like him, like Henry Cahan. Your black hair. But you're thin. Take up sports! You'll fill out." He shook my shoulder. "And your uncle? What was he like? You aren't drinking?" His insistence annoyed me. Why all these questions? He knew Aunt Laura better than I did. I didn't know what to say to this man who treated me as an equal in spite of being thirty-five and yet did not impress me like most adults. Between legs clad in silks or flannels I spotted my aunt's crocodile leather pumps. "Phone me, Greg, when you come to New York. I'll introduce you to some girls." Roger got up, empty glass in one hand, leather coat in the other, looking for the bar. Was he sleeping with Aunt Laura? What a shocking expression!

At the other end of the room Peter A was playing *Summer Time*. The clarinet drowned out the voices and its sadness reassured me, evoking familiar feelings. What was Fabien up to at this moment? Still "a little bit rich"? And Marie? Ah, I was really abroad just as I had wished! Nothing was easy. This noise, this smoke, these legs around me that hemmed me in. What an ass, Grégoire! I cleared a path to the study: full of people, beer spilled over books and notes.

"Fish are jumping and the cotton is high," sang the clarinet. The bedroom, too, was full. Even my bed had four or five people on it, sitting, kneeling, their feet on the pillow. All strangers, all friends of the two Peters, no doubt, not counting the students simply drawn there by the hubbub, the alcohol, the hope of charming one of the girls whose laughter drifted from the windows. Dreams of glory.

—Hello, Grégoire!

Among all these faces I looked for my name and found it finally in the nearest, the face of Peter B's sister, Jane. At last a landmark in the crowd. I was grateful for her as for an ash tree, a sheltering roof, a familiar crossroads in an unknown countryside. A friend, though I had seen her only three or four times, seated on the left of her father, the Reverend Graham saying grace.

—Is that the way you take care of your girl?

The boy who spoke to me, with a crewcut, was leaning against the wall. My girl? It's true that at Princeton all visitors became "my" girl, "your" girl, "his" girl, while the students, temporarily bachelors, pursued them over cocktails and through the clubs. Peter B had put his sister in my care. So, she was mine.

—From a Frenchman? It would be a neat trick to swipe his girl!

—Do you want this guy, Jane?

I pointed to the boy with the crewcut.

—Grégoire!

I recognized her shyness as, earlier, I had recognized her face. Her chin trembled at the least anxiety. Peter B, a prophet with a white brow. She, the faithful follower, resembled all the animals that run to flee: the deer, the mouse, the rabbit, the quail, the squirrel. Hair the color of bark, eyes of green, head erect to sense danger, more easily tamed than those animals that run to kill. It was enough to have kindness and patience, patience especially when the chin is trembling. In the woods at La Chêneraie, the birds don't flush unless you walk straight into them. I spoke to Jane about Peter B:

—He talks in his sleep. You didn't know that? "I'm coming . . . I'm coming . . . " Who's he talking to? Even during the day he's in pursuit of someone: on the stairways, from one room to another, on the lawns. Or else he stops dead, looks around, sinks into a book and it's the pages that dash on.

—Yes, he thinks he can never catch up to my father.

—Not God? I thought he was talking to God in his sleep.

—Oh, in our family, it's the same thing.

—But you don't seem to be late . . .

—Me? I wait. In our family, the women wait.

—Look! It's snowing.

The flakes passed by the windows. Around us the room had emptied and words, voices that were recognizable, replaced the earlier confusion. Only fifteen people remained in the living room.

—Where have you been hiding yourself, Grégoire? All these Princeton friends I invited to meet you . . .

Aunt Laura was sitting on the desk, in the midst of glasses and bottles. Peter A put away his clarinet. Perrault put on his jacket.

—You've seen the snow?

—Such a nuisance!

—Let's go to dinner.

—One last glass?

Roger did the rounds, a bottle of Scotch in one hand, soda in the other.

—Where's your glass? he asked me.

—The kid doesn't drink, said Aunt Laura.

She looked at me from head to foot, in a way that made my suit become unbearable. Was it a suit that brought back memories? A day of happiness? Of unhappiness? Was she sorry she'd given it to me? Did she want to take it back? "He's dead, Uncle Henri."

—Come on, Roger, don't force the kid to have a drink, she added.

The irony in her voice was as sharp as an insult.

"What have I done to her?" I imagined myself throwing my coat in my aunt's face: "You want to make a frock out of this?"

—There now, let him alone !

Roger's intervention calmed me like a lukewarm shower and, glass in hand, I went to sit down. What a silence! Perrault's voice imitated a hunting horn: "*Connaissez-vous la Madeleine?*"

—Let's go to dinner, said Peter A.

Poor Jane, somewhere here. Her chin was trembling no doubt but I dared not raise my eyes for fear of meeting a look, it didn't matter what look, and I was the last to leave the room. "But good God, what have I done to her?" Aunt Laura went down the stairs, her tobacco-colored hair among the other heads. The bitterness returned, this time without violence. If my aunt took a dislike to me, should I leave America? Fabien! Paris with Fabien!

—Do you forgive me, Grégoire? You're too shy to be teased . . .

She had waited for me and touched my wrist. She added in French:

—It's my fault.

There! Everything seemed to be simple now. Too simple. She was cheating.

She turned her back to me, organized the trip to Prospect Street. Helen and Jane were to get into the car with her. Slow would take them off to change for the dance. As for the men, they weren't afraid of the snow, were they?

Perrault led the march. "I'll blaze the trail." He stamped down the snow underfoot, imitated the bark of sled dogs, the cracking of whips (with his tongue). He recited Jack London, James Oliver Curwood. Roger and the two Peters were amazed by our admiration for these authors. "You don't realize how good they are!" cried Perrault. Walking backwards, he recited:

. . . he was a newcomer! in the land, a chechaquo, and this was his first winter. The trouble with him was that he was without imagination. He was quick and alert in the things of life, but only in the things, and not in the significances. (Jack London, "To Build a Fire")

At the club, Perrault asked the manager for a brush and some polish. He shined his shoes, advised us to do the same:

—Snow is the mortal enemy of leather.

—Has that some deeper meaning? asked Peter B.

—Yes! Snow makes you thirsty, said Peter A.

Prospect Street that night was an extraordinary village. The fourteen clubs were illuminated in the snow. In each club, an orchestra. A thousand students from eighteen to twenty-one and five hundred girls went from one club to another, from one dance to another. Courtesy visits, couples running through the snow, arriving breathless, wet, into the music and the warmth, throwing their coats on the arms of blacks in white jackets. Shouts, laughter, a few serious couples in the shadow of the music. Apprentices to wealth, happy, amorous, unhappy. The unattached were often drunks, dignified or noisy, diffident above all. The girls didn't know whether they ought to worry or to smile at being admired, loved, jostled by these unknown boys in gray flannels and black ties. Declarations of love on the staircases, camaraderie, marriage proposals on the sofas, an operetta in which the music varied according to the club: sambas, waltzes, jazz, paso dobles. A thousand boys and five hundred girls were learning their future roles, trying out their faces, discovering their contradictions. Children or adults? Their hopes and their despairs looked alike.

Sometimes I recognized faces in this crowd. Peter A and his clarinet:

> Let her go, let her go, God bless her
> Wherever she may be. . .

Perrault danced with Aunt Laura, Peter B asked a red dress to dance, Roger drank. I thought to myself: "Why is Peter A playing so well? No one's listening!"

— Let's change clubs!

. . . Perrault swept by with my aunt. He had retrieved all his grace. . .

—Your aunt is beautiful, Jane said to me.

—Jealous?

—Grégoire!

Jane opened and closed her hands, ten, twenty times in a row and then, as if to reassure herself, one hand stroked the other. Standing, she came up to my shoulder. Seated, she poised herself on the edge of the chair, ready to leave.

—Jane, do you have nice legs? With these long dresses. . .

—And if I had artificial legs, of iron, of wood?

She had stood and swirled around. The dress billowed up.

—You see, *Monsieur le Français*?

With her I danced easily, not thinking any more about rhythm. But I wasn't sure enough of myself to dance well with Aunt Laura who imposed her own rhythm on me and made my feet stutter again. I heard Peter A's clarinet:

St. Louis woman, with your diamond rings . . .

I was pressed against my aunt by other couples. Again I looked at the setting and its actors, happy couples, unhappy loners leaning against the wall, on the furniture, more and more immobile. Blacks in their white serving jackets gathered dirty glasses and put platters of sandwiches on the tables.

At one in the morning, the night was young but we left. The snow was falling in slow motion. Behind the wheel of the Cadillac parked in front of the club, Slow was dozing. In the back, motionless behind the glass that divided the interior of the limousine, Roger slept. Aunt Laura seated herself next to him, then Peter B, Jane and me facing them. Jane opened and closed her hands. "A lovely evening, Grégoire, thank you." In the time it took to get to the minister's house we cut up a new awkwardness into shorter and shorter sentences. "See you." "Goodnight." Peter B.

took his sister in his arms and carried her over the snow up to the door of their house.

—A nice, gentle girl, Mr. Gregory, said Slow.

—Grégoire, there's room for you back here with us!

My aunt's voice called to me from a distance behind the glass: a suggestion, an order. I abandoned Slow —good night Slow— to his domestic duties, and I obeyed, passing from one social class to another through the snow, even accepting the fold of the blanket that Aunt Laura held out to me.

—He's drunk, *ce pauvre nigaud*, this poor dope, she whispered.

Roger, legs stretched out on the jump seat, let himself be lolled about by the car, passive, ridiculous. But I envied him his sleep and her remark spoiled a moment I had been waiting for to close my eyes, to relive that evening. Forced willy-nilly into the present, I made a few movements to prove that I remained awake. Mood softened by silence, by the warmth, by the bizarre light: a countryside in negative, the sky lit up, this time, by the fields. The car was accompanied by a thin clinking of chains. The odor of my aunt's cigarettes did not cover her own odor, part female, part the perfume of lemon verbena, stronger each time the blanket shifted on our knees.

She talked on. How long had she been talking to me? Her voice barely audible above the silence. She explained to me that tomorrow morning, "in a little while," we would go duck hunting along the creek at the Port of Missing Men. "Don't forget my instructions. Always an empty shotgun when moving., an open gun except at the moment of firing." She would stay with me, she would enjoy my pleasure, she would recapture the joy of her first hunt ten years ago. Just like now, returning from a weekend . . .

— . . . and I was tired, she continued. Not from having danced, but tired of these boys and these girls that you have seen this evening. Almost the same: the nephews, cousins, brothers of the same. Worse than weary, disappointed. What had I hoped for? Keats, Mozart, Lindbergh. I am an only child, you know. Because of her bad health, my mother never went to New York. She stayed at the Port and so did I with a governess, tutors, with the library. I read everything, Grégoire, from Chaucer to Dos Passos, from Cervantes to Proust. All the novels before I was nineteen. Almost nothing since. Too disappointed. And literature, for me, is a country I lived in during my adolescence. I read novels the way one fords a stream, stone by stone, learning a few passages by heart while whole chapters floated by transparent, perhaps read then immediately forgotten. But at Princeton, on the night of that dance ten years ago, it was impossible to skip pages. To submit every minute to little men in neckties who talked only to hear the sound of their own voice. What good did it do me to know so many poets by heart? You can show me a list of the boys I met that year who have become, or will become, journalists, poets, Congressmen, scientists, intellectuals . . . too bad. They were ridiculous. Finally, I married your uncle, or rather, I fell in love with your uncle because he came from afar. A stranger to this stupidity. Do you understand why I was annoyed with you this evening? You, the Frenchman, Henri's nephew, with his clothes, his eyes, ready to become in your turn a little man in a necktie. You forgive me, Grégoire, you understand? Your two Peters, your Perrault, you, you're all better than the others. So why . . .

She drew up the blanket.

— . . . why do you let yourself live like this?

Rain now hammered on the roof of the car. I imagined the rain on the snow. How long would it take for the snow to melt?

—If you accept everyday life at your age . . . In ten years where will you be? What do you believe in, Grégoire? I asked your professor Harris: what does Grégoire believe in? "He doesn't know, he's searching . . ."

She mimicked the lieutenant's tone of voice. She exaggerated it:

— . . . "Grégoire doesn't know. He's searching." And that worries me. Have I done the right thing? It's my fault that you're here in America. It's my fault you're at Princeton. Everything is too easy for you, Grégoire. Especially your charm. Because you *are* charming . . . Haven't you noticed the look in this Graham girl's eyes? She'll get you, Grégoire. She'll make you into a man who goes from his business to his family without having had time to make a choice: A child-man. To grow older at your age ought to be by choice, not merely by the passage of time. Those who regret the loss of their youth are those who didn't make such a choice. Losers! Do you even have a choice to make?

She stopped talking. She must be waiting for an answer.

"Agreed!" I thought to myself: "Agreed, I am a failure. Perrault is a failure. Peter B is a failure. But she doesn't have the right to say so, especially not the right to lower Peter A to our level. He, at least . . ."

We arrived at the Port of Missing Men. The rain drenched the masses of rocks exposed above the snow. The car came to a halt. Below, on the invisible creek, the ducks would come. A shame that Peter A wasn't here, he would have

defended himself. Would he have shown his scar? Would
he have formulated an answer in Japanese? I followed my
aunt into the house. And what made her think she was so
superior? Her money? Basically, what game was she playing except the truth game? So, play with her and answer
her question with a question? "What choice have you made?
The choice of a life divided between New York and the Port,
of stepping stone by stone as in your reading in childhood,
with ordinary mortals wiped away, transparent, misunder-
stood by you who doesn't even understand Peter?"

I helped her out of her furs. I was silent, superior, almost
avenged by my thoughts. Roger climbed the stairs, left his
coat on the banister. "Sorry about my hangover." We
watched him disappear down the hall.

—And he, isn't he a failure?

My aunt slapped me in the face.

She went into the living room. I followed her. I carried
my slap with me, in my two hands, planted in the middle
of the room, looking at it, displaying this slap. She shrugged
her shoulders.

—But Peter A . . . You didn't have the right . . . Do you
know he was wounded in the war? That he's learning Japanese? That he stands up for the Negroes?

—How about you, Grégoire? Not everyone has a war!

Kneeling in front of the fireplace she waved a newspaper, lit the fire. Without looking back she said:

—Stop crying! *Arrête-toi de pleurer*!

Putting my hands to my cheeks, I felt the tears. How did
she know I was crying? I hadn't realized it myself. And
how would I have known, after all? I knew only the sobs of
childhood, hatred, grief, pain: not this emptiness where
tears flowed for my own death. Above the fireplace, the

stuffed teal was forever in flight, so near the stream where my Uncle Henri had killed it.

A sudden barking startled me. Médor rushed in, crazy, slipped on the rugs. At first, I refused his affection. I didn't want anyone to console me, to love me. I didn't wish to love. Médor licked me, jumped up to my shoulders. His insistence irritated me, then amused me, and at last I laughed as I had cried, without noticing it myself, his muzzle against my face, on his back, batting me with his paws; my aunt with us, all three on the floor, our hands in his black fur, the smell of the dog, and the fire.

—He knows we're going hunting in a little while, said my aunt.

When I looked at her, I was surprised at her youth.

Her youth, later, when the dawn lit her profile, attentive to the whistling of a pair of wings, her eyes following the silhouette of a mallard against the fog. The wind roughed up the surface of the water, pushed ripples towards our blind that were divided by the stems of the reeds. Fog mixed with rain, sometimes swept the waves, sometimes half revealed scenes in miniature: three reflections, a few pebbles, a branch and its dead leaves drifting. On our left a promontory several yards long sheltered a bay of calm water. There our decoys floated, well-behaved toys. Uncle George was two hundred meters away to our right. Still farther away, Slow, whom I pictured under his brown wool cap, the same brown as his skin. Daylight, when it came, confirmed the scarcity of colors. Grays everywhere: a fog of gray light, somber gray water, gray stones. Only Aunt Laura's face retained its colors, rose-orange skin surrounded by locks stuck under a wet, dark green foulard scarf. Later the reeds would become reddish brown in the sun, if the sun existed above this opaque countryside.

The arrival of ducks surprised my vigil; against my leg, the restrained eagerness of the dog: several teal, wings in a half circle, each feather spread on the wind like fingers, settled near the decoys. I trembled. Médor trembled against me.

—Look out! Ready! *Go!* she told the dog.

Médor leapt into the water. The teals took flight. I fired first, a random shot. The teals climbed straight up, one of them suspended in its flight; I heard my second shot, the teal fell.

—Bravo, Grégoire!

The dog brought me the bird, soft as a cushion. I didn't know what to do with it, put it in my pocket, lay it down, throw it away?

—Thank Médor!

I stroked his black fur.

—And now me?

—Thank you, Aunt Laura.

Shotgun in one hand, the other hand in my pocket, I grasped the warmth of my first duck.

—Think about me when you speak to me, if you please?

I let go of the duck.

—I'll train you, she said, perhaps . . .

Suddenly mollified, she showed her two cartridges intact.

—You see, to improve your chances, I didn't fire.

Some ducks turned in the fog. Two mallards from right to left: a double for my aunt. Slow fired, then Uncle George. Five ducks right over us. She killed one, I missed.

—In front, Grégoire, in front!

A female flew by, flush with the reeds. I winged her.

Médor swam toward her. Sensing her danger, the duck dove. The dog turned in the water, waited for her to reappear, pursued her again. This hunt lasted several minutes but the duck tired first. The dog had seized a wing and was dragging the bird behind him. Coming to the bank, he let go of the duck to shake himself, it slid into the reeds. In one bound, he took it in his jaws and brought it to me proudly. The duck's head, high at the end of a flexible neck, had eyes on me. My first move was to grasp her, to caress her.

—Kill her cleanly, said Aunt Laura.

I used all my strength, and the bird's head burst against a stone.

—Now you'll try not to wound them any more.

A horn sounded to the right and another answered farther on.

—Slow and my father each have their three ducks, she said. They're waiting for you.

The fog cleared away and at times a ray of sunlight touched the water. It seemed to me that for half an hour we had made an infernal noise; now there was silence. I said to myself, "She commands 'kill' and I kill." Twice with my barrels I followed some ducks within range without firing. The second time, Médor whined. Seated on her folding stool, my aunt smoked a cigarette. A mallard was swimming twenty meters from the blind. I looked at Médor: "Go!" Barely in flight, the mallard fell.

—You fired on account of Médor?

—Yes!

—You even obey dogs!

I was panic-stricken. "What does she want from me?" I had the impression of also being a beast turning in the fog, conscious of danger. However, everything had become calm again around us and we walked along the creek, in the sunlight, in a countryside more and more defined: hills of dead leaves studded with naked trees, a little snow in the shelter of the rocks.

When we rejoined Uncle George he pointed to a clump of reeds with a gesture to the Labrador, who plunged into the water. Slow came out of the woods. Jeanie ran to us:

—Greg, did you kill any? How many, Greg, how many?

The child in my arms. We all watched the dog work. He came back towards us, a duck in his jaws. As soon as he had climbed on the bank Uncle George called him, but the dog avoided him and deposited the duck at my feet. Slow explained.

—Médor, sir, he sure knows the blood of his master.

—Or his clothes? suggested Uncle George.

I knew enough to keep my mouth shut.

—No, sir, it's the blood, sir! sang Slow.

Jeanie repeated:

—It's the blood, Grandpa, Greg's blood..

Uncle George, with dignity, exasperated by this naïveté, was first to turn toward the house. His cap level with his shoulders, his body made round by his woolens, he was weighed down by waders. And I said to myself: "Grégoire, you look down on this man even though you know nothing about his life and thoughts, even though you hardly know which of his few habits have been disrupted precisely because of your being here." But this remorse did not lessen my antipathy.

This antipathy was confirmed a few hours later, at lunch, when he asked me why I had turned down a bid from Slate Club, "his" club.

— . . . Thirty telephone calls, ten letters to get you that favor.

—My two roommates are in Briar Club.

His face flushed:

—You manage very well by yourself, Grégoire. Good luck!

A silence followed this vague threat. Roger, eyes swollen, speaking haltingly, came to my defense:

—It's hard for a foreigner to appreciate . . .

—Grégoire hasn't even said thank you.

—I'm sorry.

Thinking back, I relived family scenes and Fabien throwing his bowl: "Send them my soup!" This time, at least, Aunt Laura would not accuse me of obeying everyone.

—This morning, I made a double, she said.

—Me too!

Her father's response was dry: he refused to be distracted from his bad humor, refused the salad that Slow offered him. Jeanie, a yellow dress beside her mother's green suit, was upset. Roger, absent-minded, drank sometimes his shot of gin carried in from the living room, sometimes his wine; Roger, my accomplice, the other failure.

I had put my bag on the back seat of the limousine and climbed up front with Slow. Aunt Laura hung on the door:

—I'll come to see you in Princeton soon.

The car went down the drive. The phrase repeated itself in my head: " . . . see you in Princeton soon . . . soon." A remark natural enough, but something in its tone troubled me. This was not the usual commandment. It was like a secret that my aunt wished to confide in me. About Roger? About Jeanie?

Just then Jeanie waved to us, perched on a rock. After the bend in the road she disappeared. The car ran slowly on the drive, and a mixture of earth and gravel crackled underneath the wheels. It didn't find its rhythm until it reached the main road, where joints of the concrete pavement regularly slapped the tires.

— . . . I brought your ducks, said Slow. If it's OK, Master Gregory, I'll leave them myself at the club and explain to the chef how to prepare them . . . Your friends will be glad to eat duck. They're nice guys, your friends, Master Gregory. Bob, your janitor, Bob, told me: "Nice guys, good-hearted and courteous. "

—Bob's a friend.

—You're like your Uncle Henri, Master Gregory. Your uncle, he was blind, yes, sir! Blind to a man's race, Negroes or Jews, even a Chinaman from China that he brought to the Port.

—My friends at Princeton are like that . . .

—Things are changing, Master Gregory!

An old face, the brown skin masked the shadow of wrinkles. White hair underneath the chauffeur's cap. Slow watched only the road, pale palms against the black steering wheel. A profile closer to Africa than Bob's. Race traveled in time, across generations, toward a different face.

—I'm an Uncle Tom, said Slow. A good Negro, well-fed, well-dressed, happy. Red caps, blue caps, caps are prettier than chains. Bob's right. Uncle Toms are OK for my generation. The younger ones deserve more. Yes, things are moving, Master Greg. My nephew, my brother's son, he's going to college.

With the night, neon took the place of the scenery: soon only an artificial set was left: letters in color, tail lights behind the trucks, headlights tamed by the speed limit, traveling at the same pace through dotted lines of street-lamps toward the horizon: lines bending, parallel, intersecting, the geometry of the American night. A motorcycle passed us, roaring, a red shadow, blue and yellow flames from twin tailpipes. The other America, the memory of races toward Le Havre when I wept with fear, an old dream recovered and soon dispersed in the monotonous rhythm of slow-moving cars. " I will come to see you in Princeton . . . " The voice of Aunt Laura.

And when I arrived at Father Graham's for dinner, when Jane opened the door, it was again Aunt Laura's voice that greeted me: "She will get you, Grégoire. She will make of you a man who goes from his business to his family . . ."

A blue and green living room contained this family. Above the fireplace the white crest of a wave sprayed in the wind in a gold frame. Only the narrowness of the windows was a reminder that this house was one of the oldest in Princeton. The melancholy of a Sunday evening. The pastor made a few comments on the snow, the wind, the rain. Mrs. Graham came out of the kitchen, apron in hand, eyes of green like Jane's, still good-looking. Jane would age well. "To grow old at your age ought to be a choice."

An immoveable family. I imagined their life, dormant, like forgotten waters disturbed only by the hurried coming-and-going of fish gliding nowhere. Leading me into the dining room, Jane whispered:

—Peter's told my father he's converting to Catholicism.

We each stood waiting at our place, until the pastor had ended the prayer:

—- . . . *in the name of the Father, of the Son, and of the Holy Ghost.*

—*Amen!*

115

Their drama in slow motion. Who had wept? The pastor sliced the steak. Mrs. Graham put a spoonful of mashed potatoes on each plate, another of peas. The gravy was passed around. I thought of history: the religious wars, *Chronique of the Reign of Charles the Ninth*, Saint Bartholomew, "Paris is worth a mass," indulgences. And what more?

—Grégoire, I saw professor Harris this morning.

The voice of Father Graham, low but kindly like a woman's voice.

— . . . he told me that he met your parents, when he was a lieutenant. He described your house to me, one of the nicest he saw in France.

They were already making inquiries? The minister had read in his daughter's eyes a yearning that justified these researches? Was he going to ask me my intentions?

—By the way, Grégoire, do you know that the professor will soon be blind?

My first American friend!

—Obviously you didn't know. I'm sorry.

My pain surprised me. Lack of experience. Of those that I loved, he was the first victim and now I had a better understanding of the drama in the Graham family. No more need to know who had cried. I said:

—But we saw him yesterday. He came to our cocktail party. I introduced him to my aunt . . . He said nothing to me!

—You can't announce to all your friends, "I'm going blind," said Jane. That would be horribly painful.

116

Chapter 6

—A question of imagination, said Perrault.

—No, of revelation, answered Peter B.

—There is no revelation without imagination.

Peter B had chosen Perrault to be his godfather: "I don't want to be bugged by one of those Irishmen who send you to hell for a yes, for a no." One morning, Perrault took Peter B to church. A private ceremony. A godmother chosen at random among the parishioners of Princeton because, in the Grahams' milieu, "one doesn't know Catholics." In the glacial church, dark after the blue sky of December, Jane, Peter A and I, seated at the back, followed the ceremony.

An unexpected result, godfather and godson spent hours discussing theology. Perrault, the *New York Times* forgotten on his knees, preached religious individualism from his armchair. Peter B circled around him, defending Catholic discipline "which alone creates mystics."

—And Avicenna, and the Buddha?

—I was talking about the West.

—Kierkegaard, then . . .

—A philosopher!

—What? The author of *Purity of Heart*? A mystic! As surely as you'll become a Jesuit. You're afraid of yourself.

—Why not? answered Peter.

—Then I excuse you, said Peter A . . .

He left the study and stopped next to me.

— . . . Since you're afraid of yourself.

—What is it you are excusing?

—Your conversion!

—Because . . . ?

— . . . All conversions need to be excused. The world is divided enough without people rushing to convert themselves.

—Good, said Peter B, it's one of your paradoxes!

Behind his back Peter A played a few notes on his absent clarinet.

—Not at all a paradox. Tolerance doesn't mean to put up with people while waiting for them to convert themselves, but to love them for what they are. I hope you will be more tolerant of others than of yourself.

—But since I believe in Catholicism . . .

—What were you a week ago? A Protestant who understood Catholics. Now you're just one more Catholic, that's all.

I would learn the rules of this game; the game of another truth, the imaginary truth. In the street, I repeated to myself from the Kierkegaard whom Perrault had just quoted: "Most men have traded their rationality for the phrase: to live with your times." What men? Peter B? Myself? But I'm not yet a man and I don't know my times.

—Good evening, Grégoire!

Mrs. Harris opened the door.

—Jane's already here!

Can you live with your times when you go blind? Jane and the professor were seated on the sofa in the living room waiting for me. There was a single change: no toys were scattered on the carpets. The mother must have said to the children: "Now that your father is blind, you must get in the habit of leaving nothing underfoot."

We had to come several nights each week to help Harris prepare his courses. "I'm sorry," he had said, "this malady took me by surprise. Next year, I'll be better equipped." The equipment of a blind man: a dog, his memory, Louis Braille, a dictaphone, patience. Jane worked with the dictaphone, I with the text, reading page after page of Chaucer's *Troilus and Criseyde*. My pronunciation gave the professor pleasure:

—Finally the French in Chaucer as he spoke it; *Tragédie, image, bataille.*

Around his dark glasses I saw his face, hair going gray, styled in a crewcut, a mouth thick-lipped, ironic. A monotonous voice, he emphasized intensity in the silences placed between words.

—Chaucer for the Anglo-Saxons is a language . . . a foreign language. They look down on foreign languages . . . They murder the rhythm. Even so Chaucer beseeched them:

> *And for ther is so gret diversite*
> *In English . . .*

Wait, Grégoire, find what follows, one of the last strophes.

> *. . . and in writyng of oure tonge*
> *so prey I god that non myswrite the,*
> *Ne the mysmetre for defaute of tongue.*
>
> (*Troilus and Cressida*, Book 5, strophe 257.)

There! Thank you, Grégoire. This spring, that's where I begin my course, with the end. I'm trying to make these boys understand that without rhythm, farewell to poetry, and literature, and humor. Farewell to everything, even their sacred baseball. Let's go, Jane, start your machine, we're beginning!

For the first time, I was witnessing a man working, his hesitations, his contagious love for study. I was amazed to learn that he did not repeat the same lectures each year.

—I change, he said. So do my lectures. Hold it, Grégoire, stop there! That last verse you just read. I'd forgotten it.

And Pandarus to coughe gan a lyte ...

(Book 2, strophe 37.)

Is Pandarus bashful or worldly ? Surely, both. Because of Shakespeare, we exaggerate his worldliness. His Pandarus is so cynical! Shakespeare's fame makes us forget that Chaucer's Pandarus loves Troilus. You see, Grégoire, what you read best are the actions of the characters. Better than their monologues. In the end, to read the same works too often is not such a good thing. Books become like a too familiar itinerary, some see only the road, others only the trees or the billboards. It's necessary to see with the eyes of others, to hear the reading of others. One reads the way one interprets a piano sonata, and different interpretations build on each other. To understand an author or a human being, you need to have many sides and know how to listen.

Leaning over the microphone, he resumed his lecture, asked Jane to play back the beginning, corrected himself. I said to myself: "He's right, actions are what impress me:

Peter A showing his scar, more than the story of his wound. If Harris was not going blind, would I listen to him?"

An old habit, as he spoke he played with a pencil. Watching his hands, I imagined his inner brain work, the study, the intellectual research. New to me, this world of thought seemed like a stretch of sand, a beach suspended between the three dimensions. No gravity there, no roads, no directions. No lights, just shadows. Lightning voyages, pilgrimages, expeditions, the return to this beach where time poured away like sand in an hourglass. A country that vanished at the call of a voice, any human voice.

—Grégoire!

—Yes, Jane!

—Is the professor pretending to be happy?

—I don't know.

After our evenings of work at the Harrises', I took her home. From eleven o'clock on, Princeton slept like a village. Respectful of this slumber, we moved quietly.

— ... Pretending, perhaps that's a way to become so.

—I wish they would try that in my family.

—Who is "they"?

—My father and Peter.

—He's got over it, the pastor, this conversion of his son?

—How could he? If Peter is wrong, Peter is damned. If he is right, it's my father who is damned.

—And you?

She shrugged her shoulders

—I lack ambition. I'd like to be happy.

Naturally I thought this happiness could depend on us. Nothing urgent now that we knew each other. Along the streets we talked in low voices about our reading, our friends. Why hurry? Sometimes to touch lightly on our

121

feelings. Today:
—You're not happy?
—I'm beginning to be.

She fled a single meter and closed the door of her house without a sound. I pictured her at home, surrounded by her sleeping family. One meter from our future to her past.

I walked quickly, listening to my steps, and I smiled at this new rhythm, the pace of those who have a goal, like Peter A or Harris. My goal this evening? To read Shakespeare's *Troilus*. I thought to myself: "Pace is the measure of a man's style," remembering that armies "make men march to make them submit." Therefore I ought to vary my own pace to express my freedom. The rhythm of a dance, an incredible moment. Joy took hold of my feet, reached my ears, my fingers. I was so filled with happiness for several minutes that I had to lean against a tree, my breath cut short by the surprise.

Finally I started again, worn out. "What happened?" I tried to define the impression I had experienced, to fix it in my memory. Impossible. "Is this what happiness is?"

I returned to the tree, a sycamore, and leaned against it again. I thought of Jane, of the professor, of our studies: no use, the earlier emotion had disappeared and I found only regret for this glimpse of joy. I walked slowly toward my room. "What's come over me? Why? Does this happen to others? Is this a conclusion? A warning?"

Harris would see one of Chaucer's symbols in this, a glimpse of Paradise, the measures of life set at its beginning: joy or sadness. "Would I have a choice to make?"

Whom to talk to about it?

To no one.

When Aunt Laura said, "You've changed, Grégoire . . ." I hesitated. Already I sensed her jealousy. Especially that Jane's name was not to be spoken! Here the lie began, in the car, in the night, on a road on the outskirts of Princeton.

—Me, changed?

Not a misunderstanding: a lie, because we understood each other. She regretted my youth, my weakness: as for me, I was afraid of her. Only one thing surprised me, that she had waited two weeks to come.

The car turned off the road, climbed the slope of a dirt road through the woods.

—Jeanie was sick last week, she said.

A one-story house appeared, surrounded by high grass and bushes, a house transparent in the headlights that Laura left lit, getting out of the car, crossing the grass, looking for the right key, the lock, indifferent to the light that exaggerated each of her actions. When I turned off the headlights, I was surprised by the silence.

She attended to the fire. Soon she would attend to me and I waited my turn among the objects, in the room of white walls and blond woods. She put a bottle and glasses on the table with a bag of sandwiches. She didn't come near me and when she spoke it was as much to herself as to me, her monologue like one more object in the room.

— . . . If I like you it is not because I loved your uncle . . .

From the beginning, she made this distinction between the words *like* and *love*. Less a question of intensity than of the relationship of our ages, our experiences: a difference in quality. To have a taste for, friendship for: "*like*." To love: "*love*." "If I like you it is not because I loved your uncle. *Je t'aime* —I like you—for the same reasons that made me love him. Has your physical resemblance brought back to me a kind of hope? Like him, you're different from the others and the others bore me. In fact, if I was French, perhaps you would bore me . . . "

Impossible to feel pride at this speech. I didn't win a victory, she had suffered a defeat. She outlined for me a negative love, born of death and boredom. Love in which even the verb *to like* seemed a denial. Her small voice, a murmur with sometimes those same hesitations in the choice of words that we had between students when we discussed philosophy. "Perhaps I ought to control myself . . . But, first, it's not my nature, and then you're just a boy, what's the harm in that? *Tu m'aime, aussi*—You like me, too, isn't that so? You, you risk nothing. What's the good of needless suffering? It's painful enough as it is . . . We will be careful. Jeanie and my father must know nothing . . . Jeanie especially. This will pass. Everything does except a few memories . . . You'll try to be nice. I want so much to make you a man . . . "

We no longer existed, our presence, our relationship was abandoned to these words, and I was astounded when she grew quiet. When she rose her hands were clenched in tight fists. Her fear was contagious. We were the same age: she was weakened by this fear, it made me older.

I don't know who was the first to laugh. We drank laughing, and laughing we ate sandwiches, each on opposite sides of the table that granted us a delay.

—Let's go back to Princeton, said Laura.

She prolonged the delay. Reassured, we didn't rush each other. She told me about Jeanie's illness.

—Greg! Greg! She called for you when she had fever. Médor lay at the foot of her bed for three days.

We walked on the grass around the car, quiet. A cold night, sharp. A flock of geese honked somewhere between us and the stars. Laura explained their migrations, described their invisible flight.

— ... and from above they see the layout of watercourses, lakes, bays, coasts. In the children's game of wanting to be an animal, I chose the teals.

—The stuffed teal at the Port?

—Idiot! You talk like "them."

—Laura?

—Yes, "Laura" to you except at the Port.

At the moment we parted, we regretted lost time and we were silent in the car parked a hundred yards from my room.

—Kiss me!

A return of fear, but a different fear which this time kept us from separating. For the first time I touched her hair. I carried the memory of it at the ends of my fingers, unable to go up at once to my room. By instinct I went to Perrault's, thinking that his self-centeredness would be a refuge where I could await sleep.

—*Bonsoir*, peasant! Have a beer!

On the mantel, bottles surrounded a box of canned goods open like a treasure chest and marked by a label covered with a script of fly specks: "As long as there are five dollar bills there will be bottles." I stretched out on the bed. Perrault turned around the only chair, his dressing gown of white polka dots opened on bare skin.

—It's very pleasant to speak a little French. English is all right for northerners, like fog. In English, even the best phrases—especially the best phrases—hide their heads. The head of the one who speaks. Naturally, the French hate equivocation, they don't understand anything about it. Is France beautiful in the fog? Take me! I speak English, I listen to myself, and I don't know who I am! "God" . . . Who is this, their "God"? Protestants or Catholics, converts like Peter B, they believe in a "God" whose head is bound in quarto and in several volumes, whose hands are like roots, whose heart is a piston, whose eyes are yesterday, tomorrow, never. He eats men in the sauce of despair. Me, you, all the Latins, we love a God with a white beard and a great robe. God, Grégoire, God is like Charlemagne, he smells of violets and wild thyme, and of a little heresy for us poor sinners. Find me a dictionary where this is explained! Find me . . .

Perrault had found his breath. Hands clasped on his belly, a modern monk, he compared Dante's hell to that of the Quakers.

— . . . Happily the Negroes have warmed up the Anglo-Saxon hell, cold as the North Pole. At least, they've given some rhythm to "God" and anxiety has danced to a fox trot. But the infinite wears down the best of wills, and these poor Negroes are worried. They'll end up white, just as screwed up, good for a "nervous breakdown," the purgatory of the north. Watch yourself, peasant. If you love a woman here, make love to her in French. She won't understand you? So much the better. Love in English is terrible. You don't kill. You divorce or you commit suicide!

Had he guessed? No, surely not! He brushed by me in a crashing of verbs and changed the subject.

Thinking I was tired, I went to bed. Impossible to get to sleep. I imagined Laura's body. Sometimes I hoped for the easy accomplishment of my adolescent dreams, sometimes

I foresaw a ridiculous scene, I who hadn't even known how to dance with her, and I had a premonition of my shame: a vulgar scene, vile. I recalled my embarrassment in front of Marie, reading *The Devil in the Flesh:* "the stream washes the stones," "the flax turns towards the sun."

My own bed made me sick and I got dressed groping in the dark for fear of waking the two Peters. First I ran among the dorms on lawns shining in the moonlight, then on the banks of Lake Carnegie edged with ice. "From above the geese see the layout of watercourses, lakes . . . " I could have added Laura's words to my collection of pure sayings.

I punished myself, I kept on running on the dead leaves that broke under my feet. Would I at least have the courage to confess all this to Jane? Not see her anymore? Impossible: how to avoid our meetings at the Harrises'? My legs burned. I wanted to be miserable but in my pain I was at ease. Happiness? Unhappiness? What difference did it make as long as there was movement!

—You're lying to yourself, Grégoire!

Troubled, I listened to myself. What was to be done? Seated on a rock, motionless, I waited for an answer. A few cars crossed the bridge, announcing morning. I heard a scratching. A deer pawed the grass and its silhouette was almost entirely outlined against the clear surface of the lake. There was the other America, one of animals and forests, Jane's America. With each automobile the deer raised his head. The other America? No! There is only one America: concrete in the forests, moonlight on neon, smoke in the clouds.

—What to do, Grégoire?

—I don't know. The answer doesn't come. I will wait.

Slowly, I went back to Foulke Hall. Back to an ordered life. In the bedroom the two Peters were still asleep. I lay down until they woke up so that they would not suspect my worries: it's easier to lie with actions than with words. When was my first class? Ten-twenty, McCosh Hall. "In France, people are having lunch. Do they have snow at La Chêneraie ? Who is carrying in the wood for my father?"

The first door slammed. I've come back on time. Peter A sat up in bed. Now me! Shave. Dress. It's good to have routines. To live in balance on routines.

—Morning, Peter!

—Hi, Greg!

The walk to the club, elbow to elbow, the cold air, the sycamores, all those easy things.

—Perrault has a theory. God changes according to each language.

—Tell that to Peter B.

—He doesn't even know Latin. For a Catholic ...

—God plays the clarinet.

—Blow, Creator?

On the carpets at the club, black waiters passed silently among students only half awake. "Why aren't they in our place and we waiting on them?" Fried eggs, sausages, maple syrup on pancakes. "Hunger 's another routine."

Full, almost calmed down, I settled myself in an armchair in the living room to read Shakespeare's *Troilus*. Here I found love laughed at, Hector the brave massacred by Achilles' lackeys. I came to understand the spirit of three authors and their epochs. Homer the epic poet, Chaucer the Christian, Shakespeare the poet of all human misery.

—It's too bad, I said to Harris that evening, that all writers don't have to deal with the same subject at one time in their career. A sort of exam ... Troilus by Molière, Tolstoy, Proust!

—Subjects? There's only one in any event: hope or hopelessness ...

Harris carefully wiped his glasses with his handkerchief. The smoke from his cigarette slipped from his lips with each word.

— ... Love, death and the whole parade of human circumstances are pretexts or symbols, like God and Satan.

His little girl had come to sit on my knees. With her finger she traced imaginary lines in my hand.

—That's not to say that God and Satan don't exist, Harris continued. That's another matter. Surely they exist for those who believe in them, and so for Chaucer. In reading him, let's have the courtesy to believe in Chaucer's God ...

I no longer listened to him. Why wasn't Jane there yet? At that moment I imagined that she wouldn't come anymore, that she wouldn't participate in our work. What would be my interest in it then? I wanted to go out, to telephone, to see her immediately. "Too bad about Chaucer, God and the Devil, I don't give a damn about the human condition ... "

Just then, Jane arrived, breathless, and put her coat on a chair. She leaned down to kiss the Harris girl, her face close to mine. "Good evening, Grégoire!"

We settled down to work. I summed up my stupidity. "This morning you wanted her to go looking for another lover ... "

I saw myself as an inept actor, with my pretensions, my naïveté. Fear, joy, shame all in a few moments, like the faces of infants when their cradle is handed over to adults. Impressions that were forgotten as soon as Harris began his lecture, pencil in hand, this useless pencil, scarcely hesitating in his sentences.

——*Troilus and Criseyde,* the title of Chaucer's poem, points to the history of love. In modern terms, a young man is struck by lightning, they love each other, she abandons him, he is in despair. You will see here that the contemporary mythology of love, Hollywood's for instance, copies the courtly love of the Middle Ages. These feelings have scarcely changed their clothes. Thus, Chaucer's morality will not seem foreign to you.

"In the course of the first lecture, I talked to you about Chaucer's style so that you would read him closely. The following lectures will be devoted to an analysis of the text. We may lose ourselves in the details. Today, therefore, I am going to highlight the structure of the poem, so that you can look for it as you read.

"The main idea: Troilus gives way to despair because of his weakness. Despair is the hell of the Middle Ages as it is of the modern world. Troilus is weak because he is abandoning himself to his circumstances: *Fortune,* a key word of the Middle Ages:

> *. . . Fortune!*
> *That seemeth trewest whan she wol bygyle*
> *And kan to fooles so hire song entune,*
> *That she hem hent and blent . . .*
>
> (Book 4, Prologue, Strophe 1.)

"Troilus dedicates himself to Fortune for love of Cressida. To Fortune he surrenders his fate. That is his error, his sin! To avoid despair a man must dominate himself and dominate misfortune. Chaucer's Christian must give himself only to God as the philosopher should listen only to his reason.

"Who is this Troilus? A boy of twenty or twenty-five, an aristocrat, a soldier, a horseman. When, in the first book, Chaucer shows him in the temple of Pallas ... "

Had Troilus "traded away his rationality to live with his times"? A subject for an essay that I noted on a piece of paper. Perrault would find me the exact reference in Kierkegaard. On tiptoe, Mrs. Harris came in. She sat at the other end of the room and took out her knitting. In the silence, the voice of the professor regulated even the rhythm of our breathing.

At fifteen, a few war films had served as my catechism. Chaucer now took their place. Harris was the priest of this ceremony, a calm voice, hands moving from the pencil to the spectacles to the text that he leafed through as if to confirm the existence of the work; a priest for whom courtesy consisted in bringing up only the sins of legendary characters. A scene repeated three times a week, a fixed scene of that winter. Outside, ice, rain or snow, but within always this tableau: Mrs. Harris and her knitting, Jane watching the green eye of the dictaphone, Harris on the sofa, legs sprawled out, finding his cigarettes to the right on the low table, on the left the pencil and the text, in the middle the ashtray. The same warmth and the same monotony. Ancient ideas by which to measure daily life.

As measuring an obstacle to be overcome reveals to us our weakness. For it was clearly a question of *my* weakness. No need to be an aristocrat, a soldier, a horseman, a Troilus: Grégoire sufficed. Here, I listened to reason and I understood all the better that I renounced submitting myself to it. I recognized my fault, I didn't confess it to Jane

and I was afraid that Laura would discover it. I didn't jus-
tify myself, I excused myself: since I loved them both ...

Love? I made use of them. I made use of Jane's admiration and Laura's intransigence. The first reassured me, the
second frightened me. With Jane, the game of illusions;
with Laura, the game of *my* truth. On the one hand the
hope of an easy life; on the other, anxiety, fear of my mediocrity, of Laura's mockery, fear of her now that we were
meeting each other at night.

In the night, in the dark, for Laura turned out the lights
before I came in. She did not speak, and to make love in
that way left me disappointed, disgusted. I would have
wished at least, in opening the door of her bedroom for me
in the morning, she would come out with me, that I would
meet her gaze. But I had to return alone to Princeton, or
slip without a sound into my own bedroom, if we were at
the Port of Missing Men.

In spite of all that, when she let me know, "tonight," I felt
each time the same impatience. Tonight, perhaps, it would
be different, since men like to make love, since books described it otherwise ...

—And yet, Laura and Jane have green eyes, both of them!
This observation halted me on the driveway. "What
things are green?" Water, bottles, grass, the eye of the
dictaphone, snakes, a mallard's head, a blind man's glasses,
spring, traffic lights, grasshoppers, emeralds ...

An evocation contrary to the landscape of snow, blinding
in the sunlight.

—Come on, Greg!

Jeanie called me to order; I started up again, pulling the

sled along with the laughter of the girl, her calls, her directions, and the barking Médor who followed us.

—My turn, Greg!

Going down, she took the rope. Lying on the sled, I dragged my feet so as not to overtake her.

—Greg, what are you giving me?

—You'll see soon enough.

—*Please!*

Her eyes begged me, gray blue like Uncle Henri's, my mother's, mine, like water, like the feather of a blue jay, like music . . .

—Later, Jeanie!

—Greg, are you still a child?

"Am I still a child?"

—It's such a bother, Greg, to be a child.

—Why so?

—You always have to wait.

Two children; we walked through the snow toward the house, each step very slow, then slow movements to take off our boots, our coats. To use up time, to sit down in the kitchen.

—Slow, is Greg a child?

—On Christmas Day we're all children, Miss Jeanie.

What joy to be a child and to let oneself live between Jeanie and Slow, to hope for a present, a feast! A simple moment in this room of white walls, misted windows, translucent to the northern light, the table a still life of cakes, fruits, vegetables, bread.

—Miss Laura, she'll be down in five minutes, said Slow.

He put the breakfast tray near the sink. He had just come from *her* bedroom, this room that I entered only at night, from which she never descended until bathed, made up, elegantly clothed. To see her wake up, dress herself! You're not to know her. She doesn't wish you to know her. She treats you like a kid: 'thank you, kiss me, come.'

Without a word to Slow and Jeanie, I left the kitchen. She would not find me there, among the children. Wait in the living room, a book open on my lap. What book? What did it matter? Five minutes to study indifference: the stuffed bird, the novels on their shelves, the fire laid by Slow but not yet lit. Two windows to the east, two to the west opened the room to the morning and evening sun.

—You're sulking?

In French, in the voice of her mourning. Laura with her back to a window, her face veiled by the light.

—Come, Grégoire, my father is waiting for us.

She called Jeanie. I followed them but stopped at the door of the dining room, irritated by Jeanie's cries, by the fir tree in its Sunday best, by a scene too much like the publicity photos that had been filling the magazines for the last month: the little girl on her knees, the grandfather holding out a package, gifts wrapped in multicolored paper, silver stars . . . and on the beige carpet, an unexpected beast, a black puppy in a pink ribbon with the tag, GRÉGOIRE. My dog.

—Your bitch, Grégoire.

I trembled. On my knees, I took off her ribbon. Warm. "Is she breathing normally?" New paws. New claws, new teeth. "Are you hungry, thirsty?" Let loose, she rolled in the gift wrappings, chewed on them, dragged them around.

—How old is she?

—Seven weeks. She's Médor's daughter.

Big as a cat already.

—And her name?

—Yours to choose. A name that begins with S. Sophie, Samba, Sister, Shoot, Sarah, Sarcelle . . .

—Sarcelle! Here, Sarcelle! Come, Sarcelle!

"Does she want to go out?" A black dog on the snow, running ten meters, sitting. She looked at me. "Come, Sarcelle! Are you cold?" Into my coat. Soft ears.

—Slow. My dog! Have you seen my dog?

Alone with her. I watched each movement and when she went to sleep I stretched out on the parquet floor, listening to her breathing. "Sarcelle, Sarcelle, Sarcelle," I whispered. She sighed; my face against the dog's. Everything forgotten except her, except us. This evening she would sleep next to me. In the morning, I would find her there. And the anguish of separation: "In a week, vacation's over, I'll return to Princeton. Without you!" Everything forgotten in the absence to come. I was surprised to hear sobs, to discover Jeanie crying in the hallway. I hesitated at first between the dog and the child.

—What's wrong, Jeanie?

The yellow dress fled.

—Jeanie!

She refused to raise her head, to speak to me. The puppy in my arms, I went to look for my aunt. I called on the stairs. She opened the door of her bedroom, midday sun on pale green fabrics.

—What's wrong with Jeanie?

—She's jealous . . .

—Of whom?

—Of your dog.

—She wants to have Sarcelle?

Laura was sitting at her desk (a Louis Seize desk and chair). She put on her school teacher's glasses, and I stood before her like a pupil at fault. My beret in my hands? No, a puppy.

—You underestimate yourself. She wanted to show you her new toys.

Over there, the bed was made, swathed in silk, seemed asleep.

You want me to tell you what she thinks? "Gregoire doesn't love me anymore. I'm ugly, I'm alone, I hate him, I hate myself." Children's grief is like women's. When you refuse to share their joy, they offer their sorrow, then their despair.

—I'm going to comfort her . . .

—Wait, Grégoire! Put down your dog! Sit there!

Her legs crossed; a blouse of white lace buttoned up to her neck. Laura also swathed in silk.

—I was talking to you about myself, a little . . .

She didn't tremble, her voice seemed natural but once again the difference of our ages was erased. I put my hand on her knee and I saw the emotion that the night hid from me.

—I can be jealous, too, she said.

—Even of the dog?

I felt my power, for the first time, my power as a man. All the humiliations were wiped out!

—Jealous even of a dog?

Laura smiled

—Of course not, since it was I who gave it to you.

Ek al my wo is this, that folk now usen
To seyn right thus, 'ye, jalousie is love!'
And wolde a busshel venym al excusen,
For that o greyn of love is on it shove! (Book 3, strophe 147.)

I read aloud the passage from Chaucer. Head thrown back, the professor reflected. We heard only Mrs. Harris's knitting needles. "A bushel of venom for a grain of love."

—Once again, the professor resumed, Chaucer defends the Christian point of view. Chaucer, you may have noticed, is an enemy not of love but of courtly love, the love that crushes man instead of elevating him and of which jealousy is one of the habitual expressions, the cause of hatred and of despair.

This word, Laura had uttered it on Christmas day. I saw again her lips: "despair." A word that, in English, seems like a sigh, a fall.

—Jane, are you jealous?

Later, in Princeton's sleeping streets, I asked her this question. As it was snowing, we were walking more quickly than usual.

—Wouldn't it be simpler to ask me if I love you?

The snow on her hair gave her the appearance of a young older woman.

—But it's up to you, instead, to tell me that you love me, Grégoire . . . You look panic-stricken all of a sudden!

She laughed. She did not imagine, she couldn't imagine. No suspicion, no apprehension on her face. I will not betray her.

—Of course, I love you, Jane.

And I was betraying her.

"Grégoire, you skunk, couldn't you wait? Wait for what?

137

Where? In the street, under the snow? How many months, years? How to explain?"

So much for freedom. I, who wished to lose myself! But in an uncharted country where each step would be an invention, each look a discovery; to lose only myself, and with courage! Here my cowardice split me apart, my head on one side, my belly on the other.

At least, I wasn't pleading my case. I punished myself: head and belly. In the little metallic carrel that the library provided for each student, I shut myself up for hours, nose in books read and reread aloud to force myself to pay attention; I recited them to myself walking, eating: Schopenhauer, Santayana, from aesthetics to the Treaty of Versailles, to mathematics, and from there to the gymnasium to punish the belly. Peter A, Peter B, I wore out in turn as my partners on the squash court; there we pursued a black ball rebounding from our rackets and from the four walls. In the swimming pool, the rules obliged us to swim naked. Rooms for fencing, for wrestling, for boxing. A punching bag, a friend in its hypnotic rhythm. A contest with the hiss of the jump rope. "Watch yourself," said the coach "So, you like those blows?"

The exhaustion did not comfort me and, at night, I called out to Laura, then I held my breath: Was Peter B asleep? Had he heard me?

Hours of insomnia, night after night, during which I thought only of Laura, of our next meeting: finally I will dare to turn on the lights, dare to speak to her, to demand an answer, to stay next to her. These accumulated hours created an immense obsession and tiny victories: minutes won, a profile glimpsed in the trickle of light coming under the door, I had pretended to sleep and she had called out my name. Stubbornness of a beast, a prisoner, a sick person.

Until the night when I simply turned on the light, stupefied to discover a face transformed by emotion, tears in her darkened eyes, quivering nostrils, thin lips.

She held up the sheet under her chin, her head poised in its whiteness, a trembling portrait, hands clutching the sheet. How much patience would it take to put this sheet aside? How many nights, weeks? I wanted to see her entirely.

But I was the first victim of these victories. When, after her bath, she appeared again clothed in silk, I doubted her love: I imagined that she would leave me, that I didn't count for her, so much did her appearance deny, during the day, the emotion of the night.

Worries hardly calmed by Harris's friendship and Jane's love. My violent reactions surprised her:

—Grégoire, why are you so nasty?

I wanted to hold on to Jane. I needed her because I was sure of her.

—Forgive me, I'm tired.

---You ought to sleep more, Grégoire. Peter says you're spending the nights at Perrault's. Your bed's not even slept in. You go to lectures without going to bed . . .

Perrault, my accomplice, lied for me without asking for explanations. When I asked him to act as my alibi, he'd responded with a tap on my shoulder:

—O.K., peasant! That's your business!

"What was my business? What goal? What face?"

Chapter 7

Night. Blue-black. Fifty meters from us, on the white density of the landscape,

DINER

in red on a rectangle of electric yellow.

Sixty steps from us, two hundred cubic meters of chromed warmth, an imitation railroad car standing on concrete through the speeding snow in the north wind. A pre-fab, forever temporary, dropped here one day to service the same trucks constantly renewed: MACK, GMC, FORD, abandoned this evening to the storm, silent, turned off, white.

Sixty steps from us, two cubic meters of music for a nickel dropped in the jukebox:

> Irene, goodnight. Irene, goodnight.
> Goodnight, Irene. Goodnight, Irene.
> I'll see you in my dreams.
> Sometimes I live in the country,
> Sometimes I live in town,
> Sometimes I take a great notion
> To jump into the river and drown.

From one table to another a bottle of ketchup, mustard, salt, granulated sugar; French fries, hamburgers for a quarter . . . sixty steps from us.

I am hungry.

—Let's go eat, Peter.

—Wait a bit.

Though less than a stride away, Peter A stays almost invisible under his hood.

And I am chilled to the bone. However warmly dressed, I am morally frozen because I miss Jane's smile and Laura's softness: I imagine their faces, I compose a single tableau, a portrait of family and of warmth in this windy night, silent in my solitude. "Grégoire, you're not a traveler anymore." For me, the only reason for this trip is that I don't know how to say no. So, since Peter A wanted to go . . .

Headlights float on the road. The driver feels out the weight of his trailer by tapping his brakes: twenty tons slide in the snow, find the ice, again the snow, where they dig in and come to a stop, maybe.

—Are you hitchhiking?

The driver climbs down.

—We're going to Detroit, said Peter A.

—You'd better give it up. No trucks tonight, except in the ditches. As for me, I'm through.

—I think we're going to wait a little.

The truckdriver pushes up the visor of his wool cap and walks towards the lights.

The only movement, the snow.

Sarcelle is at the Port of Missing Men where I could have spent the week, head against dog, soft nights against the warmth of her body. Poor puppy without poor Grégoire.

DINER

Over there, by the windowpanes of their imitation of a first-class carriage, snow passes on the wind at the speed of a train. Coffee, tea, a waitress at the counter, truck drivers, heads dipped toward sleep. Everywhere, no matter where, from the Atlantic to the Pacific, the same truck drivers, the same waitress.

We, alone in the cold, remain frozen in place by Peter A's patience.

La Chêneraie, Marie, Fabien in Paris. If they saw me in this snow!

— Let's go eat, Peter .

—Let's wait a bit

And then a bit more.

Until new headlights come toward us and Peter waves his clarinet case. The ghostly truck, like a dream passing on the wind and road, tries to slow down. The cab is jolted, carried along by the trailer, and we run behind, slipping, losing, gaining ground, catching up with the stopped, dazzling headlights.

—We're going to Detroit!

—Climb in!

In the warmth and the obscurity of the cab a Negro voice rings out:

—Welcome to the boys!

The motor revs up.

—I'm headed for Pittsburgh!

A voice of a singer of sentences.

—Kids, I've just come from Boston. And when I left Boston, my buddy he said

"Don't go!" he said

But "I'm going", I said
"Don't go!" he said
"I'm going! I said
"So, go drive down a ravine, ain't no one gonna talk about
you never no more!"
"I'm going! "
"Then take this bottle. You'll drink it with the devil!"
my buddy, he said
Devil or not, have a drink, boys!
Against the light from the windshield, he offers the almost empty bottle. Our eyes become accustomed to the
dark and we can make out the silhouette of an immense
body, a body like a truck, leaning over the steering wheel,
over the road, toward the snow which overtakes us, in flight
through the night, across the beams of the headlights.

Peter A takes out his clarinet. He has found a rhythm in
the running of the motor and on this rhythm he improvises. Concerto for machine and clarinet, adagio. Then the
rhythm of the wind, allegretto in A major..

—Blow, kid, blow.

The truck picks up speed and overtakes the snow which
no longer flies away, captive in the headlights. When the
clarinet pauses, the driver answers. A spontaneous dialogue.

—Negro an' two kids . . .

Cascade of shrill notes.

—In a red truck, in the snow, in the night, all alone . . .

A bass theme, repeated higher, then lower.

— This Negro here ain't no fraidy cat . . .

Baby, baby, sings the clarinet.

—It's Jim Big Jackson from Pittsburgh . . .

Triumphal march.

—Who ain't fallen in no ravine yet . . .
Funeral march.
—Ain't fallen yet in no ravine . . . .
Worried clarinet.
—With the kid who blows and the one who listens . . .
A Princeton tune, a reprise of the *Marseillaise*.
—Two young gents with a Negro . . .
Variations on the American national anthem.
—It takes the dark of night to see that . . . .
A dialogue by chance, a trip by chance having as a limit
only the darkness open to the headlights, only the rhythm
of the truck, of the wind, of the truck driver and the clari-
net
   until dawn and the suburbs of Pittsburgh
   until the next truck
   the next friendship
    and what prevents us from going to Chicago? to Fort
Wayne? Muskegon? Lansing? Detroit?
   Snow and ice, we cross a landscape in negative, touring
to see faces, the same towns, the same snow, the same roads
with their "diners" more or less new. Only the faces are
different: the mustache of a Canadian lumberjack, the scar
of a Polish farmer, the smile of a businessman, the blue cap
of a Negro.
   In Detroit, Banjo Bob's cousin trains horses. For 30 years
he has been working at General Motors, for 28 years he has
been training horses when he comes back from the factory.
One hundred and fifty square meters of sawdust behind a
three-room house. In the sawdust, two mares turn, jump,
and everywhere skyscrapers, factory chimneys, airplanes.
We spend the night on straw in the stable, next to the animals. We dine on beer and hot dogs. Peter's clarinet meets

the grocer's trumpet and the plumber's bass. The neighbors, the whole street pays us a visit, coming to see the two whites who sleep in a black man's stable. Two nights of partying and music.

In Elmira, the police chase us because Peter played his clarinet in the streets.

In Boston, Peter's mother bakes us brownies. We describe for her the mares, the truck drivers, the snowstorm. A little woman in a chrome and porcelain kitchen:

—He had drunk a whole bottle of rum? Poor boys all alone in the cold . . . . And you were comfortable, in the hay?

She is ironing our shirts when her husband comes in. The director of a shipping company, seated on a table. The smell of baking, of warm linen, of a cigar.

At New Haven, Madame de Chine and Peter discuss Chinese and Japanese literature. We drink green tea in fragile cups. Again she entrusts Perrault to my care.

—You've lost weight, Grégoire!
and she asks me about my studies.

A week of freedom, the only one, the anarchy of hours and of faces. The discovery of hitchhiking: voyages of friendship. The only ones who stop are the talkative or the tender-hearted. Wave good-by to egoists, they drive on: bourgeois enamored of their cars or their time, timid women, miserly shopkeepers, envious old men. For us, the Negroes, the generous, the poor.

Is it the presence of Peter A? We are going through a museum. Each meeting seems to be a sampling of humanity: a woman---jam, a grocer---pepper and salt, a farmer---philosopher, a magnanimous dog, the rich, the not-so-rich and he who doesn't give a damn, children with or without a ball. I had read, learned that the earth was round, popu-

145

lated. To my amazement it's true.

Hunched up in a chair, warm in the glass cage at a gas station, I watch trucks pass, I listen to the sleeping attendant.

—Peter ! Hey, Peter !

—Yes?

—What must you do to make all men happy?

—Perrault's right, Greg. You are a peasant, of a new kind: the international hick.

—Be serious.

—We're all serious!

A car pulls up. The horn wakes the attendant. We go out with him. Next to the gas pump, a man dances in place to warm himself.

—We're hitchhiking, Peter A says to him.

— . . .

—We're going to New Jersey, Peter adds. Are you going through New York, by chance?

Still dancing, the man looks us up and down. The headlights of a truck shine on him; thin hair, a beige coat, polka dot tie.

—I don't take just anyone . . . he says.

—These guys are headed back to Princeton, says the attendant.

—Oh, Princeton students. Why didn't you say so. Of course! I'm going to Philadelphia. I'll put you off at the junction. Get in, boys. You must excuse me, these days you never know who you're dealing with.

—No, thank you! says Peter A.

—Pardon me ?

—No, thank you! Peter repeats. We don't ride with just anyone.

The man's anger is expressed in an abrupt departure, tires burning on the snow.

— I'm buying, says the attendant.

From a drawer, he pulls out a flask of whiskey.

—Here's to you.

Black curls on his forehead, a sad man. He explains to us that his son studies at New York University. "He won't make a mess of his life, not him. I'd like him to meet a couple of good guys like you."

He goes back to sleep in the chair next to mine.

Later on we'll find a truck bound for Princeton. Why go back? Wouldn't it be better to continue this wandering, to go from man to man? We would tour America, the world.

And Laura, Jane, Sarcelle?

Laura would have nothing to say. Could she condemn my freedom? Jane would find herself another student, one of those straightforward Americans "who will go from his work to his family, a child-man."

My dog. Yes . . . I would miss my dog . . . .

—Let's hit the road, says Peter A. We're losing time here and we need to be in Princeton by morning.

—I'm coming.

Chapter 8

March 10, 1947

Hi, Grégoire!
The show goes on! By the way, ran into Marie Godefroy last week, she asked for news of you. Of my last five songs, two are hits: *Pocket Pea-Brain* and *Atomic Heart* (too bad, not the best ones!) You can write to me at 12 rue du Dragon, Paris 6e. I have three rooms on the fifth floor, low ceilings, a piano, two hundred records, and a bed. A luxury in old Europe. So much for your brother! Soon it will be spring. I was at La Chêneraie for Christmas. Papa is recovering from his operation. Mama writes that he is up and around for a couple of hours every day. You must listen to loads of jazz over there. My regards to Super-Aunt What's-her-name.

Fabien

An operation? What operation? When?
From a distance, this news swelled to enormous size. Why hadn't my mother let me know? Surely, he was going to die if he got up "only two hours a day." That life! All of my father's life in a nutshell: "born, lived, died at La Chêneraie." His books, his chess games, his farmers, his rheumatism, his sons.
One day he had told us: "I've had the good luck and the

bad luck of not working." What would he leave behind? A memory. Such a fragile memory: a few images and a few words that time would erode.

"For him it's too late. But you, Grégoire, how will you live to leave something more than this erasable trace, this insect trail?"

I foresaw life as too short. A moment of panic. My death surprised me. "Yet it is everywhere, in Chaucer, Shakespeare, Kierkegaard, Uncle Henri, the ducks." Other people's ...

My father's illness brought me a stage closer to death. Seated at my desk, letter in hand, I awaited the years as if they were seconds.

—You! You're beginning to bore the hell out of me with your gloomy introspection . . . Perrault said to me one evening.

For several days I'd been talking to him about my fears. He had listened with patience, patience more and more visible, more and more aggressive. We were in my room. Faint light and arched windows, a subdued mixture of electricity and the Gothic. Near me, Peter B turned (too quickly?) the pages of a book. Peter A was writing.

Perrault got out of his armchair as if from a bed, throwing aside the *New York Times* that covered him:

—Why don't you think a little more about the death of others and a little less about your own? he said in French.

Perrault repeated his remark in English, called as witnesses the two Peters, who raised their heads. They looked at me. I was the accused, Perrault the accuser.

—Do you ever read a newspaper?

—Once in a while . . .

—So, who is Anne O'Hare McCormick?

— . . .

—And Reston? Callender? Arthur Krock?

I shrugged my shoulders. Perrault distressed, sitting again in his chair, then standing, paced up and down the room, haranguing the two Peters.

—The life and death of others, that's in the papers. To read a newspaper, you have to get to know its editors, their ideas. You compare their approach, their information.

Turning to me:

—Who's the Prime Minister of France?

—Politics, always this same stupidity, the schemes . . . I replied.

—And yet you discuss philosophy, religion, ethics?

—It's not the same thing

—Are you against war?

Peter A had stood up and was watching me.

—Of course, I'm against war.

—Racism?

—Obviously.

—Then, according to you, let the Germans put all the Jews in Europe in crematoriums?

—No!

—So, there are good wars?

—You are such a pain in the ass! You think you're Socrates? And if I refuse to "live with my times." If I prefer my reason . . .

Too bad if these were clichés, I clung to them, wanting to make my ignorance an act of faith. I hated Perrault: "glib show-off." And me, always the schoolboy caught in the act. Peter B on the sofa. Peter A leaning on the door of the study. Perrault, hands raised to the ceiling, the button of

150

his blazer stretched to breaking, the fabric twisted on his stomach, eased when he lowered his arms.

—My poor old chap, that's it, to live with the times: to accept conventional wisdom, or, at least, to submit to it.

Perrault was sweating, keeping time, pacing the carpet.

—To give in to the times, to yield, not to believe in improvement. He (pointing to Peter B) goes backward twenty centuries. Why not? He (pointing to Peter A) goes forward twenty years. One searches . . . One searches . . .

Muttering, then mute, out of breath from too many ideas, Perrault collapsed into an armchair, eyes closed.

—They're fighting in Greece and Palestine, said Peter B.

—In Indochina, said Peter A.

All three against me .

—What do you want me to do about it?

—If they send you to Indochina as a soldier . . . said Perrault.

—The French won't come to get me in America.

—The Pentagon is asking for an army of a million men. You have a choice, the French Army or the American.

— But the atom bomb . . .

—Baruch says that the Russians already know half the secrets.

—The Russians are our allies.

—Are they honoring the Potsdam agreements in Poland? And in Greece, Tito supports the Communists, doesn't he? You didn't read Acheson's announcement to the Senate?

A cascade of information. How important was this jumble? Distant events made unreal by the vagueness of the articles. Countries strewn around the globe. An imaginary red thread like the one my father moved with the advance of the Allies during the war. What struck me was the passion of my friends.

Because, although their opinions differed, their passion was the same and all three considered my "indifference" an insult. They joined forces to make me read the newspapers. Day after day, at every opportunity they questioned me. In the shower: "Who's taking part in the Moscow conference?" At the end of a class: "What's going on in Hungary?" During a game of squash: "How much is Truman asking Congress for aid to Greece?"

I struggled, hating this forced education . . . and I got in the habit of recognizing the the names of characters in these different tragedies called London, Moscow, Jerusalem, Athens, Hanoi. The world emerged from the fog like Rouen seen from the terrace at *La Chêneraie*. Every morning, the paper announced the glow of fires: seventy-seven Communists killed in Greece, eight Europeans in Madagascar, twelve hundred dead at Texas City, six hundred "Viets" in Indochina, five Marines near Tientsin, strikes, Plans, conferences, treaties.

My innocence attracted my guides. Each, in turn, explained their point of view to me, leaving me alone only when they were convinced I agreed with them. A difficult task since the ideas of one annulled those of the others: Peter A pacifist; Peter B militant for a democracy which he defined as the free will of the people, and to a struggle of Good against Evil; Perrault skeptic, profiting from their disagreement.

—No one is ever right, Grégoire. War is believing you're right.

During this time came the good weather. "De Gaulle creates a political party." The trees were covered with buds. "The Moscow conference is a checkmate." The lilacs bloomed. "The World Bank lends two hundred and fifty million to France." The magnolias, the wisteria.

A spring of waiting, I live in submission to this game of *their* truth. As for my father, I had asked for details; a letter from my mother informs me that he was suffering from a stomach ulcer. The operation was followed by phlebitis. "We must be careful."

A spring of joy, above all: each morning when the sun rose, each time when I went out, even though prepared for the shock of clear light and warmth, I didn't hold back from running on the lawns. I leapt over bushes. At the Port of Missing Men, flowers, yellow, blue, pink, the creek water crossed by the white reflection of a cloud: the rocks, light gray, washed by winter's snows and rains, where moss created miniature landscapes. Sarcelle lying on the warm grass, dark eye in black fur.

Laura's dresses billowed, clinging in the wind. From winter she emerged as I had never seen her, her wrists so very thin on bare arms. She no longer feared the light and held on to me until daybreak in our house on the outskirts of Princeton.

In its untended garden, grass grew among the flowers. At six in the morning, chair in one hand, a cup of tea in the other, we looked, in our bare feet, for a spot among the shrubs. Her bathrobe was the same green as the new leaves. Some orioles had their nest behind the hedge and the male passed, yellow and black, between the apple trees. Imaginary deer, hidden in the woods, watched us. Sometimes Laura brought Sarcelle and the dog chased the butterflies numbed by the cool of the morning.

Laura's gaiety, all in gestures or in games. Laura's sadness, all in words. Laura the light or Laura the dark. Pillow fights. "Grégoire, I've spoiled you, you'll never be a man." When she laughed, she hid her mouth with both hands. When she suffered, she held her chin tightly in her fingers.

Laura of the South, Laura of Brooklyn or of London: to sing she put on any and all accents:

It's mighty strange, it's mighty strange,
No one ever says, Sylvester, you keep the change.
I try to do as folks tell me to,
But they're always absent-minded
When my work is through!

Laura was more and more cheerful, this spring; she stayed happy sometimes throughout a trip. We went to Cape Cod; she ran along the beach imitating the cries of the gulls that, surprised, turned around her. A flat land of bushes, wind, clouds. In the dunes, we made a fire and ate clams. Respectful of American puritanism, we stayed in big hotels with anonymous clients. We pretended not to know each other and I rejoined her later in her room where we spoke in low voices.

Spring gave Jane, too, a new allure: brown skin and hair cut short. She invented lives for the people we met in the street: "This woman with the grapefruit hat writes poems about birds." " The tall young man in front of the drugstore eats flowers. On moonless nights, he's the one who grazes on the flower beds in town."

One night, Jane did not flee to her door as usual. We had

returned quickly from the Harrises' because I thought she was late. Past midnight, the pastor would be worried. However, she waited there, hesitant. I recalled the impression of our first meeting—a deer, a rabbit, a quail, head cocked, an animal ready to run or to be tamed. A contagious fear. I waited for her to speak.

—Why don't you kiss me, Grégoire?

After the surprise, indignation. Kiss her? "Not you, Jane! You're not like that!"

She waited a meter from me. How could I make her understand? How could she understand that she is *the other*, the one that you don't kiss, the memory of a childhood love, the hope of a grown-up love.

I thought to myself: "The moment hasn't come, Jane. We would spoil the patience that has drawn us together built on memories of the way I wanted it to be on the terrace at La Chêneraie. Don't ruin this image of yourself. You are the refuge, the animal that one tames and that keeps a look of fear to remind us that it needs to be loved. And you would like to give an order? An order that would destroy you, destroy us?"

—You have nothing to say, Grégoire?

Silence. I had forgotten my silence. How to answer? Already her voice trembled. Say anything.

—In France, when a girl lets herself be kissed, that means to say she accepts . . . everything . . . .

But if she did accept everything ?

— . . . we don't want that, Jane. We also want to love each other later on. Please, Jane, understand me.

Her silence now. What did she understand? What did she imagine? When she began to laugh, I was sick with fear. She was mocking me? But her voice was cheerful, and tender:

— . . . My mother worries because I'm going out with a Frenchman!

My lie was accomplished, perfect. I had created for her the personage who, without doubt, suited her best: a Grégoire at once serious and romantic, trustworthy and un-expected, the "child-man" Laura had predicted.

So much the worse, so much the better. We were face-to-face. At arm's length, at fingers' length, I caressed Jane's hair. Now she belonged to me. Someone finally belonged to me, a new girl. At that moment, I remembered how as a child I put my new toys on the chest of drawers; I handled them as little as possible so they would keep, with their polish, the memory of that joy of having received them.

The next day, a return to light-hearted feelings confirmed our understanding, hands grazed as we walked together, during the dinners at her parents' or the Harrises'. We were becoming a recognized couple, almost official since host-esses invited us together to their parties, to the dances in May and June that honor debutantes. Jane, in a chestnut gown, saved me her waltzes. This rhythm pleased us.

On the "campus," I was amazed at the restlessness of the students, more noticeable each week. Meals at the club fin-ished with flying glasses of water. Groups formed: "We're leaving for New York." They returned by the seven o'clock morning train, pale and sleepy. Peter B denounced "this juvenile obsession with sex." "And you, you don't have a hard-on in the morning?" Peter A demanded. The softer the evenings, the more violent the games became on the lawns. "Spring fever." Perrault did gymnastics. Some-times, in the middle of the night, shouting announced a great concert. From the windows of the dormitories, cries answered, settled into lamentations. Rhythm of pots, of all sorts of metal objects hit over and over again, hailed by firecrackers, blasts of trumpets. From loudspeakers carried to the windows came military marches, jazz—no matter what as long as it added to the cacophony. Almost all the lights were turned on. The arrival of the proctors unleashed a bombardment: oranges, shoes, notebooks, bedding. Finally, the invasion: students in underpants, in pajamas, some stark naked, invaded the lawns, improvised a flag. Two thousand students rallied around a photo of Rita Hayworth, a chamber pot, or a bra, poured into town, stopped cars and trucks, booed the police, clamored for women, for alcohol, for freedom. And then the riot ceased, disappeared into the night, each one picked up on his way the flag, the shirt, the objects thrown from the windows earlier.

—I've got a bottle!

Peter B grabbed me by the shoulder. I stepped back, as amazed as if God had officially announced to me that He was tired. An afternoon in May, heavy heat without hope of a storm.

—Wouldn't you rather have a game of squash?

No! Peter B wanted to drink. He didn't bother to answer, brought two glasses, some water. He took off his coat and put it on the back of a chair. Seated, framed in the Gothic bay window, shoulders slumped, he contemplated the bottle of Scotch before opening it.

—Say, Peter, did you see in the *New York Times*, Truman wants to institute the draft and . . .

—Why the hell should I care?

He poured himself half a glass of whisky, a little water.
As soon as he began to drink, his forehead turned from
white to red.

—Jane will be here later!

—Help yourself!

My glass was still full, he finished his first, and prepared
a second with methodical movements that were too slow;
he was usually so hurried ... I looked out across the lawns.
Where the devil were Peter A and Perrault? Something, no
matter what, to make noise. I had never seen anyone drink
in silence.

Peter had put a foot on the coffee table; he tapped an
imaginary rhythm, regular as a metronome.

—You must be thirsty!

He had probably not heard. The foot continued, tic tac tic
tac. "He's driving me crazy." His foot stopped, he took a
swallow, the foot started up again. Each time he drank the
foot stopped, started again. "What would Peter A do in
my place? Drink with him? Hide the bottle? Talk? Wait?"

Peter B coughed. I jumped.

He poured a third glass. Sweat soaked his forehead,
formed finally a drop which hurried between his eyebrows,
then along his nose where it stopped suspended. A fly ran
across his right cheek. He looked into his glass, a mixture
of whisky and lukewarm water.

—I believe, he said, that God is sometimes wrong.

—Wrong, how?

His index finger placed on his lips, then pointed toward
the sky, he made a sign for me to be quiet. The drop of
sweat fell, the fly installed itself on his chin. He drank a
long swallow, another, refilled. We'd been there a half an
hour.

—You're going to drink the whole bottle?

—We can always buy another . . .

I, too, was sweating now. Take a shower? I dared not leave him alone. I emptied my glass. Dark patches of sweat spread out on Peter B's blue shirt in answer to the red patches on his forehead. The alcohol had done me good, I felt less nervous. "Too bad, let's go, another glass. This Scotch isn't bad, lukewarm."

—Peter, I think you have two or three flies on your chin.

—Poor beasts!

He drank in little gulps now and his glass was not so quickly emptied

—Where are they?

—Who?

—The flies . . .

—Two on your right cheek and one on your chin.

—For them, perhaps, I am God.

He closed his eyes and smiled:

— . . . But whose fly am I? Help yourself, Grégoire, we'll buy more. I would rather be a wasp. How about you?

A bee or a wasp? I meditated on this problem. Before settling myself in the armchair I filled my half full glass to the brim. Thus I would have to move as little as possible. A breath of air brought us, from somewhere, the music of a violin.

—Me? A duck!

—Oh you bore me to death with your ducks. Always in the mud. Meanwhile wasps live on the flowers.

—I'm free, am I not?

—No!

—Why not?

—The proof, you're not a duck.

—That's true!

—I told you, God's wrong.

With a violent slap he crushed the two flies on his cheek. He looked at the cadavers: "How can you expect God to resist?" The spots of sweat ran together on his shirt. The violin had stopped. Not even possible to be a duck! The armchair was suffocating me. As I was getting up I saw Jane crossing the lawn.

—Look out! Your sister!

—God save us!

Seized by panic, we stood up, emptied our glasses. Peter B snatched the bottle and we ran and took refuge in the shower room. She was already on the stairs. Her steps resounded, then her voice in our room: Peter! Grégoire!

—What is she doing?

—She's going to wait.

—You have your glass?

—Oh, shit! No.

We had left our glasses on the table. On tiptoe, with exaggerated caution in each gesture, Peter B got under the showerhead and opened the faucet. He put the bottle in the shower; a little water entered the neck of the bottle, the rest fell on him. He came back, drenched; at each step water gushed out of his shoes.

—Here, we'll take turns drinking.

Almost straight whiskey. Seated on the tile floor, face-to-face, the bottle between us, we waited. Not a fly in this white room, we were alone. Hair wet, flattened down in black locks, Peter B raised the bottle regularly, too regularly. Was he counting the seconds between each swallow? Twenty-three, twenty-four, twenty-five GULP. Twenty-five GULP. Twenty-five GULP. A swallow every twenty-five seconds. In the stairwell, Jane's voice: "Bob, have you seen my brother and Grégoire?" "No, Miss. Ain't seen 'em!" Silence. From the shower, not quite turned off, drops fell.

—Why are you drinking, Grégoire?

—I don't know.

—I know. You're drinking because I'm drinking. You are our innocent, Grégoire. Our pagan. You are the meek of the Gospels. You are in Limbo. For you, neither hell nor paradise, but an eternal waiting.

He stood up, solemn, put his hand on the top of my head:

—You permit me to baptize you?

He held up the bottle . . .

—Not the whiskey!

—You're right.

He put down the bottle, took off his shoes, which he filled with water. "In the name of the Father, the Son . . . " Coolness. Peter did not stop his coming and going, refilled one shoe and then the other, poured the water over my head. "Renounce Satan," first shoe, "and all his works," the second.

"I'm going to teach you the Pater. Recite after me: *Pater Noster qui est in . . .* "

—Careful! I hear steps on the stairs.

—It's Perrault.

—Wait until he's gone by.

—Now!

Peter took the bottle. I picked up his shoes. No need of steps to go down the stairs, we jumped from one landing to the next, falling, getting up again. Nothing hurt us. We had not conquered gravity but we had conquered pain and we flew from landing to landing. We flew across the lawns.

161

Voices called us, Jane and Perrault. Why were people stopping to watch us?

—To the tree! To the tree! Peter shouted.

He climbed it. I followed him. It was easy. Everything was easy. From branch to branch. Below us, the crowd. Peter threw them the cork and passed me the bottle. I gave him back his shoes. Perched in a fork of the tree, we drank.

—Too bad we don't have any bananas . . . .

—It doesn't matter.

Astride, he advanced the length of the limb, then let himself hang down, let go one hand, hooked by his legs, head down. Fifty feet below, a carpet of faces raised toward us.

—Come on down! Come on down, right now!

It was the voice of Mike, the university's head proctor.

—Come get us!

Peter came back toward me.

—I think, he said, that we're going to have to run. Drink up, new soldier of Christ, these heathen want to burn us at the stake.

After a religious swig, we made the descent and, six feet from the ground, we jumped. The proctors rushed forward. Somewhere, Jane's voice. We ran too fast for them, we jumped too well, over hedges, bushes. I collapsed in a clump of bushes. Kneeling at the threshold of the chapel, Peter hammered on the door with his fists:

—Open up! Sanctuary! Sanctuary!

The proctors surrounded him. They were about to take him but Peter leapt up and disappeared with his pursuers.

The coolness woke me up. It was night. My head hurt less than my arms and legs, bruised by so many spills. An end to the state of grace. I tried to get up. Impossible. Still drunk? I crawled, frightened by the slightest footstep.

Above all, I had to stay hidden. Then I remembered that Peter B had baptized me. I knelt down:

—Good Lord in Heaven, I've had enough! And I went back to sleep.

When I got back to our room, Peter B was stretched out on the floor. Peter A gave me a beer.

—Drink this and go to bed. It's midnight.

At eight o'clock, Peter B had disappeared. We found him about eleven at the edge of the lake. He was drinking gin.

He let us lead him back to the room, agreed to shave and take a shower. Then he escaped. We chased him, but he was too fast for us.

—He's going crazy, said Peter A.

—How did yesterday's binge begin? asked Perrault.

—I don't know. He just said: "I have a bottle."

It was Perrault who found him the next morning, sleeping under a car. The three of us carried him to the room. He opened his eyes, said nothing, let himself be carried. Under the shower, we had to lather him, dry him off.

—No way to let him leave anymore, said Peter A.

Jane sat on her brother's bed. When he woke up at the end of the afternoon, he seemed normal. We had dinner at his father's house, but on our return he gave me the slip. This time we didn't find him again until two days later. Beard black, clothing in rags, dirty, a gash on his forehead.

It was impossible to hold him. He took off, drank anything: beer, whiskey, wine, cognac, gin, everything he came across.

> We are poor little sheep
> Who have gone astray
> Baah Baah Baah

He had rejoined the Puritans of booze. When we heard this song at night, Peter A and I went down. If Peter B was among the singers, we would beg him to come up with us at least to take a shower and get some clean clothes, a little food. Sometimes he accepted.

By the end of the week we were resigned. Peter B was "our" drunk. A calm and humble drunk who let us bathe him from time to time. Thus he passed unnoticed, almost sober on Sunday when I took him to lunch at his father's, the pastor's, house. He became a new habit, another manifestation of this spring.

Saturday night or Sunday afternoon, dances, jam sessions were organized in the clubs, on the banks of the lake, in a rented room in town.

Coming from Vassar, Smith, Bryn Mawr, the girls arrived on Saturday on the one o'clock train. Red, blue, or yellow, dresses and silk stockings paraded between the lilacs and the wisteria. Boys lined up as they went by: the yelps and grins of young puppies. Girls who came for the first time, trembled, walking naked, transparent, clinging to the arm of the one who had invited them into this trap, often a childhood friend they no longer recognized; he also wore the mask of hunger. They hesitated in front of his room. And yet . . . they left on Sunday, almost always virgins, kissed, pawed, but intact, saved by the Puritan tradition, by alcohol which castrated the lovers, by fear of having a baby, by the jealousy of students without girls who watched the couples, not leaving them the respite for a transgression. They took the train at 5:32, crumpled by noise and emotion, nostalgia of a hangover, sadness for the party ended until the next weekend.

Saturday and Sunday, Peter A and Banjo Bob's orchestra earned fifteen dollars an hour playing dance music for their friends. Clarinet, banjo, trumpet, trombone, and piano. Whatever the club or rented room, the same people always appeared through the smoke.

> My momma done tol' me
> When I was in pigtails,
> My momma done tole me, hon!
> A man's gonna sweet talk,
> And give ya the big eye,
> But when the sweet talkin's done
> A man is a two-face,
> A worrisome thing
> Who'll leave ya t' sing
> The blues in the night.

Two or three hundred familiar faces with eyes slowed down by whisky: all met again at the gym, at the library, or in the lecture halls . . . all cousins in our white button-down shirts, on scholarships or rich, New Yorkers or Californians, descendants of Italians or Scandinavians . . . differences smoothed over by our gray flannels, by a common vocabulary. With this little guy in glasses, yesterday, I was discussing the similarities between Kierkegaardian philosophy and Dostoyevsky. "Man has lost contact with Nothingness," said he. This afternoon, he was dancing in the arms of a tall girl. I shouted to him: "Have you resumed contact?" His look did not light up in recollection.

For these costume balls we disguised ourselves as caricatures of what we were: Princeton students, like those at Harvard and Yale, the universities of the Ivy League, all cousins, all of the same skin, of the same gray flannel cloth. Peter B seated between the clarinet and the banjo, face fixed in a smile, stayed calm as long as his glass was full. Jane, at ease in my hands, ran away from her fear of others towards me. We danced in front of the orchestra and I showed her the Aesop of modern times.

—What Aesop?

— Bob, the Negro, the freed slave. He leads the dance. He's the fabler. The Negroes are America's myth makers. They set the tone. Without them, you would still be a European province . . . .

—You exaggerate!

—Always! Always exaggerate! The Negroes exaggerate. I am a Negro, a French Negro, a Norman Negro and I'll wake up one of these days with a black ear, then two. Would you love me with two black ears? Not black really, brown, chocolate . . .

Jane was glad when we left the dance. Then she dared let go of me, run ahead, turning round and round:

—Do you see my legs, *Monsieur le Français*?

We strolled along the university's paths: plane trees, linden trees, and wisteria, lawns crisscrossed by squirrels. Deserted on Sunday afternoons, because all the students had gone to a dance or home for the weekend. The professors stayed at home. A dead town in which I knew the unique survivor. We went to Perrault's room and surprised him in his polka-dot dressing gown. He gathered up the pages of the *New York Times* (ten times heavier on Sunday), took down his suit, looked for shorts, shirt, shoes, socks, disappeared with his gear into the shower room.

—Some tea, children?

Perrault, impeccable, buttered the toast, passed the cups

in this big room with curtains drawn against the sun. There on the desk, piles of yellow, pink, and green sheets of paper were the only lively colors in the room. Jane and I settled ourselves on the bed, he on the chair, he who knew that I went to meet Laura several nights a week. I imagined a reproach in his kindness towards Jane. Reproach or sadness? I smiled, happy in this quiet and empty room after the excesses of the crowd earlier. Restful politeness. A few words taking the place of the noise.

—Ah, Ramadier, Ramadier! You see, Grégoire, it takes a Socialist to bludgeon strikers! Nothing like the Left these days to beat up the workers . . . .

Perrault strode the length and breadth of the room, looking like Danton.

—I'm taking notice, Grégoire. I'm only taking notice. Opinions will come afterwards. But you must realize that the actual pay of a French worker in 1947 represents only sixty-four per cent of his pay in 1937.

I listened, convinced and compassionate, touching Jane's shoulder with mine, thinking of Laura.

Holding Laura's face in my hands. We had been walking in the woods of the Port of Missing Men; she had come to a halt:

—Kiss me!

My fingers shook. "If I held Jane like this, would my fingers shake? Can it be that I love them both? Two women, a single or two loves? A single or two Grégoires?"

—Grégoire, sometimes you worry me. I don't understand your eyes anymore.

—My eyes?

—Your look.

167

Her uneasiness was contagious and I turned my head away, looking at the trees, the rocks. "Would she be vulnerable?" She held my arm and for a few seconds I was afraid for her, a fear unknown, a fear I had never had before in my life. I thought of my ailing father, Harris blind. A moment as intense as those seconds of happiness experienced last winter. A moment of unhappiness: every human being is given to unhappiness, even Laura. I pitied her, our roles reversed.

—Look at me, Grégoire.

I didn't dare. I waited until the pity left my eyes, until this fear subsided.

—Grégoire?

—Yes.

Repeating to myself "I love her" so she would read nothing else in my look.

One night when we were in Princeton, I was working. From the kitchen I listened to Laura asleep. Beyond, through the book open before me, in "this six-inch chapter is the stoneless grave," a sailor steered his ship far from land, far from port.

. . . the port is pitiful; in the port is safety, comfort, hearthstone, supper, warm blankets, friends." ". . . in landlessness alone resides the highest truth, shoreless, indefinite as God . . .   (Chapter 23, "The Lee Shore", *Moby Dick*)

I thought: "No, Melville! No, Grégoire!" The remembrance of earlier dreams of adventure no longer seduced me. Here was the Port of Habits and this familiar breathing. Why look elsewhere? Enough light filtered through the door for me to see Laura. What lofty truths thus pursued Ahab,

Melville, and the crew of the *Pequod*? Above all don't awaken her nor Time which, like her, was motionless. "Tchang-Tchouen, capital of Mongolia, practically isolated by the Chinese Communists." This headline in the paper appeared like a post card, a red flower on the steppes traveled by horsemen. The call of a barn owl came from the garden. Laura's arm lay across the white side of the bed: later I would take the wrist and fold the arm to make a place for myself. "Grégoire, you're eighteen years and three months old. There's your shore."

But everyone wanted me to change. They wanted me to be different, each in his own way. Laura, first. Why not? I was happy, everything would be possible to me as long as we were talking: Perrault's irony, Peter A's fervor, Laura's intransigence. All except the renunciation of a Melville. Not in the springtime. Not yet. I was getting so used to lying. Besides, I wasn't lying anymore, I accepted, I believed in the beliefs of others. Such a pretty name, Tchang-Tchouen. Greece, Indochina, Madagascar: wars today, beautiful trips tomorrow. The tree frogs sang without rhythm, drop by drop. My father? With the good weather he would get up for three hours, four hours. Harris would make the best of his infirmity. Peter B would sober up someday . . .

—What are you thinking about, Grégoire?

How long had she been watching me?

—I was reading *Moby Dick*.

She raised herself, less white than the sheets, a pale shadow.

—Grégoire, which would you want to be? Ahab or Ishmael?

The one who hates or the one who bears witness?

—I haven't finished yet.

169

—Do you have to know the ending? You have to decide now. Right now.

—Ishmael, then.

Disappointed:

—In bearing witness you become accustomed, you accept. You're no longer alive.

—I don't even know whom to hate . . .

—Neither did your uncle. They killed him!

I had turned out the light. Lying beside her, I thought: "Since we've been living together, this is the first time she's spoken of him." I dared not touch her. I listened to the barn owl, the tree frogs. I listened to Melville:

Narcissus, who because he could not grasp the tormenting mild image he saw in the fountain, plunged into it and was drowned. But that same image we ourselves see in all rivers and oceans. It is the image of the ungraspable phantom of life . . . (Chapter One, "Loomings", *Moby Dick*)

My uncle, also, died by drowning. By what Moby Dick? Peter B would accuse the Japanese; Peter A, the war; Perrault, the fanaticism of reason. What's the use of seeking the truth, since it kills? Ahab's truth. I got up and opened Melville's book to his Epilogue:

"The drama's done. Why then here does anyone step forth? — Because one did survive the wreck."

Ishmael.

Would it be cowardice, the will to survive that would make me choose his role?

We were not sleeping. The whole room was oriented towards the glow of the night at the open window. Laura spoke to me—sitting up, no doubt, because her voice came down to me:

—How can you love without knowing how to hate? To know the extremes of life. Without Ahab, Ishmael would have nothing to tell, Grégoire. Witnesses are failures. Books speak only of their regrets.

She cited some examples. I dared not contradict her. With dawn, she would soften. Such exaltation would not bear the light. I listened, thinking: "This time I can't follow you."

And it was she who turned again to me, lying beside me, her hand on my shoulder.

—I'm happy anyway. I'm cold. Why is it always colder in the morning? Warm me. What time do you have to go back to Princeton?

—At seven.

When I left, she was asleep, green shadow on her eyelids. In her sleep she belonged to me. Laura without pride or silk, hands open on the sheets, an image that I carried with me on the road back. Wasn't she at least partly right? Wasn't it better to believe than to judge the beliefs of others, to act rather than to judge their actions?

I passed through the outskirts of Princeton just awakening. Wooden houses, white, blue, green, between hedges of lilacs, sycamores and ash trees, houses joined by lawns more or less recently mowed, tiny differences marking the boundaries of property. There slept the families. There I would sleep if I married Jane. While with Laura . . .

Harris and I were talking about Melville:

—Is Ishmael a coward?

—Well! There's a question!

Astonishment crossed his blind eyes. He put on his glasses.

171

—Ishmael survives by chance, Grégoire. Nothing suggests . . .

—Ishmael chose to be a witness because witnesses survive. Prophets like Ahab can't survive.

Harris had got up and was walking up and down. Did he count his footsteps or did he sense the presence of objects in front of him?

—To each, his cowardice: hate fate or fear it. Why would witnesses be cowards? Peter denies Christ three times, but he dies crucified in Rome.

—His shame had turned him into a prophet.

—Fundamentally, this contempt for witnesses, it's a fascist idea that you have there. Have we ever talked politics? Even so . . .

Standing in the middle of the room, Harris struck the palm of one hand with the edge of the other, cutting up his sentences:

—It's too easy, Grégoire, this theory. Witnesses would be cowards, writers would be cowards. What is left of a man then? Force, brutality. Hitler burned books. Ishmael survives not because he is a coward but because he is . . . sacred. Witnesses are priests, the chosen ones. Their responsibility is enormous.

He had resumed walking. I listened, again convinced, amazed at this new proof of my weakness: always convinced by the most recent words. My weakness or the strength of the words? I said to myself: "They lead you wherever they wish. But when will you learn to think for yourself, Grégoire? What does it take? What catastrophe or what revelation?

I imagined a theater where my friends would come to argue among themselves to take possession of me: Perrault,

the two Peters, Jane and Laura, my parents, Harris, Fabien.
A beautiful cacophony! And I would become the shadow
of the conqueror of this tournament . . . . I invented the
monologues of these characters, their angers, their replies.
It was a secret game which amused me sometimes, never
for very long, quickly distracted by the gestures or the ideas
of the real actors.

And I took refuge in work. For me, work was the occasion to rediscover the silent importance of books. The written word didn't require, like the spoken word, an immedi-
ate response, it imposed neither love nor hate.

As for the professors, their ideas were put away in my
notebooks. A few of them interested me, all of them amused
me. They reminded me of my passers-by of Rouen. Like
them, the professors spread out their life around a unique
monument that they described with emphasis or in minute
detail. Monuments that were immense or minuscule. One
professor had the reputation of interesting himself only in
the posthumous works of Shelley, another compared the
universe to a whirlwind of which the center was the
incompatability of egos. Harris considered every event,
written or lived, as a fable and described the Middle Ages
as a parable of modern times. Throughout my notebooks,
I reconstructed their pet theories, targets to aim at to obtain a better mark. Since I accepted everyone's ideas, why
not adopt the desired ideas at exam time?

The odor of departure: the sun dried up the grass and the
earth. The smell of the long vacation. "Long," the beautiful imprecision of the adjective, hope for quantity, hours of
space and unusual movements.

Peter B had sobered up. Out of fear of examinations? He
didn't give any explanation. The sadness of his face forbade questions.

Chapter 9

This time, I was a Negro. A sub-Negro. What work!

I was the *last* of the Negroes from eleven a.m. to midnight on Long Island, that island which starts in Brooklyn and depopulates itself in the hundred miles leading to the deserted beaches of Montauk Point. Two-thirds of the way out on the island, Southampton is a town of houses spaced far apart and as big as chateaux, built on the sand facing the Atlantic. Biblical mansions, menaced every instant by collapse into the sand and the sea, propped up by an effort paid for in dollars, constant proofs of the wealth which alone preserved them. Clubs, golf courses, tennis courts, avenues. On a lawn, in the midst of giant elms, a hotel with white columns. The shadows of the gardens attracted the coolness of the sea, which took on the taste of grass. There, guests ate quietly, here and there on the terraces. There, old ladies, gray silk and pearls, watched couples come and go on the silence of the carpets.

In the center of the Splendid Hotel, in a room without windows where the steam was heavy with grease, where the doors remained closed on the racket of the dishes and machines: one Negro, two, three and Grégoire, the dishwashers worked. The first was Washington. We sang:

> *Wash, wash, Washington*
> *Git a washin', Washington . . .*

Jefferson, the second, never took off a gray felt hat. They had nicknamed the third Truman. They didn't name me, they yelled at me: "Hey, you!"

It wasn't by chance that I was in Southampton. Laura was to come there and I had made it the end of a random trip with Peter A. Hitchhiking across the South, the Middle West, the East. Picture-postcard days, green horizons, orange twilights, the month of July in continual movement had led me at last to this cubbyhole without air and without sun.

The trays arrived through a hole in the wall. Monotony of fare and of garbage: lobster shells, clam shells, french fries, bits of meat stuck together with butter and melted ice cream, balls of bread that one swipe of the sponge sent into the garbage can. Each plate then stowed in a wooden rack, each glass, each piece of silver. Racks stacked in the machine. Oh, this machine! A steel cube, with two doors raised like guillotines, it puffed out steam. Gauges, trembling needles, Wash and Jefferson forbade us to touch it. Straddling our garbage cans, we admired it from a distance, Truman and I. It was a symbol of our inferiority, a rung to climb in this opaque cellar where the machine alone glistened, precise in the dampness. "One of these day . . . " Truman said to me. That was enough, I knew what he meant: "One of these days, Wash or Jeff will go. I'll get the machine and the ten dollars more a week." Wash had been working at the Splendid for twelve years, Jeff for seven years, and Truman for two. In three weeks I had lived their lives, except for the patience.

Then, in the cellar, I tried to imagine their patience. The stupor of my motions was a help: plate, sponge, garbage, rack. With the sponge, I wiped the sweat which stung my eyes, ran down my torso. I worked sitting down, noticing some traces of lipstick on a cigarette butt going by. "What time is it?" I worked standing. "One of these days" said Truman. The garbage can was almost full . . . a banana peel in the mashed potatoe. I sponged with the right hand. "Hey, you!" I sponged with the left hand, round plates, big, small, gravy boats, oval dishes, saucers, cups. I rinsed the sponge. "What time is it?" Again I worked sitting down. In a Kentucky field, two mares galloped with their colts.

—Truman, do you remember being free?

—Huh?

—Nothing . . .

Too much noise to talk to him, to explain my memories and my hopes of freedom. Sixteen states of the Union travelled with Peter A. Put away the sugar bowls, the salt cellars. Throw the napkins in the laundry hamper. Sponge with the right hand, then the left. Along a road in Virginia, green grass and red clay. All of July with Peter A. We didn't talk, we didn't even talk to each other anymore, we were friends. From one car to another. Through the steam, I made the journey again.

A beach on the Gulf of Mexico, swamps along Route 1, a cornfield in Ohio, and everywhere the clarinet, the trucks, the sun or the rain, night separated from day by technicolor twilights.

From Appalachicola, a post card for Jeanie.

Ashland City: "My dear parents".

Cincinnati: "Dear Jane" "Dear Laura."

The little Texan transported liquid air to Memphis at 80 miles an hour. His grandfather killed Indians.

The banker, joyous in his Lincoln.

A baby cried on my knees.

And everywhere

DINER

The memories of a white man; white hopes. Can a Negro hope to take these trips? What does a Negro hope for?

Wash, wash, Washington...

And Jeff ... and Truman .... What was it they saw through the steam of this basement? Were they like blind men? Is that what patience is? White hands shoved plates through the wall. The first teapot. Could it be five o'clock already? Rinse the sponge. "Hey, you!" Empty the garbage can. Truman and I carried it into a narrow court behind the hotel where we could have rested for a moment. But we were cold in the sun, the light hurt our eyes, and what would we have to talk about?

After so many hours of silence, I didn't know how to talk. Stripped, naked torso, naked. Every day I wrote a letter to Jane that had no end. I wrote her to write me, wrote her how to write to me, since she excused her much-too-brief letters with "I don't know what to tell you."

" ... It's easy. Start with the morning, your waking up, the noises in the house, your first thoughts. Then, dressing, what skirt or what dress, what hair style? Which did you kiss first, your mother or your father? Who smiled? What sky? The names of those you've seen, your itineraries, what you had for lunch. Was the coffee good? Were you bored, amused, what? Each move of a day, sort it out. Put it to the right for Grégoire's letter. Send it to the left to hell and gone. There you are, like God!"

All day, among my dirty dishes, I imagined the letter to Jane, as if I were speaking to her, reading those she wrote to me, longer and longer letters, moistened with steam, that

I unfolded with my finger tips to dry out in the evening in my room.

Dear Grégoire,

You tell me that you don't have time to swim or play tennis. What kind of a vacation is that! Now, every time I play tennis, I think of you and the others among their dishes and I'm ashamed. I got up at eight o'clock this morning, or rather, mother woke me because she wanted me to go shopping. Quickly, I put on my linen dress, the blue one, and then I remembered that you didn't like it. If I had kept it on, I would have had to tell you about it and you would have seen me in the blue dress until my next letter. So I put on the yellow and black one. But you don't know it. It's the one that I bought last week. So much for that. Mom called me from downstairs: "What are you doing, Jane?" Peter had already finished his breakfast. He's in very good spirits these days. I think he's a little bit in love with Gloria Dune and she with him. Do you remember? She's the one you told me has such a pretty voice. I was a little jealous. Peter goes out with her every day and when I hear her speak, I think of you. And I think of your dishes. Finally, how long are you going to stay in Southampton? Don't you think you could come back to Princeton a week early? Professor Harris has just said he would need us this fall, that we would begin work as soon as you came. And Martha Jones, Stephen's sister, is getting married on September seventh to a boy from Boston. There will be a dance on the sixth. I will wear the beige dress that mother brought me from New York. She's given me errands to do. Among other things, she wants a pink wool with a touch of yellow for her tapestry. It's impossible to find it in Princeton, even in Trenton. We'll have to write to France for it. The weather was so hot I didn't eat lunch. Nor did Daddy, although Mom made us a cold salmon salad with tomatoes and mayonnaise, everything I usually like. Now I am writing to you. It's three o'clock. I have a big glass of iced tea on my desk with fresh mint that I can smell from here. I'm wearing my green shorts. Why haven't you phoned the Alexanders yet? They have the prettiest house in Southampton. Not one of those horrors on the shore, but a little old house with trees. They're expecting your visit. Unless your horrible dishes don't leave you time for it.

I miss you.

Jane

Drying, the letter rolled up on itself. I put it under the lamp, I searched for traces of feeling: "I think of you and the others with their dishes and I feel ashamed" . . . "you would have seen me in the blue dress so I put on the yellow and black" . . . "I was a little jealous" . . . . Soon I knew each passage by heart, its place among the even lines, green ink on pale blue paper, such orderliness in the disorder of my room where only Jane's letters were put away, each one folded in its envelope, a stack of envelopes numbered by me, from one to fifteen. I was waiting for the sixteenth.

Was waiting similar to patience?

Git a washin, Washington . . .

Truman at least hoped someday to earn ten more dollars a week. But the other two; what were they hoping for?

—Truman, you're the happiest.

—Huh?

—Nothing.

Platters, plates, glasses, silver, each object had its noise. A mixture of noises and smells, steaming garbage, this room was like a garbage can where we were shut away.

"Why should I go to see the Alexanders? What was it to me that their house was little and old? I don't know how to talk anymore. They are too far away, as far as the sun and its light."

—Hey, you!

—Yes?

—The manager wants you.

What did the manager want? I was going out, Washington called me back.

—Hey, you!

—Yes?

—You can't see the manager like that!

Why not? What prevented me from seeing the manager like that? Ah, yes! The bare chest. A shirt was required to go to see these people and I put on my shirt, which because of the humidity immediately stuck to my skin. I closed the door behind me on a month of racket and recognized Laura standing in the hallway. Laura was at once precise in her green silk dress, her back to the window. I looked for the manager but he had disappeared.

—*Tu n'as pas très bon air.* (You don't look very good!)

Laura's first words were in French. I was reminded that she'd just come back from France. She'd seen my parents, Fabien, La Chêneraie. I dared not approach her, so clean, too clean to come towards me.

—Grégoire, I love you.

Her cheerful voice.

—Did you hear what I said?

She carried gloves, a purse, shoes of the same green as her eyes. She was standing six feet from me: I knew that her face came up to my shoulder.

—Are you coming, Grégoire?

—Wait for me a minute, please.

I passed over to the side of clean people, a free man. Ignoring the surprise of the manager, I left his office pay in hand, dollars stuffed in my pockets, patience abolished, discovering the joy of the emancipated.

—Just a second.

I opened the door of the pantry and I said goodbye to my three companions, realizing that here I had been afraid of the fate of others.

As if misery was contagious.

Sarcelle was waiting for me in the car. A full-grown dog now, she landed her sixty pounds on me, black paws, pink tongue, white teeth. Contagious joy. Contagious freedom, too. Laura, my freedom, my journey, my America, in a convertible with the smell of warm leather: the freedom of money and of the sun.

—Let's go swimming!

On the sand and at the sea. Sarcelle plunged into the surf, a dark silhouette in the green water. Specks of salt glistened on Laura's skin, barely shadowed by freckles. Laura the limpid, I rediscovered her in her details, fragile wrists, shorter hair and wet locks. Face-to-face, we passed from seriousness to laughter. Two months without seeing her! She's there! Shoulder against arms, my knees reach out towards hers; they had also kept their memories.

—Later.

Yes, soon. Too many people were moving about on this beach for us to dare to kiss, but we stayed, prolonging the wait. Impatience appeased by the sea. We scarcely spoke;

lying near us, the dog whined softly. One after the other the bathers went away. The shadows grew longer, accenting the relief of the sand. It took the coolness of the evening breeze to make us leave the beach,

We went through the little town and I noticed for the first time its vacation mood: cinemas, bookstores, shops for souvenirs and for antiques, merchants of the superfluous. A slow crowd moved along broad sidewalks. I lived near the station.

—You've lived here a month?

In my room, she was amazed at the disorder and the dirt, while I hid Jane's letters in the bottom of a drawer.

—You don't even have a view!

What for? I got home at midnight. From the window, I caught sight of a few roofs, some television antennas, a line of laundry drying.

—Not a book!

—Oh, when one is used to being alone . . .

—We can't stay here!

—But it's eight o'clock.

—I have so many friends who live in Southampton. They'll be delighted to have us.

—Both of us?

—You're my nephew, aren't you? Change first!

She spoke to me with the tone of reproach reserved for headstrong children, and kept to the middle of the room, set on her high heels, motionless in the midst of this squalor I was discovering. Motionless while I packed Uncle Henri's clothes in my suitcase, while I took a shower. Why was she so difficult, why did she attach so much importance to details when we had just found each other again? "She ruins everything." As soon as I had dressed and put on a tie I felt the heat. I was sweating under my jacket. How could she stand wearing gloves? Why did she so often seem to be passing through a setting that was inferior to her role?

The Splendid suited her better. I watched her come back towards me. She had left her gloves and her bag on our table; in this garden she no longer feared dirt and thieves. I rose to welcome her; she smiled, put her hand on mine for a second; I didn't know whether she was pardoning me or asking my pardon.

—I telephoned Kate Matthews. She's delighted.

The headwaiter took our orders. Of course he didn't recognize me. Had he ever really seen me? I had seen him, lording it over the waiters and waitresses, in his waistcoat, his jacket over his arm, reviewing the ranks of servants lined up for inspection.

—And for you, sir?

In vain I looked on the menu for dishes that didn't remind me of the garbage pails. There were only oysters, lobsters, and roasts. I ordered at random. The lamps in the garden went on, lighting the elms and the white columns. Laura spoke to me of France, of my father:

— . . . he gets up at noon and goes to bed at five. Your mother is less worried now.

—Did you see Fabien?

—Fabien?

She laughed.

— . . . your brother is crazy. Too bad he's not very handsome! But crazy!

Fabien, my brother, my Fabien of old times, knew all the bars on the Left Bank, all the poets, the failures, the actors of Paris. Fabien famous in a world I knew nothing about; a variation of that America I had dreamt of? They had gone out together several times. In a café, he played the piano for an hour; he sang three songs in one night club, five in another. Listening to Laura, I felt uneasy: a feeling that perhaps I was missing the adventure that Fabien had found not so far away as mine, only in Paris. Paris, was it so beautiful, so gay?

The tables in the garden around us filled up with silent customers, almost all old. I found again the old ladies in gray silks, the coming and going of the disciplined waiters, Laura's voice:

— . . . the French continue to think they are the most civilized. They look down on Americans, imitate Faulkner, jazz, hope for television. The more stupid hate us because France is twenty years behind us in our defects. The more intelligent fear us as one fears one's own future. In twenty years your compatriots will be petit bourgeois, as it is here now. In any case, I feel reassured about you. I left for France, after nine years' absence, hoping to find a generation there that would be like you. But no. You are unique, my Grégoire. All the more because you are out of your element, disabled, not yet American, no longer French. Rightly or wrongly, Grégoire, you are stateless. Not like the Negroes or the Jews, no. You, you are camouflaged. A spy in spite of yourself. A very lonely profession. Does it scare you?

Why would that have scared me? She spoke to me like a woman to a man going into battle. Instinctively I looked around us for an enemy.

In the center of the garden, a fountain was lit up. Fooled by the light, the birds didn't sleep; they sang in the trees, flew down to drink at the fountain. Sarcelle put her head on my knee; Laura's hand touched mine.

—Would you like to dance this evening? You know, Kate's a good friend. We'll be able to come and go as we wish.

She looked at me. A memory passed over her face in which I had time to recognize our nights together, her smile at that moment.

As on the beach earlier, we scarcely spoke any more. Sometimes I thought about the three Negroes. Had they already replaced me or was Truman doing my work as well? I tried to calculate the distance which separated me from them: sixty, eighty meters? I looked at the trays of dishes carried by the white hands of waitresses in black dresses, white collars, yellow aprons.

—You know, Laura, I am sixty meters from my garbage cans . . . sixty meters or a millimeter. In your opinion, what is the thickness of a man's skin, the thickness of the color of his skin?

The question rang false. I'd returned among the whites for a few hours and already my words rang false. A month of work cancelled out by an hour of well-being. Across from my three Negroes, I had looked out only for myself?

A storm was coming. The birds became silent, they too listened to the thunder in the distance. I paid the bill: a week of my dishwasher's salary. Of course Laura would reimburse me, gave me, in fact, enough money each month so that I could squander it. Was I a pimp? No, since she was beautiful. Several men turned around when she crossed the garden. I followed her. Sarcelle followed me. "Everything is in order." I thought of Jane's letters forgotten in the drawer where I had thrown them: "Never mind, she'll write others."

To go from my room to Laura's I went across a carpet. Night after night. The silence pulsed in rhythm with the waves breaking on the coast, a regular motion that toward dawn accompanied us and concealed us from the other inhabitants of the house. We loved the warmth softened by the breeze, the bed without blankets, a white rectangle in the shadow. We were blind lovers who rediscovered each morning, with the light, the tenderness of recognition. Laura left the night behind her softly: profile of her face sometimes asleep, shoulders tanned by freckles, hair the color of bread, eyebrows almost green. From the window facing southeast the first rays of the sun entered. Laura, motionless, finally opened her eyes, still motionless until her first smile.

A month of hitchhiking had tanned only my face and my arms up to the elbows.

—Look at you, disguised as a worker, she said to me the first morning.

A whitish chest. On the beach her friends were surprised at this strange uniform, a new race among their bronzed bodies. I explained to them my travels, the month spent in the garbage cans of the Splendid. They understood little of this Frenchman from Princeton, nephew of a fortune and washer of dishes. They excused me on account of my youth.

—The biggest snob of the lot? It's you! Perrault would have said.

For the first time in my life I didn't seek to make myself accepted. I, the child who didn't yet know what he wanted to hope for, had found what I didn't want. Young women, young men, the only one I knew there was Roger. He had swapped his leather coat for a leopard bathing suit. My only ally. The only one who admitted that they were all bored, hesitating between sailboat and water skis, horses and a plane. An enormous house with its thirty windows in front and its ten servants. The house and characters were interchangeable since they went from one home to another, wore the same clothes, used the same vocabulary, and said at every turn: "What shall we do?" This phrase, a memory of childhood, served as a password to this large family. At night only, they did not hesitate and we all went to dance in Southampton's only nightclub.

—What cars are we taking? asked a voice, it didn't matter whose, after dinner.

—Laura's and mine, answered Kate. You men, you drink too much to drive.

I have forgotten most of their names: the son of a New York jeweler, the heir to a soap manufacturer. They knew Paris, Rome, regretted the civil war that deprived them of Athens.

Stretched out among them on a beach chair or on the sand, I listened to their conversations, a code to which I lacked the key. I imagined a network of spies who studied all the nightclubs, from Rio to Stockholm; an organization whose adherents welcomed, everywhere, their co-conspirators. When I heard Laura's voice, I redoubled my attention; she knew how to speak their language.

How could she stand these people, she who had married Uncle Henri to escape them?

A small plane turned above the terrace, a red and green plane; probably one of the amateur pilots of the house.

I remembered the slap in the face that Laura had given me at the Port. That evening I believed it to be a punishment; she had slapped me for my own good. But was it not rather in defense of Roger? Those people, she liked them. She was contemptuous of them perhaps but all the same she tolerated them. And I had thought her intransigent! She accepted their mediocrity, participated in the gossip about the mistresses, the automobiles, the problems of absent members of the group. If I had made one of these remarks she would have turned her back on me.

Finally, I kept the nights for myself. In the meantime, swim, sleep in the sun.

—Is he asleep?

—Yes, he is.

Roger asked the question. The airplane flew away. She answered him almost in a whisper.

—Even in his sleep, he smiles.

—You really love him a lot?

Too late to show that I was listening. And I wanted to hear the answer; but Laura didn't answer. Roger continued:

—Look out for these people, especially Kate. Such evil tongues! Can you imagine your father learning that you and Grégoire are . . .

—When I see him sleeping, I wonder if he dreams in French or in English.

—In what language does he think?

—I don't know, said Laura. I'll ask him one of these days. I also want . . .

The airplane buzzed the terrace; its noise drowned out the conversation. When the roar of the engine diminished, I listened for their voices. I opened my eyes: Laura and Roger were going down to the sea. Not a cloud, not a breeze. The waves advanced toward the beach, troughs in the shade and swells in sun. Sarcelle slept under my beach chair. The plane had gone away.

"What language do you think in?" This is the question Laura would ask me: English, French?

I tried French and my thoughts formed immediately, defined by exact punctuation, thoughts of a candidate for the second part of the baccalaureate exam, philosophy section: "I think, therefore I am."

In English: "I think in two languages, I am two Grégoires."

What relationship between them? "From cause to effect, no doubt, since Grégoire-France wanted this journey" (this last phrase in French).

"What an ass!" *Quel âne!*

Grégoire–France bored me. Clearly he had not traveled. I preferred the Grégoire of America, the one who traveled on other peoples' ideas. Grégoire-France was dead, he had had his wish.

"I wished? How could I have wished for something I didn't know? Could I foresee this explosion? Could I foresee these infinite numbers of Grégoires: the student, the Negro, the nephew, the hunter, the man in love, each speaking a variation of English according to his interlocutors?"

"Too late to foresee (in English). Make the best of it, since you reason so well."

In French: "All the same, it's a pain in the ass to no longer exist. Come on, make an effort. This drifting can't go on. I ought to sum things up from time to time."

Who, "I"? Which one?

The French Grégoire. Of all the Grégoires he had lasted the longest, lived seventeen years under the same roof. A stable Grégoire for this serious moment. Let him make the effort. Perhaps by putting the question to him directly:

—Where am I?

—In America.

—And what have I found in America?

—Confusion, to be exact. Your confusion. That's what you wanted, no?

—And now?

—Continue. Go until the end.

—Until where?

—To the end of the journey. Are you afraid?

—A little.

—You asked for it.

A very French idea, this "you asked for it," which didn't surprise me.

I had gotten up and so had Sarcelle. She yawned, stretched. Paws up on the balustrade of the terrace, she looked at the sea.

—You want to swim, Sarcelle?

She licked the hand that I held out to her. We were alone. Laura, Kate, Roger and the others were stretched out in the sun; I saw them from above, separated more by height than by distance. Under my fingers, the black fur of the dog, warm in the sunlight. Since she wanted to swim, why had she not gone down with Laura? Did she love me so much?

What need did I have then of men? I understood these old maids, these misanthropes who devote themselves to a dog, a cat.

In face of the garbage at the Splendid, my contempt had grown. Was it also the patience of Negroes which induced me to be contemptuous of whites and especially these stretched out below the terrace? Among the bodies lined up I recognized Kate first, the most blonde, the most tanned; probably her prerogative as mistress of the house. At her right, the jeweler's son; at her left, a certain William; then two women, one a model, the other the sister of an important man; Roger next, and the soap heir. Finally, Laura, seated alone, enveloped in a cotton robe, straw hat. Laura was afraid of too much sun; thus different from the others, she escaped my pity, while the almost naked bodies, placed side-by-side like sticks on the surface of the sand . . . these bodies represented a pitiable humanity.

—Wait, Sarcelle!

The dog trembled but I wanted to prolong this moment. I was discovering a new mixture: the melancholy joy of compassion, pride, and love. "Grégoire, to this unhappy humanity you will teach tolerance. Now that you know the patience of the poor and the boredom of the rich, behold your mission! Behold the explanation of your multiplicity: Grégoire the Frenchman, the American, the Negro, the student . . . "

I no longer envied Fabien's adventure. I no longer feared to go to the end of my journey. Going down to the beach, my dog at my heels, I went down also towards combat. My weapons? Chaucer's charity, Kierkegaard's purity.

No one noticed my coming and I went into the sea with Sarcelle.

We had been at Kate's for five days. Faces changed; guests departed, replaced by others, nearly the same: heirs and models, the same hesitation between horses and water skis. I watched them pass by. I imagined convincing sentences about the patience of the poor. My resolutions remained a dream because I spoke only to Grégoire, only to one or the other of my Grégoires.

—Couldn't you be nicer?

Seated in front of her dressing table, Laura looked at me in her mirror. I saw her back and her face; half dressed, she was putting on her make-up, a transformation which always led to the elegant Laura that I so little understood.

—You know what they think of you . . .

I was going to answer "I don't give a damn." I kept quiet. Yes, I knew; in Laura's tone I discovered the significance of certain laughs heard behind my back, sudden silences at my approach. I who was used to being liked! I who liked them, these imbeciles!

I saw the jeweler's son again, the first morning on the beach, putting his hand on my arm; I felt his hand at the limit of my white skin: "What a funny shirt!" Laughing before the others.

Or William: his black hair against Kate's blonde hair. He whispered in her ear and she looked at me. I guessed now the disdain in her look. "Look out for these people," said Roger to Laura, " . . . especially Kate."

The late afternoon sun deepened the shadows on the waves. Sorrow and hatred in the heart. Poor Grégoire! A bunch of bastards who didn't understand. If they had allowed a little time to understand me . . . . What assholes, with their money and their boredom!

Laura put on her dress. I approached her to pull up her zipper, to catch the hooks.

—Let's get out of here.

I was ready to hate her, too, if she refused, if she dreamed up one of her theories, one of her tests . . . . After all, perhaps she thought just like them . . . .

—Yes, Grégoire, tomorrow morning.

She smiled. How I loved her smile! Already on the sea the shadows merged. Just one more night! Only the white crests of the waves marked the coastline.

Very well, since there were only a few hours left, I would

show them a Grégoire to suit them. Too bad Perrault wasn't there. He would have crushed their pride: "as in peg-leg."

I returned to my room, changed my suit and tie. My best shirt. An invitation, stuck in the mirror on the chest of drawers, reminded me it was the 6th of September. This evening, Jane would go to the dance in her new beige dress. Who would go with her? A few waltzes, a few words . . . .

On the stairway, I met William.

—Well, well, our student!

He went down before me, gray hairs on the nape of his neck. I heard voices below, a woman's laughter against the wash of the waves. William descended quickly, I went slowly; noticing details until then unperceived: the thickness of the oak bannisters, the perspective of the parquet floor out to the marble threshold, the yellow reflections of electric light on the gravel of the terrace.

They were all there, posed around the cocktail table. The women seated on the balustrades or in wicker chairs: the men stood among them, smiling. The men looked at the women who contemplated a sky still light enough to contrast with the black line of the horizon. They all seemed happy to resemble a family portrait, a portrait like those published in fashionable magazines.

—This is so pretty, Kate!

—Why, thank you, Grégoire.

I held her hand: "Very pretty, Kate! Even very beautiful!" She was surprised by my enthusiasm. I was surprised by an object, a gold bracelet, an endless thread which climbed in a spiral along her arm.

—It's a Calder. You know, the mobiles man?

She accepted my graciousness. I felt understood, admitted in ten seconds by virtue of this object. Kate turned toward the jeweler's son:

—Don't say too many nice things about it in front of our friend . . . .

—Just so! I said. He knows the difference between art and commerce, doesn't he?

Without letting go of Kate's hand, I talked to her about Virginia, her birthplace. I described myself as a lost child, hitching rides through red and green hills, admiring the architecture "whose charm reminded me of Europe." My sentences amused me more the closer they came to silliness.

The mannequin came to join us, a beige girl almost as tall as me. Thus I monopolized two of them, as Perrault had done on board the *Columbia*. What would he say to them? I imagined him in my place, I became Perrault. I invented a theory on the beauty of American women, I praised their natural and their supernatural qualities, a compliment for Kate, one for the mannequin. They laughed. This evening, this last evening, the women would be my allies: Kate, Laura, the model; Sarcelle, too, installed in an armchair, a black cushion among the green cushions.

Three steps away, William stirred the gravel with the tip of his shoe.

—Poor William, he's bored, said Kate.

—But no! That's not so, William?

He raised his head

—Kate's afraid you're bored.

Everyone looked at him.

—William certainly is not bored, I continued. (They looked at us.) The contemplation of gravel is an art of which the very complication is a remedy for boredom. And I am speaking not only of the superficial study of gravel, such as the comparison of two pebbles of the same size but different shapes . . . (I threw a fistful of gravel towards the sea.) . . . or the search for an average stone on a given surface. No! What the true amateur of gravel like William cultivates is the mystery of the meditation induced by an interchangeable relief. (I walked back and forth, my hands behind my back.) The artist loves gravel the way a child loves sand. Did you notice with what care William pushed a few pebbles to the left, then to the right? This is a connoisseur, a sensitive one. Because the way he pushes gravel about reveals a man as surely as his handwriting does.

I had planted myself between the two women, hands in my pockets, shoulders slumped, vacant eyes; with the tip of my right foot, I tenderly moved the pebbles. An imitation good enough to make Kate laugh. I sensed William's hatred at my right and this hatred excited me. His look weighed on the back of my neck. At each pebble moved, he suffered. I moved them more and more gently and Kate laughed louder. Finally, I turned toward him:

—William, would you make a martini for your student? You mix them so well.

He barely hesitated.

—Of course, Greg.

A few gulls flew through the light, created just enough movement to change the conversation. I let Kate talk. She recounted a voyage in Scotland, mountains, rain, castles. I sat next to Sarcelle, at the edge of the chair so as not to disturb her. When my look crossed William's I lowered my eyes. My knees shook; for how long? Finally the butler announced dinner.

We dined in slow motion, in rhythm with the domestic ceremony. On the other side of the table, Laura talked to

William. She smiled at me. I understood that she wanted to soothe him, to make him forget the earlier scene. I hoped she could.

Seated on my left, the model asked me a few questions about Princeton. I described for her the clubs, the dances. She had studied at the University of Michigan: " . . . especially philosophy. That's a bit ridiculous, isn't it?"

—Why?

—Oh, you know, I stayed only two years. And then, a woman reading Kierkegaard . . .

—On the contrary! Even if we grant that men are more inclined to introspection than women are, that means nothing without loyalty and women are more loyal than we are, more humble as well. To be oneself before God, women are as capable of that as men.

—But what God?

The others paid us no attention. I became again the student Grégoire. I wanted her to share my enthusiasm:

—Yours, since God is in our image. Fortunately . . . and unfortunately. Fortunately for you, your God is certainly generous. Unfortunately for Melville, because his God is a white whale and hate is his only salvation.

—But if God is a pink elephant? asked William.

They burst out laughing. How long had they been listening to me?

— . . . or a pale blue cockroach? There's also the yellow mouse and the red fly.

William recited a list of the multicolored animals of delirium tremens. At each animal, renewed laughter. They looked from William to me, from one adversary to the other.

— . . . gravel. Let's not forget the green gravel, he said.

He stopped talking; the others, too. They watched me

closely. This time, the laughs were against me. I didn't feel embarassed, I was used to it. Laura alone did not look at me. I saw a curtain stir softly behind her; I heard the waves on the beach, and I heard my voice, I spoke in a voice louder than usual:

— . . . to each his own God. The faithful of the pink elephant take communion with gin and whiskey. Their tragedy is that they confess after communion, not before, and they confess in public. Oh, their tragedy . . . Let's say, rather, the tragedy of those who must listen to them, then give them absolution and finally lead them back to their beds.

—You hear, William, said Kate. Go ahead and drink, but no confession.

The laughter passed to my side. We left the table; one after the other, we went from the parquet to the gravel, to the almost cool air of the terrace. Sarcelle came up in front of me. I should have liked to go down with her to the edge of the sea, to forget this evening. Kate called me back:

—What is your God, Grégoire?

Professor Harris, Peter A, Fabien . . . only Laura was there. Wasn't this the moment to speak of tolerance, of the patience of the poor and the boredom of the rich? To risk being ridiculous or to ridicule? I didn't hesitate.

—God? Mine? I have thirty-six. First the one in the white beard, and then the animals: the dog, the duck, Buffalo Bill's horse. Not whale nor pink elephant, luckily! Then some Negro gods, two or three paragraphs of Chaucer. What do you expect? When you're a student, God has to smell a little of ink.

Cup of coffee in hand, I drew, more and more precisely, my caricature, the caricature of my friends. What others would I to make fun of?

—We are not prophets, we are the loquacious followers of mute Gods, lined up on the silent pages of forgotten books. Ah, these books. The more obscure they are, the happier we are. In them we find bizarre, almost original, prayers. Love, Charity, Tolerance are merely everybody's ideas, too simple for us. We need gods as fragile as faded cloth . . . .

Only Laura seemed sad and in her face I recognized my own suffering . Would I be able to believe again in these myths that I distorted in public? Pain compensated for by the approval of my listeners. Perhaps they vaguely remembered having also repudiated their hopes. They surrounded me, smiled at my treason. We were finally accomplices. I was their new initiate.

—You are a good boy, Grégoire, said William.

He put his hand on my shoulder. The lamps in the house were extinguished one after another. The butler brought out the whiskey, carried off the coffee and the cognac. Lying on the balustrade, Sarcelle yawned.

—What cars are we taking? asked Roger.

—Laura's and mine, answered Kate. You men. You drink too much to drive.

Chapter 10

In front of me, on a field, two cows lying down watched a black horse run; farther away, the metal hood of a silo shone in the sun. I heard a stream hidden by bushes and I knew its shallow water flowed between the stones. I was sorry I didn't recognize the birds' song; Peter A would have said: "an oriole, a thrush, a warbler." The carillon at the University had just rung, far away, nevertheless distinct; starting now, Jane would be late.

Seated at the foot of an elm, I was happy with the sunlight, with the silence, happy to be back at Princeton and to have recovered in the last month the rhythm of classes, Perrault's friendship, the two Peters, and this New Jersey countryside which, since again I had returned to it, was becoming my countryside.

At a trot, the horse approached the fence. He stopped, whinnied. Was he asking for a treat? He was part of the country scene. My turn to please him, and I gathered a few tufts of clover from alongside the road. He sniffed at my coat before accepting them.

I stroked him and surveyed the road at the end of the path. Appearing in a curve high on a hill, the cars came down toward the river where a narrow bridge made them slow down. Jane would come in a gray Chevrolet, a make so common that several would go by, entertaining me as I waited. Finally, Jane. She parked her car near my bicycle. She walked toward me, Scottish kilt, a white blouse. I went on stroking the horse; soon she would be within hearing.

—Hello, Jane. It's pretty, this road of yours.

The horse raised his head, his ears perked up. Jane stopped a few meters away.

—Talk to him. Then he won't be afraid.

But she was silent and the horse's breathing quickened. Jane also hesitated. I felt that both were ready to flee, with me between them, wanting to calm them:

—Whoa, boy! Whoa! Talk to him, Jane! You see, it's Jane! Whoa!

The horse reared up, fled at a gallop across the field, tail erect, head high. I thought he would make a handsome pair with Sarcelle and I would have loved to ride off on him, anywhere, the dog running behind: these two black beasts in a red and yellow forest . . . .

—Grégoire!

—Yes, Jane.

She was still a few meters away, not having budged.

—Is it true that you are your aunt's lover?

My turn to run, to flee wildly across the grass . . . I stood there motionless, hoping to hold back time: a few seconds gained . . .

—Is it true, Grégoire?

—Yes.

For months I had been playing with the truth, but I had no impulse to lie. Behind me, I heard the galloping horse. Jane came forward. Was she going to slap me? She stopped very near; if I had stretched out my arm I could have touched her.

—Good-by, Grégoire.

—Where are you going?

—I'm going to college, in California, perhaps in Europe.
Fear awakened me. Now, I loved only her. Laura was
. . . something else.

—Jane, you don't understand. Laura is a woman. I didn't
know . . .

—You betrayed me.

—No! Please, Jane. Remember! I respected you because
it's you that I love.

—Or because you were already making love to her?
She wasn't crying. Why not? She must be suffering. More
than I was? "Jane, I don't know any more when I began to
deceive you. I didn't want to do it."

I held my tongue. For an instant, I listened to the birds,
astonished that they still were singing. "Grégoire, take a
good look at Jane. No doubt, you're seeing her for the last
time." Hair the color of bark, eyes of green. Her chin no
longer trembled. She was going to flee but she no longer
seemed fearful nor tameable. Had she become wild again?
Was this a mask? Later, will she cry?

—Jane, try . . .

—Grégoire, if only we had . . .
She didn't finish her sentence. She ran away and I dared
not pursue her. My eyes followed her car, the bridge, the
road up to the curve at the top of the hill where she disappeared. The horse had come back; he touched my sleeve
with his lips. I picked some clover for him.

—Here! Whoa boy! Whoa! You see how she went? Here,
old fellow! Calm down! Whoa!

—Have you seen me imitate a mouse?

Perrault lowered his newspaper. The two Peters and I looked at him, not having understood, or thinking we hadn't understood him.

— ... imitate a mouse, Perrault repeated.

He folded the *New York Times*, the polite gesture of a guest who puts away his napkin at the end of the meal. He got up, headed toward the door; majestic departure of this body ready to overflow like a balanced vase full to the brim. Silence.

—He did say a mouse? asked Peter B.

—Yes. He spoke of a mouse.

We watched the door. Was he going to disguise himself? Come in on all fours? What was he waiting for?

Peter A was the first to burst into laughter. With his finger, he pointed to the corner of the door: level with the floor, Perrault's nose posed on the carpet, a nose pink and pointed as if Hieronymous Bosch had painted it; a timid nose which barely moved forward, twitched a little. Indeed, a sort of mouse ...

Perrault's return finished us off: always dignified, he brushed the arm of his jacket with the back of his hand. He stopped, observed us with concern:

—See here, it wasn't that funny, after all ...

He took up his paper and his armchair, left us to our laughter. We laughed now for having laughed so much. A chain reaction: if one of us stopped to draw breath, the laughter of the others set us off again. The pain in the guts, in the lungs, and the pain for me of being sad to the breaking point since Jane had left me, since she had been living God knows where, for days, a week, two weeks without a letter, without news, never any more news of Jane ... and

I was angry with myself for laughing, for betraying this new suffering to which I had become attached since it replaced a spoiled love.

For I cultivated this suffering in detail. Absence of Jane in the streets of Princeton, at the Harrises', absence on Sunday and in this late autumn. I fashioned a new face for myself, traces of wrinkles between the eyebrows, longer hair falling over my eyes. I studied my silence in the noise of others, their incessant conversations, their "Good morning," their "How are you?"; the eternal discussion between Peter B and Perrault: can Christians vote Communist? "Poor humanity, I thought, don't you have the right to vote with your belly?"

It was the autumn of the Marshall Plan. Peter B read an article in the *New York Times:* to save Europe from famine, Truman had eaten on that Tuesday only cheese soufflé in the morning and fish for dinner.

—That hypocrite! cried Perrault. He gives up meat and gobbles up Communists every day.

Humanity flouted, deceived. I pitied it as I did myself. I didn't go to the gym anymore . . . A useless commotion. At balls, at the hops on Saturdays and Sundays, I didn't dance any more. Glass in hand, I sat near the orchestra to listen to the music, especially the trombone. Alcohol served me as a mirror and there I saw the reverse image of my sadness: I made a fool of myself, shame topped off my melancholy.

Peter B did not reproach me. We didn't talk about his sister anymore; finished, the dinners on Sunday evening at the Grahams', that's all. We went to the club and we returned together, shoulder to shoulder, in step. Peter went to Mass several times a week, didn't drink. Perhaps his conversion to Catholicism had helped him. I no longer heard him call out in the night. Had he become, above all, Perrault's friend? Their relationship seemed as distant as ever but they couldn't let a day go by without discussing "life, liberty, and the pursuit of happiness . . . " Sometimes, I recognized in Peter's words or gestures an expression of Jane's. A hope pushed me toward him: he was a link, through him I would find her again. I had only to find the words that would bring us together; sooner or later, Jane would reappear. What words? Anyway, I wasn't going to convert myself too or, like Perrault, read both Marx and Maritain.

It was only at the Port of Missing Men that I tolerated some moments of happiness. The happiness of a child: "Here, I *am* a child." I allowed myself to play with Jeanie, with Sarcelle. The three of us together dragged Médor and Slow onto the lawn, the old dog and the old Negro. We had invented a dance that Jeanie called "ball in the grass." We threw each other a ball that the dogs chased faster and faster, jumping to catch it in flight, all of us finally mixed up together, dogs and children and Negro out of breath, barking, panting.

We walked in the forest. I took Jeanie's hand. Sometimes her fingers scratched my palms like the claw of a bird.

—Greg, let's go see the ocean . . .

      let's go see the road . . .

      let's go see the creek . . .

I opened my hand and her hand remained there.

—Greg, Sarcelle is a little bit my dog, isn't she?

—Of course, since you love her.

Jeanie's black hair and my black hair, our gray eyes: cousin and cousin, brother and sister. Father and daughter since I was her mother's lover? No! I was unable to imagine Laura as my wife or my woman. Always higher than me on the pillow, Laura shielded me from loneliness and I made love to her to thank her for it.

These months of October and November, so sad at Princeton with the untidy fall of leaves on the lawns, with the rain on the town, with the evenings at the Harrises' without Jane when the professor repeated to me this Chaucer that I thought I knew too well. These two months I went almost every week to the Port. Dead leaves clothed the countryside, the rocks glistened with water.

We saw no more of Laura's father. He was traveling, they told me. Because he had remained a stranger to me, in my new family he was not missed. Jeanie took her meals with us at the table. Sitting on the stairs, Médor and Sarcelle watched us eat. Slow all but brought in his own plate. He stayed standing at Laura's left and gave the latest news of the creek:

— The barometer's rising, Miss Laura. Tomorrow morning will be a cold morning with fog and I saw three flights of mallards. In town, they even heard a few geese . . . For those who aren't afraid of cold mornings there will be some ducks on the wing . . . .

—Slow, light the fire in the library.

—Right away, Miss Laura.

—And prepare thermoses of hot coffee.

—Sure! Miss Laura. I sure will be glad to do that.

The thermoses announced the hunt. Tomorrow we would carry them in our knapsacks, for each his share of warmth while waiting for daybreak. I had my own blind at the end of the creek, alone with Sarcelle.

My dog.

Slow had trained her. Lying down in front of her dish, she would not touch it without a command. He taught her to heel, to sit, to lie down, to leap. It was me, though, that Sarcelle recognized as her master; she obeyed me even better than she did Slow. Repayment for my love for her? My hands searched for her fur, her look awaited my look.

—Do you love me as much as your dog? Laura demanded.

I looked for an answer: "Of course," "It's different," "That depends."

One Saturday in November, Sarcelle brought me my first duck: a double baptism, consecration of her chosen name since she placed in front of me a teal with blue wings. I patted the dog; the broken bird spoiled my pleasure, reminded me that Sarcelle would not live forever and that death would separate us, like this death delivered by my gun.

That evening Jeanie was already asleep and I was sitting with Laura in the library, the wood fire, the two dogs, the books around us.

—Grégoire, do you know why my father doesn't come to the Port any more? (Laura asked me the question in French.) He's found out that we sleep together.

I heard the horse gallop in the field and Jane's voice: "Is it true that you are your aunt's lover?" Laura got up. Back to the fireplace, her legs silhouetted against the fire, she explained to me in English:

— . . . There are eight million inhabitants of New York. But the rich are like a village and everybody ends by knowing everything. These people from the Social Register, there are some of them who have nothing to do, who spread news of the miseries or the happiness of others . . . .

So, "everybody" knew. Laura's concern did not touch

me yet. I had lost Jane; what could be worse? I imagined these unknowns talking about Laura and her French nephew: faces seen at dances, lawyers or brokers met at the Port, young bourgeois of Southampton, and especially Kate, whom Laura shouldn't have trusted.

—What did your father say to you?

—He is rather mad . . . . I think we must be careful.

Leaving the fireplace, she took my arm, her hand trembled.

—Be careful of what? Since everybody knows.

—Grégoire, if the rich are a village, I live in this village. Jeanie too.

What's the good of these riches? And her so-called independence? What's the good of her refusal of everyday life, her cult of prophets and of Melville? Hadn't she accused me of being a coward, one night?

—I know, Grégoire, I know.

A year ago, she had slapped me to defend Roger and the people of her village. *"Stop crying."* Her turn to cry. Shame?

—I have Jeanie, my house, my father. You, you're young, you're free.

She clung to me. The dogs were worried. Sarcelle came to us; Laura pushed her aside with her foot.

She called the dog back and caressed her.

—I'm sorry, Grégoire.

I pitied Laura. For the first time in my life, I felt pity for a superior person, one of those "grown-ups" for whom my childhood had bequeathed me an image and a need. I felt delivered from bondage, and a little more alone.

On the post card, a fisherman was sitting at the foot of a cathedral: "The Seine at Notre Dame."

Hi, Grégoire. Back from La Chêneraie where our father is in good spirits. The little song is making me a capitalist. Unbelievable! When are you coming back? Merry Christmas.

Fabien

I propped up the card on my desk. Peter B appeared with his suitcase. "Have a good Christmas, guys!" and disappeared ... replaced by Perrault, breathing hard, also with a suitcase. He was spending the holidays with Peter A in Boston.

Groups of shadows on the snow went down towards the station and the five o'clock train; for each shadow a goal, father and mother, a family at the end of a few hours of travel. Soon, Slow would come to get me and it would be my turn.

—How about a drink, Greg?

Banjo Bob entered with a bottle.

—Sure, Bob! Come sit down.

He didn't talk about his sadness but he didn't hide it either: we were young, we were white, we were leaving for the holidays: he would stay in the empty rooms ... he would stay there until his old age, until life no longer made sense.

—Merry Christmas, Greg!

—Merry Christmas, Bob!

He was wearing khaki pants and a shirt with a button-down collar. Was he imitating the way students dressed, an unconscious imitation after so many years? Or were these clothes tips, old hand-me-downs, carefully patched by his wife?

I looked at his face. Like so many American Negroes, a white face rubbed with a light shoe polish: long nose, thin mouth, forehead sloping back to black crinkly hair. How different from Slow! Slow seemed to have come straight from Africa. Banjo Bob had made a hundred detours, by way of the Antilles, Virginia, the North; each time cross-bred, a quadroon, the face of a Scotsman, negrofied, and yet as much a Negro as Slow: made Negro by his crinkled hair, by his patience.

What will happen the day they lose patience? Will they cease to be Negroes?

Bob wanted me to tell him about France, and I described our house, our churches, the fields, the hedges, the slow and narrow rivers, Norman France with ash trees and red bricks, cows, hay stacks and slate roofs.

Outside, night was falling, held back by the whiteness of the snow. No longer anyone on the walks. A calm and deserted campus. Bob's friendship and some frost on the windows.

Slow was late. Had he had trouble, an accident? He was always punctual. "When he comes, I'll offer him a drink with us. Will he dare? What's the distance a formal servant keeps?"

—Greg, I got to get home now.

Of course, Bob went home at six. Another small glass to drink a last toast. I looked for words to detain him. Slow would come and I would not have to be alone.

—Good night, Greg.

—So long, Bob.

Tranquillity or silence? I saw Bob go up the path, then up the steps of Blair Tower. Darkened windows everywhere, a few of which reflected street lights. I toured the apartment to light the lamps, even in the bedroom and the study: let our windows, at least, announce a presence: "Grégoire is here, Jane. I am here."

Bob, good old Bob, had left the bottle on the table and I served myself. "Well, well! This is the first time I drink alone." I sat in Perrault's armchair, the *New York Times* carefully folded to a headline announcing the Christmas present of the United States to Europe: five hundred and twenty-two million dollars.

If Jane was in America, would she return to Princeton for the holidays?

Surely not. Jane would return only married, or engaged; wound healed, a happy woman followed by a man surrounded by suitcases knocking at the door of her father's house.

Too bad that Slow was so late. We would almost have arrived at the Port! I imagined the snowy driveway, the black shape of the trees, the last curve: the gray house in the headlights. An image so sharp that I was astonished to find myself in this chair, whisky paled by melted ice. On the rug, my bag awaited its trip, a short trip. Fortunately! This evening, I wanted neither exodus nor odyssey, nothing but a return to my American family. A second-hand family? No! A reinvented family, built on tenderness for a woman, a child, a servant, a dog. While Jane . . . it's my fault she's spending these holidays alone.

I contemplated the harm I had caused: Jane a stranger among strangers. How cold she'll be! Inwardly, I asked her pardon; I cried out my remorse: "Jane, forgive me!" Did she hear me? In a room or in a station, on a ship or on a road, Jane raised her head: "Where is that voice coming from?"

"Idiot! She hears nothing. She remains alone and it's your fault. You who wanted to evangelize humanity. Humanity was her, first of all!"

Below, the door opened. High heels on the stone steps of the staircase. A woman was coming up. "See my legs, *Monsieur le Français?*" I tried to recognize the rhythm of this step but I heard only my blood beating in my ears. Too long a wait, too short.

—Aren't you going to kiss me?

She sat at the end of the sofa, the beaver coat half opened on a tailored suit of dove gray cashmere, ankles in silk. Oh, so completely Laura! Calling to me with her gestures and almost motionless, impatience controlled by a smile:

—I've made you wait? A drink, please?

I went to the bathroom to wash two glasses, to splash cold water on my face. "Yet, Laura is beautiful, more beautiful than Jane. And then, you're going to see Jeanie and Sarcelle. Perhaps we'll go hunting tomorrow morning ."

Laura had just come from New York. Two hours to get to Princeton.

— . . . This traffic is impossible. Twenty minutes for the tunnel. If I had known, I certainly would have taken Slow with me. He is so great, Slow. An hour, two hours of driving without moving, it makes no difference to him. Such patience! I get nervous when nothing moves . . . .

To take off her coat, she stood up and so did I like a good student from Princeton, half gentleman, half dog, receiving into my arms the fur with its lemon verbena perfume, receiving her look:

—Do you love me, Grégoire?

—Yes, I love you.

Thinking: "Why don't we go? We're already late enough!

We'll never get to the Port in time for dinner."

—This traffic has worn me out.

"What an egoist I am! Poor Laura!"

I brought her a glass.

—Would you like some music?

It was Monteverdi, by chance. I turned out most of the lights in the apartment. In the middle of the rug, my suitcase upset the neatness of the room and I pushed it behind Perrault's armchair with my foot. Laura lit a cigarette and I put an ashtray next to her.

—Grégoire, do you love me?

—Of course. How's Jeanie?

—Very well . . .

. . . a distracted murmur. She put her hand on my wrist.

—In New York, I had lunch with my father. We have made up.

This sentence was spoken in a solemn tone. Yet I still was not on guard. I imagined them both in the dining room of the house in New York, tablecloth and drapes of horizon blue, like two actors on a set, waiting for the butler to go out to continue the dialogue. A play in one act, an old-fashioned play in the manner of Ibsen or early Bernard Shaw.

—Could we spend the night here, Greg?

—But we ought to . . .

The disappointment prevented me from finishing my sentence. I stood up and so did Laura. Face-to-face. She held something toward me, her hand trembled.

—Here! It's your Christmas present.

I did not see the object. I saw only her eyes, which were full of tears. Now I understood, I waited for her to say it, impatient to know what words, what tone, she would choose . . .

—My father is coming to spend the holidays at the Port. Don't be angry with me. Please, Grégoire. I'll come to Princeton, every time I can . . . .

"And you, you stay here." She hadn't dared to say it. I wasn't listening to her any more. Goodbye, my American family. Goodbye, Sarcelle, we will not hunt tomorrow. No more walks with Jeanie and Slow. Alone in Princeton. Alone like Jane. But her father, what the hell is he to her, Laura, her father? This stuffed duck? Her, Laura the free, Laura the prophet, Pythia, Cassandra, the daughter of a duck? I felt like laughing. I laughed. Laura cried and I laughed louder. We were ridiculous. My little suitcase all ready behind the armchair and Laura with the present in her hands that she didn't know what to do with. I heard myself laughing. How funny: no need to speak when laughing. No need to explain with words. No more need to lie.

She came toward me. Her lips moved but she didn't speak. Again the chorus from Monteverdi. My laughter had ceased. I was afraid, afraid of what would be said or heard, afraid of us since we now knew the measure of our love. The door was open, I ran away. A sonorous cavalcade in the stairwell, then silence on the snow. Why run? She was not following me.

"How stupid they seem, women in the snow!" I watched Laura leave, a silhouette in a fur hood, and I imagined her high-heeled shoes on the icy ground. She had waited almost an hour for me to return; from a distance, I watched the door. "Is she going to make me cool my heels here forever?" Furious, I hoped that she was unhappy, that she missed me, that she was sobbing. "The bitch, she can wait all night if that makes her happy."

When I went up to my room, the phonograph was still turning; Monteverdi was over, finished; the needle scratched the record: skiss . . . skiss . . . skiss. Laura had not touched her drink. In the middle of the sofa, she had left her present and a blank sheet of typewriter paper with *Grégoire* followed by three question marks which took up almost the whole page.

What a beautiful signature. Instead of Grégoire Engivane, Grégoire ???

—What's your name?

—Grégoire???

This mimicry was worth being worked on. At the moment of ??? I would raise my eyes to the heavens, shrugging my shoulders, a surprised face, perhaps a questioning grunt, that is to say, a passing from a low to a high note.

In one hand, I held the paper; in the other, the present. What could be in this box? Not big, square, relatively heavy, wrapped in pale green paper. "If you open it, you keep it." Curiosity. Blue ribbon, gray box, white tissue paper: a gold watch and chain. The watch hung at the end of the chain, round, flat, gleaming, symbol of everything bourgeois, treasure of the rich and dream of the poor:

> . . . put a twenty-dollar gold piece on my watch chain
> So you can tell all the boys I died standing pat.

What time was it? Nine o'clock, at a guess. I opened the window the better to hear the carillon at Nassau Hall when it rang. The winder. Tic-tac-tic-tac. "It's working."

In the case, I found an inscription:

Grégoire Engivane
au Port des Absents
Noel 1947

When she bought the watch, Laura still thought I would
be at the Port for Christmas. So, today, at noon, my fate
was decided in the course of this old-fashioned play, this
pale blue comedy in the dining room.

I put out the light. The tic-tac of my watch was easier to
hear in the dark. At the Port, on Christmas morning, I
would have looked under the tree, on the beige rug. Last
year a black dog, this year a yellow watch. "Look, Jeanie."
Jeanie put the watch against her ear, against Sarcelle's ear.

Shit!

The carillon rang nine o'clock. Get up? Turn on the light
to set my watch? Never mind. "Ten minutes is close
enough. What's the difference, since I'm all alone!"

" I have Jeanie, my house, my father. You, you're young,
you're free."

Free, or alone like Jane? Two women and, within a month,
none at all. Why? Gossip. "These rich are like a village
from the Social Register," as Laura had said. Some hasten-
ing to tell Jane that I slept with my aunt, others informing
Uncle George . . . a little crowd of gossips, standing, glasses
in hand . . . ants scattered about who returned at night to
the ant hill pulling, pushing enormous news: Grégoire
sleeps with his aunt . . . nibbling at my name on the telephone.

"If I ever meet Kate again, I'll slap her so hard!"

No satisfaction: in vain I had invented a room full of
people and brightly lit. The sound of that slap brought me
no comfort. I thought instead that Laura, in her car, was

approaching the Port. What would she tell Jeanie? "Grégoire is spending his vacation somewhere else . . . " Jeanie would see it as a betrayal. Sarcelle would softly sniff Laura's clothes looking for my scent.

Was it necessary to write a letter and return the watch? Or better to pretend to be dead?

"But, Grégoire, you forget that she pays the bills from the University, that she also forwards a hundred dollars to your account each month. Do you pay dead people? In February it's the end of the first semester---the club bill, the dorm rent, tuition, books to buy."

I turned on the light. A pen: three hundred dollars here, plus one hundred and twenty, plus two hundred and fifty, plus thirty . . .

"So much the better, I'll earn some money. I'll have a little reserve at the bank, do without all of them and hold on until June, until my diploma. After that, I'll earn whatever I want. What's left . . . let's see . . . two hundred and thirty-four dollars. At least three hundred more to hold on."

On the back of my checkbook, I compared the plus column and the minus column. I boxed in the results with four lines of ink: three or four hundred dollars to hold on. Play dead and earn some money. That's freedom, the only one.

—In one way, it's not a bad time, said Banjo Bob.

Seated in Perrault's armchair, I had just told him my story. Why not? Since New York and the Social Register knew it already . . . what was one more Negro?

After a long night, of little sleep and beautiful resolutions, I got up early, profiting from the luxury of the others' absence: apartment, bathroom, a whole dormitory to myself. A quarter of an hour to sing under the shower, variations on the second movement of Beethoven's third symphony: Papa Pam . . . Papam Papam Papaaam . . . Poum! Resolutions accompanied by a clean shirt and a vest for my new watch.

Bob arrived and we found ourselves seated facing each other as on the night before, but playing different roles. My turn to wait in empty rooms. My turn to be sad, but I tried to hide it. How had I treated Bob last night? Pity, condescension? The Grégoire of the morning had trouble remembering the one of the night before and distrusted him.

—You're lucky, Bob continued. The holidays, that's when people entertain. Dances, dinners! Greg, you've eaten in the homes of the rich, you'll know how to wait on them, won't you? Yes, madam. Yes, sir. Push the French accent a little. That's worth two dollars more an hour by itself, just the French accent before you pass a plate.

—And you really think . . .

—When the noon bell rings, come up to town with Bob, Greg. My pals and I, we'll fix you up.

—Thanks, Bob, thanks a lot!

—There'll be Social Security. Maybe a problem since you're a foreigner . . . . We'll fix that up, too. You're a student, right?

A foreigner, I was a kind of Negro. However, I didn't find any trace of pride on Bob's face. Not even a protective air when he introduced me to his friends a few hours later.

And the next day, I was working.

In the beginning, my new occupation amused me. I pretended I was an actor: black tie, white jacket and the trousers of my tux. I discovered that some guests were scared of me; quickly spotted, they blushed at each look. To compensate for my youth, I said little. When my bosses for the evening had their own servants, I only had to wait at table; otherwise, I also washed the dishes. The first night, my first as a servant, I found the lady of the house unfolding a red cloth on the table.

—If Madam has a green tablecloth, it will go better with the curtains.

A woman without pretensions or rancor, she let me set the table. A fascinating placement of plates and of glasses, of silverware, I spent an hour at it; a few flowers, not too tall; positioning the salt cellars, adjusting the napkins. My reputation was made, my work assured for the vacation.

Banjo Bob laughed:

—Greg, you amaze me. You have these dames in the palm of your hand.

—I tell them to change tablecloths.

—Sure, Greg, sure! When you don't need this bread to live on, that lets you say a lot of things . . .

From Trenton, from Morristown twenty miles away, they came to get the French butler. Houses of pink, blue, green . . . pastel houses in the snow. I entered by the kitchen, the back door. Judging from the sink, the pots and pans, the refrigerator, I pictured the living room, almost always mistaken in the beginning, discovering that taste bears no relationship to wealth. Most of my hosts let their wives furnish the house. Thick carpets, deep sofas; comfort replaced charm. No taste, a few errors of taste, but the first cocktail hid this banality snug and warm behind the double windows.

Several times I met people I knew, more embarrassed than me, especially the young, especially the girls. I laughed at this under my mask of gravity. Didn't they know that the distance that separated us was easy to bridge? Swap my white coat for black and I would be with them. Why do it? I had no desire to.

Toward midnight or one in the morning, when I'd helped the last guest put on his coat, the master or the mistress of the house drove me back to Princeton. No longer a servant. I abandoned the third person and I invented a Grégoire who talked hunting, sports or philosophy with his boss of the moment, often a little drunk. If Madam drove, I courted her discreetly and, the moment the check came, I buried it with two fingers in the pocket of my vest, without reading it. Then I took out my watch: "Already?" My embarassment thus disguised, I spent amazing days between my bed, work and the bank. Christmas Day for me was a holiday only for other people; three temporary jobs, eighteen hours of work at double pay and fat tips, seventy-seven dollars more in my account.

But after Christmas, the atmosphere changed. The closer New Year came, the longer the evening's work, noise replaced conversations. Never before had I watched drinking without drinking myself. The complicity among drinkers, the opaque wall that separated me from them, through which they became a spectacle, actors that were more and more obviously outside their usual role. If the better part of the guests were quickly numbed, there were others who seemed to seek my approval. That began with a look: "Did I give a good answer?" Worried that I didn't play the game with them, attracted without doubt by this witness who didn't drink, their only public, they sometimes became hostile or angrily humble, tried to get me on their side of the imaginary scene in which they felt themselves observed.

I kept silent, useless because they often guessed my contempt. On these evenings, I would have liked to be a Negro.

Disgusted to be a servant with a face, I missed the anonymous dishwashing at the Hotel Splendid. My hibernation was finished, it had not lasted ten days. Troubled sleep, hours of insomnia were dominated by almost unknown characters; they were like summaries, anthologies of drunkards. Laura and Jane circulated among them, points of reference who ignored each other or became reconciled, fitting badly in my dreams, becoming accomplices of the others. A nightmare recurred often: they accused me of being crazy. How to prove the contrary? This anguish extended into the day to become an obsession. "If this cop arrests you, what are you going to say in your defense? How do you prove to him that you're not going to do something stupid? Break a window, slap this woman coming along?"

Without reading them, I had torn up two letters from Laura. I was sorry I had. I would read the next . . . she wrote no more. Slut! Bitch! Her love wasn't worth three letters. She was probably sleeping with this airhead Roger while her mallard of a father shut his eyes. Were they hunting this morning? If they were hunting they had taken Sarcelle, my dog who trembled near them, for them, for the dawn and the whistle of wings on the creek.

Harris was not at home.

—They went to the grandmother's! a neighbor called to me.

He swept snow from the sidewalk and I waited in front of the green door, right hand, ungloved in the cold, on the button of the doorbell. Was it any of the neighbor's business? If he had said nothing I could have rung for five minutes, hoped for five minutes, returned this afternoon.

A ball for the boy, a doll for the girl, I put the two pack-ages on the veranda. Too bad if someone stole them, these children should have stayed at home; I didn't want to go through town again with these gifts, useless now in their star-sprinkled paper.

And what to do? The whole day, ten hours to waste until this evening. Bob had advised me to get some sleep: "The New Year's Eve party at the Harrisons' is a handful of work. Grab yourself a nap!"

I wasn't sleepy. A book? I knew them all, useless to read others; what good were they? Even Chaucer, Melville and Kierkegaard . . . their sentences, their chapters weren't worth anyone being there. A heap of paper good for stud-ies, useless texts when you needed them. Could I have recited Conrad to Jane, or skipped along behind her shout-ing out Rimbaud?

Music? I put on a record. A Mozart concerto for clarinet. I didn't listen to it, nor to the Beethoven quartet which fol-lowed. Their gaiety, their sadness: noise.

Copies of the *New York Times* were stacked on a chair. Stalin and Truman would do without my advice for a few days; the world would turn without me, and I waited for seven o'clock. Then I would wash, shave myself as slowly as possible, to gain some time, to lose it.

In the middle of the afternoon, I got hungry. Eat alone in town? I knew the restaurants and their tasteless cuisines, the sadness of a sandwich, the expanse of a white table-cloth with a single place setting. Resigned, I left for Nassau Street and the inevitable swill. Why inevitable? Walking along, I had the idea come to me from food glimpsed in the shop windows: smoked salmon, fois gras, caviar. I began to run. First to the bank, a bite out of my savings. Black bread, white bread, butter and lemon, a red lobster, boxes with labels in French — "the best of the best" —, some champagne: the most expensive. Two napkins, knife, fork, even a champagne glass; why drink Dom Perignon in a toothbrush glass? And some plates, some flowers for Grégoire Engivane.

On my return I first put the champagne at the window, to chill and to calm itself from my running. Now the table: a napkin in the guise of a tablecloth, a bouquet of flowers, the champagne glass, the contents of the boxes emptied on the plates: pink, black and beige food, surrounded by green salad, yellow butter and yellow lemon, red tomato. Music: Handel. Dinner is ready! "Long live me, I am eating! Wisely, carefully." A spoonful here, a slice there. Caviar first, then the salmon, the lobster. Drink slowly. "I am alone. All for me. Screw them all!" Good warmth, good meal. "This table is my island. I am the castaway, the Robinson Crusoe of the lobster." The claws crack under my teeth. Eat more and more slowly. Wash my hands, rinse the plate and the fork before moving to the fois gras. To savor it, wait until it melts on the tongue until only the truffle is left. "Another slice? I can't! In a moment, perhaps?"

When I woke up in Perrault's chair, eight o'clock was ringing and I had to run to the shower, run up to town, take a taxi to the Harrisons', happy to be rushed, to regain a few of the minutes which had seemed to be unbearable that morning.

Banjo Bob was already setting up the bar. Someone else lit the fire in the stone fireplace. On the four walls hung the stuffed heads of moose, deer, foxes; furs on the parquet; wreaths on the beams.

—Greg, you set up the tables . . . leave room for dancers.

Ten round tables, I positioned them between the sofas, four places at each table. The musicians arrived, five Negroes in straw hats shaking the snow from their coats.

—Hey, boys, you think it's Easter?

—Banjo Bob! Banjo! You here?

Reunited in friendly shoves, Negroes arm in arm, interrupted by Harrison.

Silence.

He inspected the room and its details. Small feet, bow legs of a horseman, carnation in the buttonhole of his dark jacket, not a word until his speech:

—Boys, my New Year's Eve parties have their reputation. Liquor, music, I'm counting on you. You're the Frenchman?

—Yes, *Monsieur*.

—You'll wait on the tables. The first guests will arrive in twenty minutes.

Exit.

—Just twenty minutes, repeated the trombone player.

The trumpet played the call to charge which transformed itself into *Do What Ory Say*, taken up by the others. Bob stood on a chair:

> You don' do like Harrison?
> Why don' you do like he say?
> If you don' like what I do,
> Do what Harrison say.

The others took up the chorus

> Say what to do, Harrison!

Bob improvised:

> If you don' like what the Frenchie do,
> Make the Negroes do it, Harrison!

In chorus:

Make the Negroes do it, Harrison!

Twenty minutes of jazz. Bob, beside the pianist, playing four hands: *Panama, Dr. Jazz.* "Go, man . . . go!" Twenty minutes of recreation before the arrival of the whites, the real whites, the rich. *Alexander's Ragtime Band. Five Foot Two*:

Five foot two,
Eyes of blue . . .

The piano, one of those uprights with a metallic resonance, gave rhythm to the racket. The guests entered, silent at first, new to the scene, feet in fur boots and women with bare shoulders hesitating between the wood fire and the shelter of the sofas. Then, the best places taken, they occupied the tables, the buffet, the bar. Indecision about the first drink: gin, whiskey, champagne? An irreversible choice, in principle, on which perhaps the whole evening depended; those who hoped for joy, those who wished to last for as long as possible, those who preferred the taste of Scotch... The couples recognized each other, left their places and regrouped with their friends. People from twenty-five to forty years old, almost all married. Among the men were many graduates of the University; they had not wanted to leave Princeton, their youth, their memories, *a la* Fitzgerald. Working in New York or Philadelphia, they had made this college town a bedroom community for businessmen and lawyers. There, they lived among their own, drank among their own, talked of the good years before the war when they danced the Charleston. Had anything about them changed in ten years, in twenty years, apart from their waistlines and their wrinkles? So polite! They asked my first name: "Grégoire" here, "Greg" there. Soon, the work absorbed me. I saw only empty glasses to refill. "Two Scotches, a Tom Collins, three champagnes ... Watch your back, sorry! ... Coming by, excuse me! ... Two bourbon and gingers ..."

For an instant, the music stopped, revealing the hubbub of voices. Already, a few guests raised their heads, concerned. But Harrison scurried toward the orchestra:

—Give us *The Saints*!

... as if he were afraid that his guests would be frightened by their own noise.

Oh, when the Saints
Oh, when the Saints
Oh, when the Saints go marching in
I want to be in that number ...

The clarinet, sometimes hesitant, with some successful riffs, didn't have Peter A's flowing rhythm. Better? To each his own style. I could hear only the clarinet. Only its clear notes pierced the thick layers of voices and smoke. If I were a musical instrument, I would be a clarinet ... an animal, a teal ... a writer, Chaucer ... a plant, a dandelion ...

—Greg, some champagne!

... But no, it's stupid, a dandelion! Pushing up dandelions? Then why? Remember: tufts of seed you can blow away: "I sow to the four winds." I pour champagne and Scotch for all comers. Bottoms, hips, dresses, arms, a limp countryside, a forest. "Imagine a rabbit there! I am rabbit, the orchestra is my thicket, the bar my burrow. No dog! No more carrots." Oops! Crash! ... a broken glass: the rabbit goes on all fours to gather the fragments on the fur of the bear.

Suddenly, the lights go out and the forest shouts "Happy New Year!" Here comes the New Year on all fours. Guests were running in all directions and I took refuge under the table, a shelter from kicks. Above, they called to each other, clinked glasses, kissed. Here, I was safe, and when the lights came on I felt the urge to stay there. If only I could get rid of these fragments of glass cupped in my right hand . . . .

—Happy New Year, Greg!

Brown hand on my shoulder.

—Thanks, Bob. Same to you!

Some guests departed, replaced by others who maintained the balance between noise and smoke. They had been drinking for hours: many were beginning to get drunk. I hardly noticed, or rather it seemed to me natural. Without having drunk, I felt a little tipsy; not only from fatigue, but by contagion perhaps, as if the opaque air contained fumes of alcohol and of nonsense. I spoke to the guests, equal to equal, I interrupted conversations to give my opinion. One couple seemed to me to be particularly sympathetic, both small, blond, twins in love with each other. Several times I sat at their table; he had been in the war and stammered a few words of French. Filled with wonder, she listened to him say: "I love to walk in the "wheels" *(roues)* of Paris."

This evening the nasty drunks didn't annoy me. I poured some champagne into the whisky of the most obnoxious and soon, with Bob's help, I put him away behind a sofa, head on a cushion. Only his feet stuck out.

> Gonna take a sentimental journey,
> Gonna put my heart at ease . . .

The orchestra played slow music. A dozen couples danced cheek to cheek. Almost no one was left in the room; even Harrison had gone. Only the happy pair remained and I watched them, having no more work to do. I imagined their happiness. If it was anything like the beauty of the girl, my twins were winners: she was the only one almost as beautiful as Laura. Why were their eyes closed? What were they thinking?

> You ain't been blue
> No No No
> You ain't been blue
> 'til you've had that mood indigo.

—Bob, think I could have a Scotch now?
—Sure, Greg, sure!
Never had a whisky seemed to me to be as well deserved. I'd paid an indefinable price for it that I looked for in its color, its transparency, its smell . . . .
—Are you sad, Greg?
Holding her husband-twin by the hand, she leaned over me:
—The poor boy, he's sad. If Greg has a girl, he's sad. If he doesn't have a girl, he's still sad, isn't he?
This kindness confirmed the pity that I felt for Grégoire-the-lonely. Basically, I preferred aggressive drunks; they didn't oblige me to speak. To be sure, she was beautiful, sympathetic. So what? Impossible to gain anything from that, except to share a vague emotion which would hurt me more than it did her; especially later, in my empty bed.
I remained on the defensive. Sensing that she had nothing to fear, she became almost tender and I thought: "Look!

Charity! Not *Caritas* . . . not the charity of Chaucer . . . but modern charity: to have pity on a dog, a lost child, a man one will not need to love for long."

—You're not listening to me? she asked.

—Yes I am!

—What were you thinking about?

—Chaucer:

> *Delyte nat in wo thi wo to seche,*
> *As don thise foles that hire sorwes eche*
> *With sorwe . . .*   (Troilus and Criseyde, Book 1, strophe 101.)

—What does that mean in today's English?

—Oh, something like this: "Delight not in woe thy woe to seek, as do these fools that add to their sorrows with sorrow..."

—You're French and you know all that?

This admiration seemed overly naive to me. Basically, if I had wanted to love her, already I would no longer love her. But I felt the emotion of this possible adventure. A voyage missed. Is that it, Don Juan? Never refuse a voyage? In the place of the husband . . . A decent husband! He was half asleep in his armchair, smiling, a little drunk. If Jane could see me! Jealous when I told her that Gloria Dune had a pretty voice . . . .

At the bar, the musicians and Banjo Bob gathered around a bottle. Only the pianist played:

> I've found joy,
> Happy as a kid
> With his new toy . . .

—What's your name?

—Liz! Not very exotic . . . .

"If I asked her to dance anyway? What's the risk?"

I leaned toward her. I was going to speak when her husband woke up. A decent guy! I admired his luck . . . or his instinct perhaps? In this case, he deserved to keep this woman from unfaithful curiosity. He had beautiful hands. While chatting with him, I watched them: hands slimmer, more feminine than Liz's: mobile fingers, antennae which had warned him earlier of a vague danger.

We talked hunting and Liz, in her turn, dozed off. Or was she hiding her deception? All she said was:

—What? You kill birds too?

—I like the waiting in hunting, that sort of hope.

He lived near Red Bank, not far from the Port. Had we shot at the same flock of ducks? The solidity of the mallards, the rapid grace of the teals . . . But he talked particularly well about sailing. Brought up in Maine, he had always loved the sea and the near silence of sails. When he retired . . .

—You're not thirty!

It didn't matter. The day he retired he would buy a sailboat, he would cross the Atlantic, sail around Scotland, down the coast to Gibraltar . . .

—And Liz?

—She doesn't like the sea much. She'll get used to it.

Sitting on the arm of Liz's chair, he caressed her hair, repossessing her with his hands; gestures so gentle they upset me, informed me of my coming solitude. I questioned him, I animated the conversation, dreading that he would take advantage of a pause to decide to leave . . .

—Time to go, Liz!

—Wait for me! I'll leave with you. That won't put you out? You'll leave me off . . . the Port is on your way, hardly a ten-minute detour . . . .

I'd spoken without thinking. A decision already made without my realizing it.

—Bob, can I go?

— Sure, Greg! Sure!

He drove so slowly! What time was it? Four o'clock by my watch, her watch. The car was barely moving on the snow. Sometimes, other headlights lit up the twins, blond head on blond shoulder. Before leaving them I would ask for their address. Where are we? A town. There's the Ford garage! Ten minutes more. How nice they are, these two.

Too nice! They wanted to enter the driveway, take me up to the house.

— I swear to you it's not far. With the snow, the car won't make it. You need to know the road.

I got out, shoes in the snow, almost annoyed with worry: if they continued to the house, the headlights would wake people up, the dogs, Laura's father. I needed the walk to think things over.

Finally, the car drew away. When it disappeared, the calm. And I was afraid, a feeling of uncontrollable anguish. "Why just then? You've never been afraid of the dark!" It made no sense, since the night was clear. "Fear of the silence?" However, I had only to close my eyes to hear the orchestra at the Harrisons': *Saint Louis Blues* and the clarinet

> Saint Louis woman
> With your diamond rings
> Got that man of mine . . .

230

I sang. I talked out loud. Enough to wake up the whole house! "Fortunately they're still far away. Watch yourself, old man, you're drunk!" Drunk from alcohol or from fatigue? I scrubbed my face and the back of my neck with a fistful of snow. Already wet feet, cold hands. "What would my mother say?"

First the drive went downhill. I followed the car tracks, two furrows barely covered by the last snowfall. "The snow is a sheet, a shroud, a cotton coat, a white negative under the trees, a post card addressed to Grégoire. Is that me, Grégoire? Yes, since I'm walking in a furrow of snow. Left foot, right foot. You're going to raise a hand. Give the order . . . it obeys. Your hand exists."

I didn't believe it. How could I convince myself? "If only I were at La Chêneraie!" That forest was a part of my life, while America . . . "But you are in America, State of New Jersey, New Year's Eve 1948. You walk, you breathe in America. You are there because you hoped for it, wanted it, succeeded in it." With Fabien, we would have run through this forest, run so much that we would have learned it by heart, by night and day, blindfolded, blind. Does Harris know a forest by heart? Did he have the time to learn one, before? His eyes against the light: "You must go to America, Grégoire. You will help Americans understand the French and when you come back to France . . . " Help whom? Jane, Laura? Did they understand the French better? Who is French? Am I French? Not as French as Perrault . . . even when I say "Yes, *Monsieur*." Besides, Perrault wouldn't say that. He would rather die. He, he's French and he knows Jack London by heart; he recites him while walking in the snow, he improvises: "Snow is the mortal enemy of leather." That evening, I had met Jane

231

and been slapped by Laura. More than a year ago! The snow is always there, in spite of the trip to the Gulf of Mexico with Peter A, in spite of getting drunk with Peter B, in spite of the dishes at the Splendid, in spite of . . . everything, we are all still in the snow.

The third or the fourth turn? "Who knows? That will teach you to not learn your forests by heart!" A forest to recite as if it were Chaucer, each tree a strophe, each branch a line with leaves that fall in the winter so that the poem is without words . . . hence the silence. Silence which doesn't frighten me anymore. I am at peace with myself. I babble. Warm feet, burning ears, I talk to myself. Sometimes, one talks to oneself out of worry, sometimes out of gaiety . . . "Oh, don't ask too much of me! I'm not a Negro, not yet." When I am a Negro, I will go back to France to help the French understand the Negroes. I'll go to Marie Godefroy's house, I will play the banjo for her, I will sing her the blues. When I have the patience of the Negroes . . . .

Ah!

The house! *Bon Dieu*, there's the house and I still haven't thought about anything, decided anything. The house is there on a snow-covered lawn under the bare elm. Over there, Jeanie is asleep, Laura is asleep, they all sleep except, above the fireplace, the teal in flight. But what to say to them, *Bon Dieu*, what to say to them? I'm not the prodigal son, since they have driven me out. I'm not a shivering dog hoping for a pardon; they don't chase away dogs. Then, Grégoire, what are you doing here? Run away before they wake up. Run away quickly, before daylight, before a blunder, before shame . . . .

Bitch! Does she think I am afraid? That I'm a quitter? No! I'm not a coward. She must know that. How do I let her know it? A stone! Where to find a stone in this snow? A stone of contempt, not too light, not too heavy. Where to dig? Here? The gravel is so stupid. Throw the watch? Of course! With the chain. There's her window. One move and the house lights up, window after window, a house of winter evenings lit on its lawn of snow. A warm house, stones pierced by light. How I love this house, *Bon Dieu*! How I love this lawn and the creek and the forest, and Slow and almost all those who sleep there.

What time is it? Five o'clock. I put the watch away in my vest pocket. Even if I throw the watch I'll have to run away, and run all the more quickly if I throw it. Run at the first sound, at the first light . . . while if I wait . . . the house stands there, and me too, the others sleep.

I hear a noise, a moan perhaps. There is no wind. Who stirs? Who is crying? Is it a flight of ducks? No! The noise comes from below, toward that door. Listen. Come near! It scratches, like an animal. It cries like a child. Who is it? Is it you? *Bon Dieu*, is it you? You say it's you! I'm coming! Say nothing! Not a sound! Wait, I'm opening the door! Wait, Sarcelle, my dog, *Bon Dieu*! Come, girl. Let's leave quickly before they wake . . . without a sound. Wait! Your collar is not mine, and neither is the watch . . . . You, you belong to me. The rest is theirs, we leave it behind. We are not thieves, hey, Sarcelle? The collar, the chain, the watch, hang them all on the doorknob. They will understand, Laura will understand . . . Slow, too, the poor soul. The watch is for him. I will send a telegram to Laura: "The watch is for Slow. "

Come now. They're sleeping. They will sleep for another two hours and we will be far away. For always, Sarcelle. You and I together.

We both ran. We weren't running away, we were dancing.
I ran on the driveway and Sarcelle traced black circles in
the snow with me at their center. Each circle was a sentence:

    . . . Grégoire, why have you taken so long to come?
    . . . Grégoire, don't leave me anymore . . .
    . . . Will we go hunting?
    . . . I'm yours . . .
    . . . A rabbit went that way . . .
    . . . Later I will be dignified . . .
    . . . Why doesn't Jeanie come too?

That last question, Sarcelle had asked it sitting in the road
whimpering, off again soon for other circles, scarcely
slowed by the unevenness of the terrain, jumping over a
dead tree, buried in the soft snow, her coat powdered with
white, then with a shake, changed back to black:

    . . . A man and his dog . . .
    . . . Live, live, live and run . . . .

black between the silhouettes of trees and rocks, film in
black and white of a run for joy up to the main road where,
wisely, she lay down to wait for me.

—Sarcelle, heel!

Disciplined: her muzzle level with my left knee, as in the
manuals of dressage, she studied my pace to regulate hers.

Soft: she licked my hand with her tongue from time to
time.

Attentive: she lifted her head each time I looked at her;
certainly she understood my words:

—We have left the Port. From this road on, it's the world.

234

You have to beware, my dog. It's lucky that it's still dark, that it's snowing, and people are sleeping off their New Year's partying. But the daylight will come with thousands of cars on this road. Stay next to me, you'll have nothing to fear. Never anything to fear. Although . . .

I would have loved to take you to my home. But that doesn't exist yet, or anymore. I had oak woods, I had the Port. Now, I have only Princeton and the University has a rule that forbids dogs to live with Grégoire. But you will go to the Harrises' house, or to Banjo Bob's house. Which would you prefer? The blind man or the Negro? Both are my friends, our friends, I'll come to see you every day, several times. I'll take you for walks on the banks of Lake Carnegie. We'll wait there for spring. You'll help me write my thesis. This devilish thesis! You'll help me, won't you, Sarcelle? A hundred pages on Kierkegaard and on love; intelligent pages in which I quote Chaucer, St. Bernard, and Melville . . . I, who don't even believe in God . . . It's crazy, isn't it? To believe or not to believe in God when you love as I love you. You will lie in the grass at my feet, I will read *Purity of Heart* again and when I need an image of God, I will pet you. You'll replace Him, a bit. Why wouldn't He be a Labrador, or a teal in flight? Is He simply a reason to love, to hope, to caress, to walk in the snow at dawn with my dog step by step you lick my hand to hear that I love you and that we will find somewhere another Port, another Chêneraie for summer or for winter since there will again be snow and sunlight, night and leaves day after day at each step of my dog my blind man my Negro my girl . . . .

III

—What is the purpose of your visit?

—The marriage of a cousin.

—Passport, please. Someone will call you shortly. Number eighty.

Answering "thank you," I'm sorry that my voice is never normal when I am summoned to appear before bureaucrats. Where does this unease come from? I know perfectly well that all over the world every day people wait by the thousands for a visa, answer personal questions posed by indifferent officials. Most of these people have other concerns than a marriage . . . "Exiles, expatriates, my voice imitates your humility. I would like to assume your fears and your hopes!"

It's the only explanation. Because this visa has little importance since Jeanie will come to France after her marriage. I will meet her husband, I will get the latest news of Laura, the Port, Slow.

Some thirty persons are seated in the waiting room of the consulate where the clatter of a typewriter rhythms the silence. Only my neighbor has brought his newspaper. A few of the curious leaf through the propaganda scattered on the tables. The others wait patiently, and their eyes fascinate me. What are they looking at so fixedly? Do they see the secretaries, the American flag, the photographs of landscapes in Vermont, in Texas, in the Rocky Mountains? Or do they see only themselves? Memories of abandoned homelands, here a Portuguese, there a Pole, and this old Jew who strokes his gray beard. What language do they speak? Whom do they speak to? To those they have left? To those they will see again tomorrow? To their missing or to their dead?

To speak to the dead, what a temptation! Advise Caesar to beware of Brutus and remake history. Speak to the missing, to objects, to landscapes. I walk through a garden killed by those who have given it a new life by planting tulips in place of hollyhocks, by pouring gravel on grassy paths,and by seeding lawns where kitchen gardens used to be. Some men think thus to be reborn and disguise themselves in the fashions of the day. We bury only their neglect, knowing they will perhaps say one day: "What a shame! I was too busy. I would like to have seen you more often." Perrault raises an arm and leans over my tombstone; the wind lifts his graying hair; dressed like a president, he speaks to my corpse without the mob's thinking him eccentric.

—Seventy-two! Number seventy-two!

A black gets up and goes over to a secretary. A round head, pointed shoes, where has he hidden himself so that I have not noticed him? Ivory Coast, Senegal, or the Cameroons, under what circumstances does he want to rejoin his American brothers, Banjo Bob, Slow, Wash-Wash Washington?

I was walking in the neighborhood of Yvetot. Crossing a village, I opened the gate of the cemetery. At the fringe of the usual gravestones, behind a boxwood hedge gray crosses were lined up decorated with rusty rosettes and with the inscription: "France Remembers". Fifty-three burial mounds rounded off by heavy rains. On the road I met an inhabitant.

—Hi, there!

—Good evening!

—In the cemetery, are those Negroes?

—Yes, *monsieur*, the Negroes of June '40.

The road left the plateau with its lines of winter wheat and went down through a wood to the valley of the Seine. I spoke in Negro: "*Loumbabamoum togonyika caméghana djuda tchombé.*" That meant: "Worthy Negroes, I hope at least that your sergeant wasn't a son of a bitch." Some Senegalese lifted me up in their arms, *Y a bon Banania*. I sang in Negro:

> When the blues jump the rabbit
> They run it for a solid mile.
> Well, the rabbit he turn over,
> An' cry like a motherless chile.

Light-colored palms, pink nails, brown hands throw dice against a wall, sevens and elevens rolling on the crumpled dollars. Negroes from Africa and from America, Negroes imported for war or for growing cotton, summer Negroes, winter Negroes, my Negro friends, truckdrivers, musicians, infantrymen, janitors, dishwashers . . .

—Numbers seventy-three, seventy-four and seventy-five!

They were three women who went towards an office, or rather three copies of one woman---a mother and two daughters. Not only did they look like one another, but they followed one another like an allegory of the fate that will soon make this child of thirteen a young girl in heavy make-up, then an older woman overweight. Father Time sits beside their three chairs and the Fates disguise themselves as ordinary people in one of these modern films that draw their inspiration from myths.

I enter a room with collections of ancient books. Louis Quinze armchairs are placed on the pink and green Persian rug. A woman materializes. She is dead. Dead with her teapot. A barber has cut off her braids. She dies with her sugar bowl, with her pretty, fashionable figure. I haven't seen her since Rouen. Did she have breasts then? I lend the look of a child to this woman who offers cookies, and her body tosses and turns like a rude joke.

—You used to be more talkative!

It is Marie's voice and it has not changed. If I closed my eyes, the smell of tea and toast would remain. It's impossible and I wait carefully for the moment to depart, fearing the clumsy action that would tie this happy winter of my childhood to the ridiculous present. I call up the silhouette of Marie upright on her bicycle with the upturned handlebars. For her I had exposed my pride on a scrap of paper. The wind blows the rain on a plowed field, the earth softens, forgets the plow, becomes again a plain on which faces, some tiny, some without limits, overlap one on another, streaming with water.

In a few weeks I shall see Jeanie again and already I am preparing myself for possible disappointments. Whom will she look like? Her mother? Mine? She had, she will always have, the gray blue eyes and black hair of my family, but Laura's spirit is contagious, even a Laura grown older, married for twelve years to that worthy Roger, her protégé, her victim . . .

—Number seventy-six! Seventy-six, please!

The typewriter clatters on. I've been waiting for a quarter of an hour and I have the impression of having nothing more to say to myself. Must I, too, leaf through the embassy's brochures to keep from being bored? No. This literature, wherever it comes from, exasperates me.

I should have brought my dog to keep me company. Do they allow dogs, these bureaucrats? She would have put her muzzle on my thigh: "Good dog! Good Sarcelle, Flaque, Quetsch!" So many names, so many dogs, and that same softness of skin behind the ears when one caresses them. "Do you remember Sarcelle's first duck, one morning in November? And the thirteen snipe killed at dawn with Quetsch? The pheasant, head high, that Flaque retrieved from the other end of a field of alfalfa . . . " Three generations since that Christmas morning, black puppy in a pink ribbon on a beige carpet. Sarcelle died of old age at twelve, Quetsch killed at five by a viper's bite, I still caress them all, hands full of their fur. What grief for these lost friendships!

My neighbor puts down his newspaper. The first page lays out its evaluation of famines and wars, accidents at work, automobile accidents. Not one of these sufferings causes me the sorrow of the death of my animals. Why? How to learn oneself and teach other men to weep for a thousand deaths a thousand times more than for the death of a friend or a brother? I know they're not worth much, those for whom the death of strangers remains unimportant.

And the old shame creeps over me: how have I become this almost indifferent bourgeois? My Norman countryside, my family, my horses and my dogs, my tranquillity in the shelter of the hedges and curtains of elms and ash. The usual shame, I know the answers: "I, too, could have . . . should have . . . I had read Saint Bernard, Chaucer, Melville, Kierkegaard, and Marx . . . I had to plunge ahead, burn my bridges . . . but I am like Ishmael who wants to survive the shipwreck . . . I don't know how to hate, I don't know how to love . . . It isn't in me to be angry!"

—Numbers seventy-seven and seventy-eight!

Two young people get up. I look around me. No one is angry, not even the old Jew, nor the Negro, nor the type-writer, nor the President of the United States whose photograph watches over the sleeping flag.

—Number seventy-nine!

—Number eighty!

"Is that my number? Yes!" And my heart begins to pound, particularly because the voice which calls me is not the usual secretary's voice. A man is waiting for me at the entrance to a corridor.

—The Consul wishes to see you, Mr. Engivane.

I follow him. He points to a door and I enter a dark room. Between the curtains on the windows, I see the courtyard and on the other side of the courtyard, sunlight.

—Sit down, please!

Behind a desk cluttered with documents, badly lit by a small lamp, the Consul smiles at me. A comfortable chair, he waits while I settle myself.

—Mr. Engivane, you have asked for a visa to attend your cousin's wedding, am I right?

He speaks English, I answer him in English:

—The wedding takes place in two weeks . . .

—Three years ago, they refused you a visa . . .

—That is true, because of an election.

Somewhere else, I would have burst out laughing at the mere thought of that electoral campaign. Charles Perrault de Peygues (as in peg-leg) Progressive candidate. Deputy: Grégoire Engivane, farmer. We had travelled all the Norman roads in my old Citroën, explaining to farmers the benefits of an enlightened collectivism. They listened more politely than I would have believed, out of deference, it seemed to me, for Perrault's aristocratic name, for his portliness and his accent from the Midi. We had even won three or four per cent of the vote. Perrault was triumphant. The day after the elections, he had hugged me on the station platform: " You damned peasant!"

—You understand that in spite of recent liberal measures, it will be difficult to obtain your visa in time because only Washington can decide these special cases and this procedure, even though it is only a routine procedure . . .

" . . . given the third line of the twenty-second paragraph of the treaty on regularization of the sale of cornfed chickens during leap years . . ." This man speaks like the fine print of a contract, and I improvise a text that I could recite to him if I were sitting behind his desk and he were in my arm- chair. When I sense that he is going to end his speech, I listen to him.

. . . three weeks at a minimum.

Forget the wedding. I had hoped to see the Port, flowers everywhere, Laura with tears in her eyes, Slow moved, Jeanie glowing . . .

—Well, let it go. It's not worth the trouble!

A fit of temper, I get up. I have no desire to beg favors. Am I a child to be deprived of candy on the pretext that I've not been a good boy? They can go fuck themselves with their visa! As for this poor bureaucrat, pale as a slice of veal, in his office without light, I look for a cutting phrase for him, the stroke of a spur or of a riding whip . . . But no! When a horse refuses, the fault is with the rider. I smile at the Consul. He smiles at me. He seems gentle and embarrassed. He wears the green and blue tie of Slate Club members.

—What year were you at Princeton?

His astonishment almost consoles me for the spoiled wedding.

—I finished in '52, he answers.

—Then we couldn't have met each other. At that time I'd already worked three years for the *Herald-Tribune*. Oh well, delighted to have met you, sorry the circumstances are so boringly official . . .

I left. I have only one wish, to return to the sunlight. As soon as I reach the rue Saint-Florentin, I turn to the left. I walk across the Tuileries. The chestnuts are in flower; yesterday's rain has surely made the boxwood green again. There will be tulips but no children. I don't know the children of Paris anymore; Marie and I always stay home on Thursday's school holiday, because of our two daughters. They have their dance lessons in the morning in Rouen, riding lessons in the afternoon, sometimes the dentist, shopping, and Marie spends her Thursdays chauffeuring these young ladies. After dinner, as soon as the children are in bed, she tells us all about it: the little one dances better on her toes than the big one but the big one's progress on horseback is such that the riding master lent her Mistral who reared up twice and the big one had not been at all afraid, she had lowered her hands, she had . . . My mother insists on the details, again, again. I doze thinking of tomorrow's work; sow barley in Long Riages, in Moulins, roll the field at Bordes. Later, when we are alone, Marie tells me:

—You know I passed by La Chêneraie. They've planted tulips all along the terrace. It's delightful.

—And the hollyhocks?

—Ah, there were hollyhocks?

Of course, she cannot know. And then, what does it matter? When we had to choose, at my father's death, between La Chêneraie and the farm, we sold La Chêneraie and I don't regret it. I don't regret Paris, or the newspaper, or the apartment in the rue Vaneau. This isn't much to pay for a life of freedom. I have always preferred tractors to Cadillacs. All the same, someday I would like to know why? How is it that all my ambitions are reduced to clods of earth, to flax and rape flowers, to alfalfa and clover? Was it worth the trouble of going all the way to America in order to return to Normandy to plant cabbages?

"Oh, if you had known, Grégoire, if you had known at sixteen, how you would have despaired!"

However, I'm happy. Happy? Let's say, content! The difference is not great, and only Harris would understand that no man is happy in the present. The happiness of a man is judged in the past, after his death. Harris will be, without doubt, a happy dead man, he who's not an unhappy blind man. I'll write to him tomorrow, I promise! Of all those on this aborted trip I will miss him the most. It's not like Laura and Roger who often come to France, Peter B who lived three years in Paris... Harris stays in Princeton where his blind movements know the sidewalks and the distances, where his hands easily find the buttons of the tape recorder. Before leaving I had recorded all of the *Anthology of Arland*, plus *A Season in Hell*, *The Songs of Maldoror*, and some poems of Apollinaire:

Let us rejoice not
because our friendship has swelled like the Nile,
Rivering our lives with everything men long for...

(Guillaume Apollinaire, translated by William Meredith)

In the end, of all these friendships there is only one I don't miss, Peter A. Since his death in Korea, I think of him so often that I don't miss him. Wasn't it a little for Peter that I was a candidate in the elections? But try to explain that to a consul, even an old Princeton man and a member of Slate Club . . . he'll believe you're political . . . he'll believe you insult his flag . . . he'll believe . . .

—Mister! Please, Mister!

. . . that you're a dangerous provocateur paid by Moscow and Peking . . . Worse! He'll imagine that you work for nothing, pushed by a fanaticism as incomprehensible as the dance of the whirling dervishes . . .

—Please, Mister! Can you fix my bicycle?

What bicycle? Let him go ask his consul! What's the point of consuls if they're not there, here, everywhere, ready to repair the bicycles of their young nationals?

—Don't cry, Bud! Cry no more, son, you've had the good luck to stumble on a specialist! When I was young, I fixed flat tires in three minutes . . . Where's your mother? She leaves you all alone in these forests? Oh, the beautiful tack: do you see it? Look carefully, it's a carpet tack lost by workers of King Louis the Thirteenth the same night a certain d'Artagnan arrived in Paris. *En garde!* A scrape of the rasp before the patch . . . Stuff this tack carefully in your pocket and you will trade it at school for seventeen marbles, a pocket knife with six blades, and two cookies.

The kid looks at me dumbfounded. An American angel, face blond-blue-pink for a full-color photo in *Life*, he has never heard anyone speak so fast. I lay it on thicker, speeding up the words and gestures, pumping air into the tire:

— . . . and when you return to New York, your country without cows and steam locomotives, you'll tell your buddies in Central Park: "I have Parisian air in my tires, air from a springtime afternoon in the Tuileries, come sniff the chestnuts and the roses."

—Thank you, Mister!

He gets back on his bicycle and flies away pedaling furiously, leaving me alone with my dirty hands. What's more awkward than dirty hands when you're all dressed up? You carry your hands at the end of your arms, far from pockets, far from trousers. Fortunately there's a big basin where I wet my fingers, I dry them with my handkerchief and I am sorry . . . how sorry I am! . . . not to have a pretty sailboat to put on the water.

—Thank you, Monsieur. That was very nice of you . . .

After the child, here was the mother, so young. It's true that now all women under thirty seem young to me. Laura must have been her age when I met her.

—It's beautiful here! she says.

. . . and she's right. I look first towards the Place de la Concorde and l'Etoile, then toward the Carrousel.

—Yes, very beautiful.

The chestnuts are in flower. I had come here on purpose to see them but it took this woman to make me lift my eyes to look at them. They ought to put foreigners everywhere, on the Acropolis, on the Campodoglio, in the courtyard of the Louvre . . . Not tourists, but only one or two foreigners: a woman who knits without taking her eyes from the equestrian statue of Marcus Aurelius, a Chinese transfixed in front of the Parthenon. The disillusioned natives would be inspired by these fervors.

The woman and the boy move off. They are a little bit mine. If I had stayed in America, if I had married one of these girls, if one put Paris and New York in the same bottle.

Finally the image of the Consul fades away and I find my America again: a red motorcycle on a gray road, a black horse in a green field, a blue teal on the snow: "America, can you forgive me? Ah, forgive me for having abandoned you!"

After five years, I returned to France as a foreigner. I, too, looked at each stone of these monuments, each tree in these gardens. Did I have an accent? The waiters in the cafés answered me in English. It's true I still wore some of Uncle Henri's suits. Several times I almost went back. If it hadn't been for my father's long illness... I wrote to Laura, I wrote to Jane, even though she was already married. I waited every morning for their answers as a summons to life: America was not forgetting me.

Fabien and Perrault joined forces to make fun of me, to strip me of my Anglicisms, of my prudishness, of my habits, of all this youthful love. I still remember humiliating scenes that they have certainly forgotten, that no doubt would seem funny to them if I conjured them up. In a café on Saint-Germain-des-Prés for example there were ten of us sitting around a table and Perrault cried out

—Grégoire hasn't yet seen Micheline's breasts!

—What? The most beautiful breasts in Paris...

—Micheline, show him your breasts!

A blouse opened and the breasts were displayed, as if placed on the table, slightly paler than the tanned torso.

—Touch them!

—You feel how firm they are?

—Oh, the asshole! The dirty old man, he's blushing! Look at Grégoire blush!

But there is the Seine and I'm on the Carrousel Bridge. A tugboat lowers its stack, plunges under the arch and disappears, followed by one, two, three barges loaded with sand; the wake reaches the riverbank, then the water becomes calm, black and soft.

> I spit in the spring,
> On the fish that flee,
> It makes funny rings
> And that comforts me.

Marie taught me this song as she taught me to play patience, piquet and slapjack.

—You're too serious, she said.

—Me? Not at all . . .

—In fact, you seem entirely too serious.

Has she changed me? Probably not. I don't think people change. They evolve in one way more than another until a certain age. Then they freeze. The trick would be to freeze at the instant of a smile so the snapshot is always a pleasant one to see . . . especially in my case. For those who have neither the anger, nor the superior look of the prophet, there remains only the smile.

. . . and I smile going back up the rue des Saint-Péres. I greet an old lady, I admire a baby, I avoid the Regency armchair brandished by an antique dealer, I accept a prospectus announcing the end of the world and the reign of Jehovah, I show two young Germans the way to the rue de Verneuil, I estimate the number of steps remaining to get to the boulevard Saint- Germain . . . sixty . . . I count forty, fifty, fifty-eight , fifty-nine, sixty, sixty-one, two, three, four . . . I am a bit off, but I cheated a little at the end by lengthening my pace.

In a few minutes I shall see Marie. When I tell her of my

disappointment, she will feel sorry for me. I will think: "Basically, she's happy that I'm not going without her to the country of my other loves . . . " But I will pretend to believe her and in ten sentences we will play at this game of fibs and tenderness, this game that is more real than the game of truth. What truth?

—Engivane! Engivane!

Perrault is seated at his usual table, at the back of the Café de Flore. The back of his neck rests on a mirror, a head with two faces like Janus'.

—It's very good, Fabien's song.

"Very good" is articulated with emphasis. Perrault sings off-key but sings the refrain all the same:

> Since one and one make two
> When I'm in love with you . . .

As he has forgotten the rest, he sings tra-la-la-la. His small mouth is rounded. He sputters in telling me about my brother: Fabien has a feel for dialogue even in his refrains, the theatre is waiting for him, the honors. According to him, plays pay better than music. Fabien will write a tragedy and Perrault will recite it, hands shaped in the form of a tulip: a monologue in Act II, a dialogue in Act III. I'm no longer listening to him. He would better have said to me: "Your brother drinks too much. Why is he so unhappy? Can one help him?" While Perrault the Useless babbles on, I have a conversation with Perrault the Useful. Both of us would take Fabien to Greece: summer, the monuments, the swimming and Fabien tanned, sobered up, full of work. But Fabien will never agree, he doesn't like trips.

And yet he's gone so much farther away than I have ever

been, in an unimaginable country that he refuses to describe. What irony! It's I who's succeeded our father, while the elder, the redhead, the true Engivane has withdrawn from the world.

—Listen, Grégoire!

Perrault calls me. I listen since he wants me to. Tired of standing, I sit next to him so he doesn't see my eyes: no need to hear him. Take care of Fabien by force? For a minute I pound the table, I think I am fighting with Fabien. Then I leave off: how can I reform others, I who have accepted everything?

— . . . and since you've been growing wheat, you seem less like a peasant, says Perrault. Excuse the paradox, but in the end, of all of us you're the only one who's done what you wanted to do. Well! Here comes Marie!

Always adroit, Perrault has slipped his belly over the table, among the bottles of beer and the empty glasses. He presents a cheek and Marie kisses him, asks about his health, invites him to come to Normandy, as at each meeting. Old friends, old dialogues . . . .

— . . . you are a mother to us all, you, who are almost a child and our mother all the same. How are your girls?

Ten minutes later Marie and I leave the café. She doesn't look back, she knows I am following her. To cross the boulevard Saint-Germain, I take her by the shoulder. Marie is not tall, she is made for lawns and for flowers, too tender for this macadam, these trucks, this racket. I clasp her tight against me, I guide her, I protect her, I hold her. I love her I love her I love her and I pity her amidst the cars.

BIOGRAPHICAL NOTE

Alain Marc Prévost 1930 - 1971

Alain Prévost grew up in wartime France. His father, Jean Prévost, was a famous author and critic in the thirties who became a leader of the Resistance and commandant of a company in the *Armée Secrète*. Jean Prévost was killed, at 43, in a German ambush in the Vercors, a rugged, mountainous region near Grenoble. Alain's mother, Marcelle Auclair, was a well-known journalist and the biographer of, among others, Saint Teresa of Avila, Jean Jaurès, and Bernadette. She raised her children---Alain, his brother Michel, a poet, and his sister Françoise, a noted film actress---in the environs of Paris.

Alain came to Montreal in 1946 to attend a Jesuit school and obtain his baccalauréates. Sponsored by his parents' friend, Alan Stuyvesant '27, Alain entered Princeton in 1947. He took to the University with his customary zest for life and soon made a wide circle of friends, not only among his undergraduate colleagues at the Nassau "Lit", MSS, the Rugby Club, and Key and Seal, but also with members of the Princeton faculty: R.P. Blackmur, John Berryman, and many others.

After graduation Alain worked for a year in New York for *Agence France Presse*, the French version of AP or Reuters. In 1952 he married Helen Alexander, the daughter of Archibald Alexander '28. They returned to France for Alain's military service. He then began his writing career which was to produce six novels, four children's books, two works of non-fiction, and many articles and short stories. His first novel, *Le peuple impopulaire,* was published by Éditions du Seuil in 1956. *Le Monde* praised it as the work of "...a vigorous talent that bursts forth on every page." *Grenadou, paysan francais,* Alain's study of a farmer friend, was a best seller in 1966. Like many of his works, it revealed his preoccupation with the experience of working men and women, whose integrity and friendship he treasured.

In 1967, *Le port des absents* was published. This novel, with Princeton as its main setting, was reviewed by Pierre-Henri Simon of the Académie Francaise: "What might seem too intellectual or too genteel in this story of the privileges of birth, intelligence, and culture is saved by something of quiet and uncommon quality that seems to spring from Alain Prévost's innermost nature: a preference for simplicity, for the appeal of a child or an animal, a liking for eccentrics and misfits, a need for good friends, good fellowship, and even affection, and a taste for the good life as well."

In the early morning of December 19, 1971, at St. Loup just south of Chartres, Alain walked into his fields with his English setter, "Pixie", suffered a sudden heart attack and died instantly, at the age of 41. A fine collection of his short stories, *Adieu, bois de Boulogne,* was published posthumously in 1972. It confirms his place as one of the most prolific and distinguished writers among graduates of Princeton. Even so, his writings cannot fully convey the qualities of this exceptional man, his devotion to his family and friends, and his outrage at injustice which was so well expressed in his life's work.

Alain is survived by his widow, Helen Alexander Prévost, who lives with her Labradors and her horses at their home in Saint Loup; by their son, Jean-Victor, an international lawyer in Paris; and their daughter, Lauré-Hélène, a doctor of medicine and the mother of their three granddaughters.

TRANSLATOR'S NOTE

The rough translation of *Le port des absents* was drafted by Ralph Woodward '51, who takes full responsibility for any errors in rendering or interpreting the text. Careful readings and detailed assistance from Helen Prévost and from William Clary to clarify Alain's intent and to correct and refine the English translation were essential to the project. Their collaboration is gratefully acknowledged.

The text of this book is set in Palatino, a modern font of harmony and elegance.
It was designed for the Stempel foundry in 1950 by Hermann Zapf.
One of the foremost typographers of the twentieth century, Zapf created more than fifty
typefaces including Aldus, Melior, Mergenthaler, and Optima. His Palatino is a roman style
with broad letters, strong serifs and handsome proportions.

The design of the book and its cover were created on PageMaker 6.5 software by the translator.
The book has been printed using digital print-on-demand technology under the supervision of
Steve Lewers, Chief Trade Book Officer of booktech.com, www.booktech.com.
Five and Ten Press, Inc. is the imprint of Robert V. Keeley '51, publisher.

For information concerning this publication, contact:
Ralph Woodward
45 Wayside Inn Road
Framingham, MA 01701
508-877-5328 naipr@aol.com